Renev
by int
in per:
by ph

SPECIAL MESSAGE TO READERS

THE ULVERSCROFT FOUNDATION
(registered UK charity number 264873)
was established in 1972 to provide funds for
research, diagnosis and treatment of eye diseases.
Examples of major projects funded by
the Ulverscroft Foundation are:-

- The Children's Eye Unit at Moorfields Eye Hospital, London
- The Ulverscroft Children's Eye Unit at Great Ormond Street Hospital for Sick Children
- Funding research into eye diseases and treatment at the Department of Ophthalmology, University of Leicester
- The Ulverscroft Vision Research Group, Institute of Child Health
- Twin operating theatres at the Western Ophthalmic Hospital, London
- The Chair of Ophthalmology at the Royal Australian College of Ophthalmologists

You can help further the work of the Foundation
by making a donation or leaving a legacy.
Every contribution is gratefully received. If you
would like to help support the Foundation or
require further information, please contact:

THE ULVERSCROFT FOUNDATION
The Green, Bradgate Road, Anstey
Leicester LE7 7FU, England
Tel: (0116) 236 4325

website: www.foundation.ulverscroft.com

Over fourteen million people tuned in to see Nadiya Hussain win 2015's *Great British Bake Off*. Since then, she has captured the heart of the nation. A columnist for *The Times* and *Essentials*, Nadiya is also a regular reporter for *The One Show* and presented a two-part series, *The Chronicles of Nadiya*, on BBC 1, and has been named as one of the top five most influential Asians in the UK.

You can discover more about the author at www.nadiyahussain.com/

Follow her on Twitter @BegumNadiya

THE FALL AND RISE OF
THE AMIR SISTERS

The four Amir sisters — Fatima, Farah, Bubblee and Mae — are as close as sisters can be, but sometimes even those bonds can be pushed to their limits. Bubblee is finding herself increasingly unable to produce artwork that she is happy with, while Mae heads off to start her new life at university. Becoming a mother has always been Farah's dream, so when older sister Fatima struggles with a tough pregnancy whilst Farah has trouble conceiving, she can't help but be jealous. A plan is formed that will break a huge cultural taboo in the family and give Farah a renewed hope of having children with her husband Mustafa: using a surrogate. But nothing is ever that simple. As tragedy strikes in the family, can they pull together to rise again?

Books by Nadiya Hussain
Published by Ulverscroft:

THE SECRET LIVES OF THE
AMIR SISTERS

NADIYA HUSSAIN
WITH AYISHA MALIK

THE FALL AND RISE OF THE AMIR SISTERS

Complete and Unabridged

CHARNWOOD
Leicester

First published in Great Britain in 2019 by
HQ
an imprint of HarperCollins*Publishers* Ltd
London

First Charnwood Edition
published 2020
by arrangement with
HarperCollins*Publishers* Ltd
London

A catalogue record for this book is available from the British Library.

ISBN 978–1–4448–4348–4

Published by
F. A. Thorpe (Publishing)
Anstey, Leicestershire

Set by Words & Graphics Ltd.
Anstey, Leicestershire
Printed and bound in Great Britain by
T. J. International Ltd., Padstow, Cornwall

This book is printed on acid-free paper

'I want to be an archaeologist,' I said. 'You can't be an archaeologist, your parents are not rich enough, it will be a miracle if you make it to university.' I didn't become an archaeologist or go to university. I did something else. I remembered her words and followed every dream. Unkind words bloom the unlikeliest of passions. This is dedicated to the dreamer in you.

1

Farah liked bustling around. She was perpetually busy when not at her job; her hands at work on a curry, washing clothes, fluffing pillows and inspecting areas of her now smaller home. *At least it's easier to manage.* She was going to be positive. She paused to try and listen for what Mustafa might be doing upstairs. Maybe he was still lying in bed. It was ten o'clock in the morning but his sleeping habits were never predictable any more. Or perhaps he was just looking out of the window, like he'd taken to doing. There was a time when she'd have asked what he was thinking. Now she wasn't sure whether she wanted to know.

He came downstairs, managing to grunt a good morning as he opened the fridge.

'Why is it stacked with so much stuff?' he asked.

Farah was spraying Pledge on to the coffee table, wiping it down with a cloth.

'For the sandwiches I'm making for Mae's party later,' she replied.

His brows furrowed as he snapped: 'Where's the mango juice?'

Farah swept into the kitchen and looked inside the fridge with him. 'It must've been finished.'

He slammed the door shut and she jumped. 'For God's sake. You have the thing heaving with stuff for Mae but no mango juice.'

She folded her arms and clenched her jaw, looking up at him. Her husband was a stranger to her in these moments, because, before the accident, in all the years they'd been married, he'd never lost his temper with her, or anyone for that matter. It hadn't yet failed to surprise her when his mood took a turn. He opened the fridge door once more and slammed it shut again. His face was enraged as he glowered at her but she didn't move an inch. She waited. He stood there for a few more moments before thundering out of the room and she heard him slam the front door behind him.

Farah took a deep breath, because the last thing she needed was increased blood pressure. *My husband is alive.* She repeated this to herself every time she thought of him lying in his coma after the car accident. He had been punished enough for his mistake. Mustafa had crashed his car after finding out that her brother Jay had lost all of the money he was supposed to be investing in their business and now here they were, living with the consequences of Mustafa's ongoing medication. The doctors had said it'd affect his moods — to be careful of him falling into a kind of depression, but Farah couldn't quite separate the man from the drugs. Aside from that, this little flat wasn't theirs. She missed the open spaces of their five-bedroom semi-detached place. Farah liked having a guest room in case one of her sisters wanted to spend the night, or they had family or friends visiting. She took comfort from the idea that there was another room that would make the perfect nursery

. . . but she had to let go of that dream anyway. Looking around the small living room, the light wood laminate flooring, wallpaper they couldn't afford to change and paint instead — apart from her parents, who had wallpaper now anyway? — she took a deep breath, closed her eyes and opened them again. Still, there were things to be grateful for — being alive was one of them.

⋆   ⋆   ⋆

When Mustafa returned an hour later he came into the kitchen. She pretended not to notice him as she made a start on the sandwiches.

'You can feel summer coming to an end,' he said.

She ignored him.

'Can I help?' he asked.

She got the butter out of the fridge and slammed the door shut, pointedly, looking at him.

'What do you think?'

His face fell. The way he looked at her always reminded her of Jay and it managed to soften her heart.

'You'd just slow me down, anyway,' she added.

He smiled and looked at the ground, nodding. This time his chosen mood was martyrdom: the long-suffering husband of a wife who he couldn't seem to please, even when he tried. He left the room without another word.

Farah listened to him going into the bathroom to take a shower. She heard his footsteps come out and go into their room. He stayed in there for two hours. Farah walked towards the bottom of the stairs and paused, caught between fury and guilt. Fury won. Mango juice! Of all the things in the world that he could get angry about. The sheer audacity of it! Here they were, living in this one-bedroom flat because of his inability to manage money. Because he decided to squander it on some half-baked scheme, cooked up by Jay, and all he cared about was the contents of the fridge.

Farah went back into the kitchen and finished making the sandwiches. After she'd scrubbed down the kitchen tops she squinted and knelt down to take a closer look behind the standing lamp. Her intuition for cleanliness had become quite remarkable.

'Sandwiches ready, or are they hiding behind our lamp?' Mustafa's voice came, soft and sheepish.

She frowned when she looked up at him. Farah noticed his smile falter and tried to rearrange her features.

'It'd be a miracle to hide anything in this place,' she replied.

He cleared his throat as he looked over at the platters in the kitchen. She began wiping the floor as she heard her husband's body shuffling around.

'Come on, no one cares about some dust in the corner,' he said. 'You can't even see it.'

'*I* can see it,' she replied without looking up.

There was a pause.

'Maybe you need the opposite of glasses?' he suggested.

She sat back and looked up at him. What was the point? He was trying — he always did. All this anger just exhausted her, and she was bored of being tired and frustrated — all of the negative feelings, which seemed to wash over her on a daily basis.

'Something to blur my vision?' she asked.

Mustafa took a second.

'Exactly.'

Joking was good. Joking is what Farah's sister, Mae, did all the time and her life seemed to be a lot less complicated. Except Farah had read that it wasn't good to compare your life to another's — she wondered if the same was true if all you wanted was to emulate them.

'At least then I wouldn't have to see everything — you know, just let some things go,' she added.

It all felt too loaded. She needed to master the art of saying things with lightness — her words should be like froth, not lead.

'Are you ready?' she asked.

'Yeah. I'll put those in the car,' he said, indicating towards the trays.

He walked over as Farah got up and brushed down her skirt. She watched his now bulkier frame as he made sure the cling film covered the sandwiches. Despite the weight, there was still something commanding about his figure. The new beard suited him, though he'd let his hair grow longer than she liked. Mustafa looked at the two trays as if confused about how to take them to the car. He put one on top of the other and Farah stopped herself from shouting out that he'd squash the ones at the bottom.

'I'll take that one,' she said, rushing towards him. 'Thanks,' she said, as he handed the top tray over to her. 'I can't believe Mae's finally going to university.'

'She used to be such a cute kid,' he said.

Farah bristled. What did he mean *used to?*

'We all need to grow up one day,' she replied.

She and Mustafa stood opposite each other, trays in hands. Farah remembered, as Mae got older and went to school, learned new things, that Mustafa being their first cousin from their mum's side was not normal for non-Bengalis. Farah recalled the face she'd make as if she were about to throw up. Even now, years later, Mae would sometimes comment on how Farah was cousins with Mustafa one minute and then *sleeping* with him the next. It was usually accompanied by a shudder. The whole thing seemed to perplex her completely. It was a different generation, thought Farah. Things which seemed so normal in their culture had changed so much within the space of a decade.

'Yeah,' said Mustafa, bringing Farah back to the present day. 'I'm just saying.'

He was always *just saying*, not thinking about his words — about the effect they could have on the people around him; namely Farah.

Mustafa added with a smile: 'And at least she's not like . . . ' He paused and seemed to think better of finishing his sentence.

'Like?' Farah asked.

'Nothing.'

'*Like?*'

'Bubblee.' He raised his eyebrows, knowingly, as if this was an inside joke of theirs.

But Farah knew what his jokes really were. They were grievances from before the accident, which he'd remained quiet about, but which somehow now came to the surface.

'I mean,' he added, 'at least Mae likes me.'

Farah avoided his gaze. Even she couldn't lie about how Bubblee, her twin sister, felt about him. He was on medication, he wasn't stupid.

'I don't know who's going to keep Mum and Dad company when Mae's gone,' she said.

'Right.'

'Dad's going to miss her so much.'

Mustafa gave her a sad look — as if he wished she'd contradicted him, told him that was nonsense and that of course Bubblee liked him.

'They'll be fine.' He smiled. 'We're here, aren't we? And anyway, look at it this way, she'll be making trouble elsewhere.'

Here was the problem: Farah thought she had forgiven him for his mistake, for the way in which he'd changed their lives. Being able to feel his arms around her again, it had been impossible not to. At the time. That was the other problem. Time had a way of making things changeable, including feelings, and God knows, hers never seemed to stay the same. At least that was something she and Mustafa had in common.

'Mae doesn't make trouble,' replied Farah.

Mustafa gave her an incredulous look, but flinched, closing his eyes as if in pain.

'Are you all right?' Farah took his tray from

him and put hers down too as she looked up at him.

'Yeah,' he said, shaking his head. 'Just a weird twinge.'

He put his hand to his temple and opened his eyes. She saw the emergence of a smile.

'Why are you smiling? You just looked like you might faint.'

'You look worried,' he replied. He took her hand.

'Oh, you like my face like this, do you?'

Where exactly had this new snappiness come from? She reminded herself more and more of Bubblee by the day. She guessed it was the result of living with the new and not-improved Mustafa.

'Only when it's for me,' said Mustafa.

Farah smiled and shook her head. 'It's a lot easier being worried about you when you're in *this* kind of mood.'

He looked embarrassed. 'I know. I'm sorry, babe. I don't know . . . Sometimes I don't know what comes over me.'

Mustafa kissed her forehead as she forgave him again, because Farah realized that you can't forgive someone just the once. You have to do it every time the same resentment hits you.

'I know,' she said.

They picked up the trays again and made their way towards the car. Farah sat in the driver's seat and took out her phone.

Bubblee: Where are you?? We're all already here, waiting.

8

Mae: Bubs is in cntrl mode. Hurryyyyyy

Fatti: Our baby's going to uni!

Mae: Lol. Im rolin my eyes. N jus so u kno im a woman nw

Bubblee: One who can't spell properly.

Farah: On my way. Mae, honestly. Sometimes it's worth listening to Bubblee.

Farah looked over at Mustafa, in the passenger seat, staring blankly out of the window and tried not to think about how Bubblee felt about him. About them.

Farah: Only sometimes, though.

2

Mae had to listen in to her parents' room. She almost hesitated, as if she were already at university and weaning herself off the habit. She crept along the corridor, bending over the bannisters to make sure the others weren't going to see her, and leaned in to the door. Silence. Why couldn't her parents make eavesdropping easier for her? Then she heard her mum.

'I am just an old woman now.'

Weird. Her mum's tone wasn't resigned, it seemed to ask for a reaction. But of course this was her dad they were talking about. Dad was about as responsive as a tortoise.

'We are both old,' he replied.

Mae rolled her eyes and ambled down the stairs, biting into her home-made cacao-and-chia-seed almond ball. Maybe she was imagining her mum's behaviour becoming erratic. She'd probably taken a leaf out of Mustafa's book. God, her family needed to take a chill pill. All this angst made Mae twitchy — as if she couldn't really concentrate on her own angst, and, hello, she had plenty if this lot would ever allow her to really worry about it. She felt a rush of excitement at the idea of the unending possibilities university would bring. Her life stretched out in front of her into this magically unknown place. She forgot about her parents, her brother-in-law, Mustafa — everything family related — and skipped down the last few steps, accidentally dropping her cacao ball. Oh, well, there were worse things she could let drop.

★ ★ ★

'Fazaroona and Mussie Mustafa. Enter, please.'

Mae bowed down low and outstretched her arm for Farah and Mustafa. For some reason Farah felt tears prickle her eyes. She had an overwhelming feeling of love for the lightness of Mae and prayed that university wouldn't change her.

'Salamalaikum, Mae,' replied Mustafa.

Farah wished he'd joked back with Mae, done a little skit with her, the way he would've done in the past. Now Mae seemed to annoy him. He'd say things like: *Not everything in life is a joke. When is she going to be serious about life?* Despite the fact that Farah would sometimes share this sentiment, she wondered why everyone had to be so serious, anyway. Mae cleared her throat and looked solemn.

'Mustafa Bhai. Deep gratitude for the sandwiches. Very much obliged. I will be eating the filling, these are defo not gluten-free.'

He handed the tray to her as he walked into the house. Mae widened her eyes at Farah as if to say: *Your husband — what a trip.*

'The clan awaits,' said Mae as she and Farah followed Mustafa into the living room.

'Well, it's about time,' exclaimed Bubblee. 'I can make it from London on time but you guys, who live ten minutes away, are late.'

'Nice to see you too, Bubs,' said Farah.

'Bubblee, let your sister sit down before you start shouting at us all,' interrupted their father.

Their mum gave him a long look, and her voice softened as she spoke: 'Listen to your abba.'

But their dad didn't seem to notice their mum staring at him as he took Mustafa's jacket and went to hang it up.

Bubblee embraced Farah in a rather sturdy hug. 'Sorry. Bloody neighbours have a new baby that cries all hours into the morning, and I haven't slept for days.'

Farah looked at Bubblee properly and could see what she meant. She had dark circles, her hair looked as though it needed a wash and without any make-up on, Bubs looked older than usual. Older than Farah did, she was sure, and they were twins.

'The poor baby,' said Fatti, who pushed herself off the sofa. 'You should offer some help to them, you know. I mean, I know you're busy, but if you're tired imagine how the parents must feel.'

Farah observed her oldest sister, Fatti, who was looking rather well. Marriage agreed with her. It looked as though her husband, Ash, was thinking along the same lines. Every time Fatti spoke, he seemed to think it was the most important thing being said. That's how Mustafa used to look at Farah when they got married. She felt a pang of loss in the face of Fatti's gain. *Must not compare lives. MUST. NOT. COMPARE. LIVES.* If only the heart could do what the head told it to.

'Fats,' said Mae. 'I'm sure the parents of the newborn have got enough troubles without you springing Bubblee onto them.'

Bubblee smacked Mae around the head as their mum said: 'Fatti, you must think of having your own babies and stop worrying about someone else's.'

Fatti just looked at her hands.

'Salam, mate,' said Ash, shaking Mustafa's hand.

Farah had to take a minute and appreciate the moment. After everything they'd gone through in the past few years, they were all here together. Apart from Jay.

'Your brother is out making a delivery,' explained her mum. 'He is working very hard now.'

Farah had to admit that it was better than him sitting around, waiting for someone to fix his life. Even if she wanted to she couldn't give him money. And she wouldn't want to — not after he'd turned their lives upside down.

'We should find him a nice wife now,' her mum added.

'Who'd wanna marry him?' exclaimed Mae. 'He's a proper loser.'

'*Mae.*' Their mum narrowed her eyes at her.

'But it's true though, isn't it? I mean, he probably needs another five years before he can even support himself, let alone some poor woman who's got to stay married to him for the rest of her life.'

'Five *years?* A man has *needs*,' said their mum,

pausing meaningfully, looking around the room before her eyes rested on her husband. 'Everyone does.'

The room paused as her family looked at her. 'Eww,' mouthed Mae to her sisters. 'Gross.'

Bubblee and Farah exchanged looks and Fatti never could hide her blushes. Their dad laughed nervously as he said: 'Yes, yes, Jay's amma. Very good. You must be hungry, Mustafa? Hmm? Ashraf? My daughter is feeding you well?'

Farah expected Bubblee to have something to say about a woman having to feed a man — as if they were incapable of doing it themselves — but she stayed quiet.

'Can't you tell?' said Ash, patting his stomach.

'Oh, please,' replied Fatti. 'There's nothing there.'

Mae laughed. 'Yeah, that's because it's all there.' She gestured at Fatti's robust frame, which hadn't diminished with marriage.

'Mae, you could probably do with some of this yourself. Look at how skinny you are. It's not healthy,' replied Fatti, unmoved at the attention brought to her wide hips and thick thighs. She didn't seem to care whether her stomach protruded any more, and she looked the better for it. She no longer slouched or fidgeted with her hands. Farah noticed that Fatti never looked sideways any more before answering a question, as if she wanted to run away from the pressure of giving an answer. Today she was wearing a long burgundy chiffon top over a pair of tapered black trousers. She no longer wore things that were either too tight or too loose. Somewhere along the way she had managed to balance her wardrobe as well as her life. Her hair was loose and curled and she wore the golden bangles that Mum had given her when she got married, rings scattered on her fingers. Farah noticed she was even wearing earrings.

'Fatti's looking well, isn't she?' commented Farah to Bubblee as they went into the kitchen while the others tucked into the buffet already laid out on the table.

'Yeah. Though not sure about the contents of Mum's jewellery box being tipped over her.'

Farah simply sighed. Wearing a pair of dangly earrings might make Bubblee look a little more approachable. She watched her sister's movements as Bubblee put some samosas in the microwave. Farah uncovered the sandwiches.

'Are you okay?' Farah asked.

'Hmm? Yeah, fine.'

'I mean, marriage has completely transformed her,' added Farah.

'Not marriage, Faar. Love. Apparently there's a distinction.'

Farah felt uneasy. She began opening the cupboards but forgot what she was looking for.

'Stupid, anyway,' said Bubblee. 'As if you should need another person to make you feel better about yourself.'

Farah wondered whether having another person was exactly what Bubblee needed. Not that she could tell her that without an argument breaking out.

'What about you?' asked Farah. She lowered her voice, to make sure their parents couldn't hear, although there was enough chatter coming from the living room. 'Are you . . . you know . . . seeing anyone?'

Bubblee flashed her a look.

'I'm your sister,' said Farah. 'Aren't I allowed to ask?'

'As my twin, you should know that such things are low on my list of priorities.'

Bubblee took out some glasses and seemed to avoid Farah's gaze.

'Okay then.' Farah leaned against the kitchen top and folded her arms. 'What is important to you?'

Bubblee's eyes flickered. She placed the glasses down carefully, each one next to the other.

'I'm serious. I'm asking you,' added Farah.

'Being . . . ' Bubblee itched her head. 'Being, you know . . . For God's sake, just *being*.'

Farah paused. 'You know, your life in London as an artist has made you . . . '

'What?'

'Nothing. Is Jay behaving himself here?'

Bubblee shrugged. 'Mae's the one to ask about that. I haven't even seen him yet. Mum and Dad say he's working hard and Mae hasn't contradicted them, so maybe he is.'

'That boy used to tell me everything,' said Farah, staring into space.

'But now you don't want to know. I mean, he never did deserve being your favourite, and now he definitely doesn't.'

'No,' replied Farah.

'It's really quite amazing that Mum and Dad

never seem to mention how he messed up this family. Especially when Mum still hasn't let go of the fact that I decided to move to London for uni and never came back. That was ten years ago.'

Farah gave a vague answer in response and went to leave the kitchen with the sandwiches laid out on plates when Bubblee asked: 'What about you?'

'What about me?' said Farah, turning round.

'What's important to you?'

Bubblee's look seemed to be challenging Farah to something, though she wasn't sure what. The chatter from inside got louder as she heard Mae laugh.

'Family, of course.'

Bubblee raised her eyebrows and for a moment Farah wanted to slam the kitchen door in Bubblee's face. Because she didn't want to admit that her words seemed hollow. That even though her answer was honest, there was something gaping in it. Instead, she tried to look resolute before turning around and walking out of the door.

★   ★   ★

The truth was that Bubblee had just wanted a reaction. She knew she gave everyone a hard time and that it somehow distanced herself from the family — shaped her as the black sheep — and yet she couldn't help herself. She was, as one would say, her own worst enemy. Perhaps it wouldn't have annoyed her as much if she didn't want to be a part of what seemed to be everyone's camaraderie. She listened to Mae's cheer as Farah must've entered the living room and thought about the question her sister had asked her. *What's important to you?* She used to think it was her art. She would spend every day trying to create something innovative and brilliant, and after so many years in London, after so many tried and failed starts, she realized the stark truth of it all: she was a hack. She put her hands to her eyes because the last thing she needed was to fall apart in her parents' kitchen. Bubblee was no longer sure whether she was ashamed because she'd failed herself, or because she didn't want to hear *I told you so* from her family. The two had somehow become inseparable and she wasn't able to untangle them, or herself, it seemed. She thought of Fatti, the one who'd probably gone through the most in the past few years, only to come out on top, really. She shone. The one who used to cast shadows now cast light. Bubblee laughed at the ironies of life. The sheer inconsistencies that could make a person stumble from the shock of change.

'Yo! Bubs. You gonna stay in here all day? Thought you feminist types hated the kitchen.'

Mae was chomping on a celery stick.

'Just eat a samosa, you brat.'

Mae laughed. 'No, thanks. I'd rather let my arteries breathe.'

'Arteries don't breathe,' replied Bubblee.

'Whatevs.'

Bubblee regarded her little sister. So slight and pretty, pixie-like — full of energy and life. She

18

envied the way the future was laid out in front of Mae. There was no doubt she'd thrive. Things would fall into place for her because nothing seemed to bother her — there were no insecurities, no second-guessing. God, how depressing. Bubblee wanted to *be* Mae. She shook her head.

'Are you, like, having a spasm?' said Mae, scrunching up her face.

'Shut up and take these samosas in.'

'Sure thing.'

They were leaving the kitchen as Bubblee asked: 'What's wrong with our mum, by the way? She's acting a bit weird.'

'God knows.' Mae gave an exaggerated shiver. 'Ugh. *Needs.* What was that?'

It was odd, but then people were always going on about men's needs. No one else's seemed to matter. Bubblee scoffed. It was just typical. Bubblee noticed the colour had risen in Mae's cheeks.

'I hope university opens up your mind a little to feminism and sexuality.'

Mae looked at her, hesitating. 'Bubs, can I ask . . . Have you . . . ?'

'What?'

'Have you . . . had *sex*?' whispered Mae.

'That's none of your business,' said Bubblee, raising her head.

Mae stopped. 'But you're not married.'

Mae seemed to consider it, looking by turn amazed and bewildered. Living in a small village with her traditional parents had done nothing for Mae, but Bubblee couldn't help her own heart from beating faster.

'We're not talking about what is, essentially, a person's private matter,' replied Bubblee. She walked past Mae, into the living room, adamant that she'd not let her flushed face prevent her from acting normally.

⋆　⋆　⋆

They'd all eaten, cleared the table and were sitting around, drinking tea and eating jalebis. After so much gabbing and noise that was brought about by too many people trying to fill their bellies, a quiet calm had descended upon them. Farah felt content as she watched Mustafa talk to Fatti. It wasn't as if they had a new-found bond since discovering they were actually brother and sister, but there was a respect that they showed each other, which Farah felt comforted by. Their dad stood up, unexpectedly.

'Okay, okay. Listen now.'

Everyone turned their heads towards him. He brushed down his brown trousers before patting his dyed jet-black hair.

'Mae is leaving us.'

Farah noticed Mae look at Fatti.

'I'm not dying, Abba,' said Mae.

'Tst tst, such things you say,' said her mum. 'You will give yourself the evil eye.'

'Mae is leaving us,' repeated their dad.

'Yeah, rather unfairly since none of us were allowed to leave home for university,' said Farah.

She'd have liked the chance to be alone and independent. Fatti never seemed to have the desire, but if Farah had known it was within the realms of possibility there's no way she'd have passed up the opportunity. As for Bubblee, she didn't care about whether the opportunity was there or not — she created it for herself, no matter how much their parents, especially their mum, had told her she couldn't.

'Can you let Dad speak?' said Mae. 'Finally it's something about me rather than you lot. Go on, Abba.'

Mae settled into the sofa, curling her feet under her and holding on to her mug of hibiscus tea.

'Mae, we hope you will be a good girl and come home every weekend.'

There was a pause.

'Is that it?' Mae asked.

Farah had to suppress a laugh. Their dad cleared his throat, seeming to struggle for words.

'Uff, Jay's abba. Hurry up,' said their mum.

'Study the media well,' he added. 'It is very bad and maybe you will fix it.'

'God help us if Mae's about to help to fix the world,' retorted Bubblee.

Mae leapt off the sofa and gave her dad a hug. 'Thanks, Abba.'

He held on to her and kissed the top of her head. Farah noticed Mae looking at Fatti again. Farah glanced at Fatti who was shaking her head.

'What's going on?' asked Farah, her eyes darting between both of them.

'What? Nothing,' said Fatti.

Only now Ash was looking at her too. Fatti seemed to be suppressing a smile as her hand went to her stomach.

'Well, the thing is . . . '

'She's only preggers, isn't she?' interjected Mae, beaming.

Their mum and dad seemed confused.

'With a baby, Amma and Abba,' explained Mae. 'Up the duff — having a baby.'

Mae gestured a large curve around her stomach with her hands. Their parents looked at Fatti as Farah saw her mum's eyes fill with tears.

'Allah, you are great,' exclaimed her mum.

Before Farah knew it everyone was standing up, hugging each other. Mustafa gripped Ash's hand, a constrained smile on his face as Bubblee kissed Fatti on both cheeks.

'How come she got to know before the rest of us?' said Bubblee, pointing at Mae.

Mae put her arm around Bubblee and said: 'A, I am a very approachable person, thank you very much, and B, I'm her favourite sister.'

Mae went and took her place back on the sofa.

'I'm only three weeks,' said Fatti. 'I don't even have any symptoms yet.'

'We mustn't tell anyone,' their mum said. 'Not until after three months or you might get the evil eye.'

Farah realized she hadn't moved from her spot when Fatti looked at her. She got up as quickly as she could to hug her sister.

'Congratulations, Fatti.'

Farah felt a lump in her throat. Something pushed up through her chest and caused tears to surface; she wanted to run out of the room and cry in the bathroom, on her own. She blinked them back before anyone could see but caught Mustafa's eye.

'It's *such* good news,' she added, releasing herself from Fatti's grip and grabbing on to her arms.

'Thanks, Faru.'

Fatti stared at her for too long. Farah saw the pity in her eyes so starkly that it didn't matter how much she blinked back her tears, they still fell down her cheeks — no amount of smiling could hide them.

'I'm sorry,' whispered Fatti.

Farah just shook her head and tried to laugh. 'What for? This is great news.'

Before Fatti could say anything else she was swept away by her mum who began to give instructions on how to be pregnant. There was something not quite right about their mum's excitement in telling Fatti what to eat and what to do when she had never actually carried Fatti. Surely Farah's parents' first grandchild should've been hers — the daughter their mum held in her womb. Farah instantly regretted the thought. Fatti was their sister! Even if it was their mother's sister who had given birth to her. It was amazing what an unfulfilled desire could do to a person; how the tendrils of jealousy and resentment could so easily dig into a person's mind. Farah thought she was better than that. She was meant to be the contented and sensible one, after all: the glue that kept them all together. But somehow, with time, the role had been co-opted by Fatti and neither of them had even realized it.

'I'd have bet good money that Fatti, *of all people*, would have been the first one of us to have a baby,' laughed Farah.

It was meant to be a joke but everyone's voices quietened as they looked at Farah. She realized the joke wasn't actually funny, but had to maintain her smile. Fatti was staring at her, but with the same pity she'd shown earlier, and it made Farah want to shake her and say: *You weren't always this good and happy. Have you forgotten who you are?*

'We never thought she'd even find anyone to marry her,' added Farah.

The words were right but the order was coming out all jumbled, or the intonation was wrong. Ash's face was no longer open and kind — it seemed hard, daring Farah to continue.

'Not like that. I mean, then she found you, Ash. And you took her off our hands.'

'Far . . . ' Bubblee was looking at Farah. Her sister's exhausted face seemed fully alert now.

'What? I mean he did, didn't he?' Farah laughed again. 'Remember Fats and her stuffing Primula cheese down her face? The mashed prawns and secret stashes of food in her bedside drawers? You know prawns aren't allowed when you're pregnant?' She paused, the silence oppressing her. 'Maybe Amma's already told you that?'

'I think you should stop.' Ash was staring at Farah, his eyes intense, hands gripped together.

'No,' said Farah, trying to make them

24

understand she wasn't saying anything wrong — just pointing out the irony of it all. 'We're all *happy* she's pregnant. A few years ago the only thing she had in her life was her hand modelling and now look . . . a husband with his own driving-school business — working with him like they're a power couple, a whole new *look* as well.' Farah's smile was faltering; she could feel it strain under the pressure of appearances. 'You all remember how Fatti was, don't you? It's against all the odds.'

'Farah . . . ' began Mustafa.

'I'm just — '

'*Stop*,' exclaimed Ash.

'All right,' said Mustafa, shooting a look at Ash. 'There's no need to use that tone.'

His voice rang out as clear as Ash's. It was the most emphatic Farah had heard him.

'Then she should stop.' Ash was looking at Mustafa now too.

Before anyone could say anything else their mum clapped her hands together as if giving a round of applause. When she didn't speak their dad said: 'Who wants more tea?'

'Jeez,' muttered Mae.

'I'll have one,' said Bubblee, still looking at Farah. 'Ash?'

He was rubbing his palms, eyebrows knit together. 'No, thank you. Perhaps it's time for us to go.'

Farah's stomach had turned into knots of anxiety as she looked at Fatti. *Please don't leave. I didn't mean it like that.* But the words — the ones she should actually be saying — failed to come out. She hoped her look said it all. Farah waited for Fatti to speak. The seconds seemed to stretch into hours.

'No, we'll stay,' replied Fatti. 'I'll have one too. Peppermint.'

Fatti walked into the kitchen with Bubblee, leaving Farah behind in a room filled with silence.

★ ★ ★

Bubblee turned around and faced Fatti. 'You know it's because — '

'I know,' replied Fatti.

Fatti had been aware that it wasn't going to be easy, not with Farah having wanted a child so badly, but she'd thought that perhaps Farah had now accepted it and let go of that want. Of course, you can't let go of it because it's not in your control. It holds on to you, not the other way around.

'And she didn't mean — '

'Yes, she did,' said Fatti.

Fatti turned her back to Bubblee, filling the kettle with water. The truth was that Fatti knew she'd never escape who she used to be, but at the same time she didn't want to. It was fine with her that she used to be nervous and shy and never felt as though she belonged. It made the place she was in now all the more miraculous. What she didn't like was the idea that her sister thought the old Fatti was still inside her somewhere. As if Fatti's happiness, her whole persona, was a phase. Because she didn't feel

26

that different. It was more like being stripped of the negative stuff rather than it being buried. Fatti had peeled back the unwanted layers of who she was. And though she felt bad for Farah, surely Fatti deserved some sympathy for finding out her parents weren't her biological ones, for going to meet them in Bangladesh, only to find out they didn't regret giving her up one bit. But Fatti let go of that because she no longer wanted to be unhappy. Having Ash helped. It helped a great, great deal.

'Okay,' said Bubblee. 'That wasn't — '

'Forget it.' Fatti turned around and gave Bubblee a smile. 'Let's just forget the whole thing.'

Bubblee began warming some milk in a pan. 'So, you and Ash are helping to overpopulate the earth then.'

Fatti saw Bubblee was smiling.

'Yes. I'm sure you disagree.'

'How does your stepson feel about it?'

'You know, I think he's actually excited,' replied Fatti.

Bubblee looked incredulous. 'Excited? Sounds a bit far-fetched.'

'Well, he didn't stomp off to his room or tell Ash how much he hates him, so I'm going to take it as a positive sign.'

'Gosh. I guess so,' said Bubblee.

'You're going to be an aunt,' said Fatti.

Bubblee's smile met her eyes. She really was so beautiful, even if she wasn't looking her freshest.

'Will I have to babysit every time I come to visit?'

27

Fatti shook her head. 'But I am going to make sure my child likes you the least.'

Bubblee looked so genuinely hurt that Fatti laughed and gave her a kiss on the cheek.

'We weren't made to be alone, Bubs,' said Fatti. 'Don't try so hard to be different that you end up not getting what you actually need.'

Bubblee put teabags into the mugs. 'Oh, right, what do I need then?'

Fatti considered her younger sister. There was so much there, if only she'd stop being so . . . well, *Bubblee*. As much as Fatti hated to admit it, who would put up with someone so difficult? Bubblee was lucky she was beautiful because Fatti supposed it'd make it easier for her to find a husband. Probably not Bengali, though. No, Bubblee would have to marry a non-brown person. Fatti would help her when it came to Mum and Dad. It would be good if she managed to find a nice Bengali boy, though. Someone who loved Bubblee for who she was. She'd never have said all this stuff out loud, of course — it made her sound positively backward — but she couldn't help feeling it. Happiness comes from the people who love you, and who you manage to love back. It's just the way it is.

'Well, you'll know when you find it.'

Just then, they heard Jay's voice break the silence in the room as Mae told him that Fatti was pregnant. He appeared at the kitchen door, tall and slim, wearing a sweatshirt and trainers, hair flopping over his eyes.

'Congratulations, Uncle Jay,' said Fatti.

28

He smiled and hit Fatti on the arm before hugging her. 'Better steal some of those kids' toys I deliver then.'

'*This* is the man Mum wants to subject some poor woman to?' said Bubblee.

'How's . . . ' He cleared his throat. 'How's Farah taken it?'

Fatti just gave a simple smile.

'Always asking the right questions, Jay,' said Bubblee with barely hidden sarcasm.

'And how long are you planning to stay?' he asked her.

She looked away, turning the heat down on the hob. Fatti just about made out Bubblee shrugging before they were called into the living room by their mum. The three entered the room, puncturing the silence, as Bubblee wondered how long she could stay without her family asking her questions about where her life was going.

⋆ ⋆ ⋆

That night, as Farah got into bed she thought over the evening's events. Why had she said those things? She turned over and looked at Mustafa, his back to her. He'd hardly said a word when they got into the car and she drove them home in silence. Since the accident Mustafa was no longer allowed to drive, in case he had a seizure — just another one of the many changes their life had undergone. She looked on the other side of her bed, at the empty space where a baby's cot would easily fit. The light on her phone disturbed her as she checked it and saw the messages.

Fatti: Goodnight. Xxx

Mae: Nyt losers xxx

Bubblee: Goodnight. Mae, I can hear you on your laptop from here. Mum and Dad probably can't get to sleep because of you.

Mae: Whatevs. Usin da old folks as an xcuse cos u hv ears lyk a bat.

Farah: Goodnight. I am happy for you, Fats. Xx

Fatti: I know xxxx

Farah is typing . . .
I'm dying a little inside. I want to be happy for you. But I'm too sad for me right now. I can't find the light at the end of this tunnel.

★   ★   ★

Farah then deleted her message and turned around in bed, hoping for sleep.

3

Farah was happy for Fatti. At least she would be just as soon as her own life caught up with her sister's. She put her phone away and reached over for Mustafa.

'Are you awake?' she whispered, putting her arm around him.

There was a pause. 'Hmm.'

Farah stroked his chest. She knew he liked the way she curled his hairs around her fingers. Farah used to like it too, until it became a bit arduous; another hurdle in the obstacle of impregnation.

'Want to try and make a baby?'

He turned his head. 'What?'

She attempted to give him her most seductive look.

'Are you all right?' he asked. 'You look like you might cry.'

She paused, biting back her surge of anger.

'Cry?' she carried on whispering. 'Only if you make me.'

Her hand slid down his torso when he turned around towards her fully. 'I'm not in the mood, babe.'

He brushed the hair away from her forehead and planted a kiss on her brow.

'What about me?' she asked.

She was no longer whispering, but she tried to keep the accusation out of her voice. He looked at her for a moment and gave a tight smile.

'It's been a bit of a night,' he said. 'Aren't you exhausted? Let's sleep.'

How was her slim chance of getting pregnant ever going to happen if her husband didn't sleep with her? Mustafa turned his back again but she pulled him towards her. All it took was one time. This night had to be it. It felt fortuitous with Fatti's pregnancy. If she could get happily married and start a family, then Farah could surely get pregnant and happy too. If only her husband would let her.

'All the night's made me want to do is . . . '

She put her hand between his legs, but he moved it gently away.

'Come on, babe. I'm serious.'

One time. Just the once and they'd be done. Her family would stop looking at her with such pity, and words that didn't seem to belong to her would stop spilling out of her mouth, causing other people pain.

'So am I.'

She pulled his face towards her and kissed him. His mouth tasted minty and his beard bristled on her face. She had a memory of the way they used to kiss and it stirred something up inside her.

'Farah,' he mumbled.

'Mhmm.'

'Farah, stop.' He pulled away, looking at her. 'What's got into you?'

Why was he being so difficult? After the way the night had gone, how could he not want to make it better by giving her just *one* chance?

'*Me?*' she said, sitting up. 'I'm your wife. How are we ever going to get pregnant if we don't have sex?'

He took a deep breath and sat up with her. 'I didn't know we were trying again.'

'We should *always* be trying.'

'Listen, I know this thing with Fatti must be hard for you right now, but I told you, I'm not in the mood.'

'Oh, of course, your mood.'

He rubbed his forehead. 'If this was the other way around you know that I'd never force you.'

She scoffed. 'I didn't realize sleeping with me was such a task.'

'I didn't mean it like that.'

Farah tried to relax — tension didn't help getting pregnant, that's what numerous articles and bloggers said. It's all about de-stressing as well as things like ovulation and science.

'Well then?' She put her hand on his face, stroking his beard.

He patted her hand and went to move it away, but she kept it there, forcing it to his face.

'For God's sake, Farah,' he shouted.

He pushed her away and leapt out of bed. She leaned back, pulling the covers over her. Mustafa's shadow seemed to her foreboding and foreign in that moment, and her heart began to thud.

'Mustafa . . . '

'What the hell are you playing at? What's *wrong* with you?'

He said it with such a look of disgust it brought unexpected tears to her eyes. *Everything is wrong with me. I'm a woman who can't even have a baby.* She knew she shouldn't think like this because that's not all a woman is, but she couldn't help feeling it. She'd wanted a family of her own since she could remember. So many years had been spent trying and dreaming of what it would be like that she didn't know how to want anything else. It'd be like teaching herself not to breathe.

'Don't make *me* feel bad, because *you* can't conceive,' he added.

Before she could even take in the words he'd spouted, he'd left the room, slamming the door behind him.

'Oh, God,' she whispered, putting her hands to her face and letting the stream of tears come out.

That night she sobbed herself into a dreamless sleep.

★　★　★

When Farah woke up the following morning her eyes felt sore and her vision was blurred. She reached out to Mustafa's side of the bed and when she realized he wasn't there the preceding night came back to her. She closed her eyes again and put her head under the cover, trying to block out the all-in-one shame of rejection and accusation.

Did Mustafa not want a family any more, or did he just not want her? Did he really blame her as much as she blamed herself? She hadn't ever imagined a Mustafa who'd say such a thing. All this culpability really did exhaust her. She kept her eyes closed until she fell asleep again.

This time Farah awoke to clattering. It was coming from the kitchen. As she swung her legs over the bed she still couldn't open her eyes. She grabbed her dressing gown and pulled it over herself, trying to steady her feet. The words beat in her ears: *Don't make me feel bad because you can't conceive.* She opened her eyes as her face flushed in anger. She didn't need her husband to feel the same way she felt about herself. That's not how it worked with them. It never had and it wouldn't damn well start now.

She ran down the stairs without even brushing her teeth or washing her face, the gunk from last night's make-up gathered in the corners of her eyes. Farah burst through the living room that led to the kitchen, ready to point her finger at Mustafa and shout at him. She wasn't sure what she'd say yet, but anger was best served improvised. She stopped. He was hunched over the hob, frying some eggs. Their small table was set with two plates and cutlery. Mustafa turned his head towards her, giving her such a sad smile that all her anger fell away.

'Hi,' he said.

She looked at the table again.

'I made us breakfast,' he added when she didn't speak.

'I see that.'

He went to the fridge. 'Juice?'

She shook her head.

'Coffee or tea?' he asked.

'Is this — '

'I'm sorry,' he interrupted. He paused, looking dishevelled in his shorts and T-shirt. 'I don't even know what I said.'

'You said not having babies was my fault.'

Mustafa bowed his head. She thought he might let the carton of juice fall to the floor the way it dangled in his hands.

'I lost my temper,' he said, head still bowed.

When he looked up Farah saw tears in his eyes. She had the urge to go up to him and hug him, but couldn't bring herself to move.

'Yeah, you did.'

She saw the flash of something in his eyes — was that anger again? Mustafa looked as though he might say something.

'What?' she asked.

He paused. 'Nothing.'

She went and took a seat at the table. 'Go on,' she encouraged him.

'It just . . . forget it,' he finally said.

He put the carton down and brought the rest of the breakfast to the table, setting his pills beside his plate. They ate in silence for a while. Farah kept looking at her husband, biting into his eggs and toast, taking a sip of tea with a faraway look. He downed the pills.

'Do you still . . . ' Farah gripped her mug of tea tighter. 'The baby — you still want one, don't you?'

'Hmm?' Mustafa looked up at her.

'It's like you're on another planet,' she said. 'Did you hear me?'

She couldn't quite read his expression.

'Sorry,' he said.

36

'Do you still want a baby?'

Mustafa leaned forward and took Farah's hand as she put her mug down.

'I want *us*.'

She looked at him, confused. 'We have us. Us is sat right here.'

But even as the words came out she knew how hollow they were. Mustafa let go of her hand and just gave a small smile.

'Fatti and Ash seem really happy, don't they?' he said.

She nodded.

'She deserves it,' he added.

'She does.'

Farah played with the toast in her hands.

'You want more tea?' he asked.

Just then the phone rang. Farah went to pick it up and it was Bubblee.

'You all right?' Bubblee asked.

The scene from Mae's party pushed itself to the fore of Farah's brain.

'Yeah, great. Fine. What's going on?'

Bubblee paused. 'Not much.'

'What time are you leaving for London?'

'You know, I thought with Mae leaving at the end of the week and all . . . I thought I might as well stay,' replied Bubblee.

'Oh. Right.'

Bubblee paused again. All this pausing didn't suit her. Farah glanced over at Mustafa who was stabbing at his eggs and realized she wasn't listening to Bubblee's response.

' . . . another week or so.'

'Okay. What about work?' asked Farah, turning

back so Mustafa stopped distracting her.

Pause.

'I've got some holidays. Plus, Sasha can cover for me at the gallery while I'm here.'

Farah wondered why Bubblee would forsake an extra week out of London to be in Wyvernage with her family, but she looked over her shoulder and Mustafa was still staring at his plate. She told Bubblee to come over later — better than going to her parents' house and risk seeing Fatti — and put the phone down.

'Do you want to go to watch a film later?' she asked.

He looked up at her and smiled. 'Yeah. That would be good, I think.'

Farah went back to the table. Perhaps if the film was good and put Mustafa in a better mood, he'd sleep with her and she'd get pregnant. Farah knew that the key was to try and make Mustafa feel *normal*. Those pills didn't help, but they were necessary. Yes, they would come back from the cinema, have sex, she'd get pregnant and then all these problems would go away. With that thought Farah finished her breakfast, enjoying the toast a lot more with the hope of what was to come.

★　★　★

Bubblee knocked on the door.

'Oh,' said Farah, opening the door and looking surprised. 'Oh, yes, sorry. I knew you were coming over.'

She looked at Bubblee as if she wished she'd

do an about-turn and leave the way she had come.

'You're going out?' Bubblee asked.

'To the cinema. Come with us,' said Farah, smiling widely.

She was rushing around the house, fluffing pillows, getting her keys and purse, talking to herself: *Dishes washed, laundry out, vacuum done . . .* Farah surveyed the place around her, looking pleased. But there was something twitchy about her movements. She looked far too keen and chirpy.

Bubblee stared at Farah. 'Not really in the mood for it.'

'To be honest, babe, I've kind of lost interest too,' replied Mustafa, taking his jacket off.

Bubblee sat on the sofa as Farah stood in the passageway door. Bubblee looked for signs of disgruntlement. Interfering was Mae's job but with her going away and the image of poor Fatti's face when they were in the kitchen last night — well, Bubblee had to do something. Even if it was against her better inclination.

'Come on, you guys,' said Farah. 'It's meant to be a psychological thriller. Mus, you love those.'

Bubblee looked over at her brother-in-law whose back was turned as he'd gone into the kitchen. Even his gait annoyed Bubblee. She supposed that once upon a time he'd have been called 'jolly', the way he'd waltz into a room, slap people on the back and laugh so hard that his shoulders shook. Now he was like a retired comedian, or circus clown. Yes, it was a mean thing to say, but that didn't make it any less true.

Plus, at least Bubblee didn't say it out loud. It wasn't her fault that her brother-in-law had descended into being pathetic.

'Would you like a drink?' he asked her.

'No, thanks. Bought any nice new things?' Bubblee asked Farah, bouncing up off the sofa with uncharacteristic alacrity.

'What?' asked Farah. 'No.'

Stupid question to ask because Farah couldn't even if she wanted to — not with their dire financial issues.

'Show me.'

Bubblee jerked her head towards the stairs as Farah looked on, confused.

'I don't — '

'Great,' interrupted Bubblee, pushing past Farah and up the stairs already.

'What was that about?' asked Farah as she walked into the bedroom after Bubblee.

Bubblee folded her arms and looked at her sister.

'First tell me what yesterday was about.'

Farah's eyebrows knit into a frown as she looked shiftily around the room.

'Well?' said Bubblee in the face of Farah's silence. 'Listen, I'm all for straight talk but you should apologize to Fatti.'

Farah paused. 'Oh. Did she say something to you?'

'Come on, it's Fatti, she'll never say anything to anyone. Anyway, does she really need to?'

'I wasn't being offensive,' Farah replied as she walked over to the blinds and began trying to fix them.

Bubblee raised her eyebrows.

'Not on purpose,' Farah added. 'God, you're making it sound worse than it was.'

'I think the blinds are straight enough,' said Bubblee.

'Me and Mus were meant to go and see a film.'

Bubblee watched Farah pause and sway so that she thought she might faint. But Farah just went and sat on the edge of the bed. Bubblee noticed she was still looking at the blinds.

'They're still not straight,' said Farah.

She went to get up again but Bubblee was blocking her way.

'What is wrong with you?' said Bubblee.

'Nothing, I'm . . . ' Farah's voice wavered. 'It's just . . . oh, Bubs — why can't I have a baby?'

The tears began to stream down Farah's face as Bubblee sat next to her and put her arm around her. She sobbed into her arms for such a long time Bubblee worried that Mustafa would come up and ask what was going on.

'Shh, it's okay,' said Bubblee.

She looked at her sister's tear-strewn face and felt several pangs of sympathy.

'It must be hard,' Bubblee offered.

'*Hard?*' said Farah, wiping her eyes. 'It's . . . it's . . . ' Farah looked around the room, frantically, as if she'd find what it was in their bedroom. Her eyes settled upon Bubblee again.

'But you don't get it, do you?' said Farah. 'You've never really cared about having babies.'

It was true. Finding prolonged sympathy for Farah's problem was going to be difficult — but she could understand the feeling of loss, of not getting what you want. Wasn't every single atom of passion that she poured into her work — her labour of love — amounting to nothing?

'No. They cry an awful lot.'

Farah shot her a look.

'Well,' said Bubblee. 'I just don't understand the need to have them, but I do get what it feels like when you can't have what you want.'

Farah looked at her. 'Were you seeing someone?'

'No. Not everything has to do with relationships.' Bubblee looked at the ground. 'Things just aren't really working out. With the art scene.'

As soon as the words escaped her Bubblee knew them to be true. It was a long-held secret that could only become fact once she'd said it out loud. Now, expecting to have felt a release of some kind, Bubblee just felt numb.

'It's the only thing I thought I was any good at and now . . . I don't know what I'm meant to do with myself. My whole life. So, no. I don't get the need for babies, but I get the idea of needs.' She turned to Farah. 'That gaping hole.'

Bubblee could finally share this with someone, and what's more, she could share it with her twin sister, who'd always been so different from her.

Farah's brows twitched. 'Bubs, it's hardly the same thing.'

'Sorry?'

'Not being able to make sculptures isn't the same as not being able to make babies.'

Bubblee felt the warmth of her blood rushing to her face.

'I mean, I'm sorry to hear it. I know what it meant to you, of course. But you can't tell me not having a family is like no longer being able to . . . ' She waved her arms around, scrunching up her face, presumably to impersonate what was Bubblee's livelihood. ' . . . you know.'

Bubblee's tongue felt glued to the roof of her mouth. A barrage of things to say were exploding in her mind, but couldn't make their way out as she stared at her sister: the one she'd shared a womb with, birthdays and playtimes as they grew up; the person with whom she'd shared her secrets.

'I'm sorry,' said Bubblee, her voice even and cold. 'I didn't realize your husband wasn't your family.'

She didn't even care about Mustafa. She never thought he was good enough for Farah when they got married, and he certainly hadn't improved in her estimation since he'd lost their money and had that godawful car crash. At least before he was tame and negligible. Now you never knew what might come out of his mouth.

'Husbands don't make families — children do,' said Farah.

Farah's eyes went to the bedroom door, and there was Mustafa, standing with his hand on the doorknob.

'Sorry,' he said. 'I just wondered what you guys were doing.'

Bubblee saw Farah swallow hard.

'I'm going to go out, okay?' he said.

Without waiting for a reply he turned around and closed the door behind him.

'Oh, God, do you think he heard?' asked Farah, looking at Bubblee in despair.

'Doesn't seem like you really care either way.'

'What? Of course I care. I just need more than him. Is that so bad?'

Bubblee barely recognized her sister. When did she go from being the foundation of this family, the go-to person with the ever-straightforward-yet-wise advice, to this woman who couldn't see past her own ovaries? Bubblee stood up and went to leave.

'Where are you going?' asked Farah.

'Home.'

'Are you annoyed because of what I said about your art stuff?'

'You feel how you feel.' Bubblee looked at her sister. She wouldn't waste time trying to justify her needs and wants and losses. 'I don't know why I'm expected to feel more for you, though.'

She followed in Mustafa's footsteps, out of the bedroom, closing the door behind her, before leaving the house.

★　★　★

Mustafa didn't come home until late and Farah was already in bed, pretending to be asleep. She felt him slide in beside her and wondered if she should turn around and say something. What would she say, though? Sorry? If he had any sense in him he'd know what she meant, and he couldn't possibly feel that just the two of them was enough. Not any more. It was a missed opportunity in terms of trying to have sex, but she couldn't bear looking at his doleful face. Tomorrow Farah would go to the doctor because every problem has a solution, and she had to find theirs.

⋆ ⋆ ⋆

'Have you considered other options?'

Farah wished the doctor was female. The greying man looked at her as if he were her teacher and she hadn't prepared for her class quiz.

'I know you tried IVF before, but you might like to — '

'No,' interrupted Farah. 'We can't afford to try again.'

She remembered the hormone injections, the failed pregnancy tests, the spiralling of hope that would expand and contract but never amount to anything. The doctor cleared his throat and adjusted his navy tie.

'What about surrogacy?'

He wasn't getting it at all.

'Our finances. We can't.'

And another woman carrying her child? No, thank you.

'Well,' he continued. 'Let's put you in for a transvaginal scan. The last lap-and-dye wasn't successful, but let's check that again and see what results we get. In the meantime, take some time to think about what I've said. Speak with your partner. Also, here are some leaflets with numbers for counselling. Trying for a baby can take its emotional toll on a couple.'

I don't need more leaflets; I need you to tell me how to conceive. Maybe the results this time would be different? Her heart beat faster at the thought — a knot of anxiety forming in the pit of her stomach. She took the leaflets he was handing to her and left the surgery.

Farah looked out into the cloudy sky and the town that seemed as oppressed under the bleakness as she felt. She took out her phone and waited a few moments before pressing on Fatti's name.

'Hello.'

'Hi,' Farah replied.

'How are you?' said Fatti, as if nothing had happened between them.

Farah had to admit her sister was a better person than her. She really did deserve to be happier.

'Fine, fine. You?'

'Not so — not so bad. Good. Oh, God, sorry . . . '

'Hello? Fatti?'

Where had she gone?

'Fatti? What's happening?'

Farah hung up and then dialled the number again. She had to do this a few times before Fatti picked up.

'What happened?' Farah asked.

'Sorry, it's just this . . . morning sickness,' she mumbled.

Farah stood by her car, ready to open the door, but paused. 'Oh.'

'Sorry.'

She leaned against the car door and closed her

eyes. This couldn't go on indefinitely. She was going to be an aunt.

'Don't be, Fats. I'm sorry you're getting sick.'

'It's fine. Part and parcel of it,' replied Fatti.

There was a long pause.

'Well, I'd better go,' said Farah.

'Where are you?'

'Just some errands before getting back to work. I wanted to call and see how you were.'

'Oh, God, sorry. I have to go again.'

Before Farah could say anything Fatti had already hung up, leaving her with the taste of bile in her own mouth.

★ ★ ★

That evening Farah went straight home after work, rather than popping in to see her parents, which she often did.

'What happened at the doctor's?' asked Mustafa when he walked through the door.

'More tests.'

Mustafa threw his house keys on the table as he collapsed on the sofa. The smell of manure had already reached Farah who was standing on a chair, dusting the curtains. Every time she looked around the living room it seemed so worn, no matter how clean she kept it. The black leather sofa had rips in it and the flooring was scratched and dull.

'You need a shower,' she said. 'Maybe you should try and see what other jobs there are. You know, instead of cleaning out stables.'

'What else is there around here?' he said.

Farah paused. 'I don't know. We can have a look.'

When there was silence she looked over her shoulder and saw that Mustafa was staring at her.

'You know you'll be all right,' he said.

If he could just have said *we'll be all right*, she wouldn't, that moment, have wished he hadn't bothered to come home at all.

'What's for dinner?'

He went into the kitchen and saw that there was no dinner. She'd started cleaning as soon as she got home and wasn't even thinking of food. Farah was about to retort with something when he said: 'Don't worry. Shall I make us some pasta or something?'

This was the thing: at times like these he was so different from what anyone would expect from a typical Bengali husband that she couldn't be annoyed at him for too long. His moods were just a glitch. This was the real him. Farah got down from her chair and sat on it.

'The doctor said we should think about IVF again,' she said.

She decided not to mention the counselling. They'd get through this together. He was about to say something when she added: 'Don't worry. I've already told him we couldn't afford another round.'

Suddenly, she realized Mustafa's eyes were filled with tears.

'Sorry, babe,' he said, wiping them away. 'I just never thought it'd be this hard, you know?'

She went and put her arms around him — he

did want a baby, after all. It was 'we', not just her.

'I know,' she said into his ear. 'The doctor even suggested surrogacy if we have no luck.'

Mustafa looked at her and frowned. 'That would be weird. I don't like the idea of some stranger carrying our baby.'

'No,' she agreed. Still, she half wished he'd try to talk her around the idea, but who knew what the test results would show? Perhaps they would get good news after all.

'No, you're right,' she added. 'Nor do I.'

Mae: Its lyk no I evn cares im leavin in 5 DAYS.

Mae: Helloooooo??

Mae: None of u can com to my campus.

Fatti: Been sick all day. In bed. Will come and see you on Friday xxx

Bubblee: Mae, stop being so dramatic.

Mae: I think Im gonna take a module in drama

Bubblee: God help us all.

Mae: Helloooo, Fazzler? Rmba us? Ur sisters?

Farah: Had errands. I'll pop over Friday too. GTG X

4

Mae opened the door and saw Farah shifting on her feet, carrying a box.

'Why didn't you just use your key?' said Mae, rolling her eyes. 'I've got too many boxes and Mum says I can't take my juicer. I mean, hello? It's not like any of you lot are going to be making kale smoothies.'

Farah walked in and simply greeted this with: 'Oh.'

'Thanks for the sympths. Hope your packing powers are better,' Mae said, striding up the stairs, leaving Farah behind.

'Well, she's here at last,' said Mae, going into her room where Bubblee was throwing some of Mae's clothes into a black bin bag for charity.

'Oi, no! I want those,' exclaimed Mae.

Bubblee held up the beige cargo pants in disdain. She just shook her head and chucked them back in the cupboard. Fatti was lying down, her eyes covered with her arm and a leg dangling off the edge of the bed.

'I'll be better in a minute,' she mumbled.

Mae went over and put her hand on her forehead.

'She doesn't have a temperature,' said Bubblee. 'She has a baby.'

Mae looked at Fatti, her brow knitted in concern.

'You were all right last week,' she said.

'Evil eye.'

The three girls turned around to see their mum looming at the door and watching Fatti with a look Mae didn't quite recognize.

'Yeah, thanks, Amma. That's gonna make her feel loads better,' retorted Mae. 'And who's given her this evil eye?'

As if on cue, Farah appeared next to her mum, holding a box and looking into the room. Under normal circumstances Mae would've laughed. Only, it was a bit of a coincidence and it made her feel uneasy. Because Farah was not being Farah. That wasn't to say she was going around cursing people with bad health, obviously, but still.

'You've not got very far, have you?' said Farah, eyeing Mae's room: the empty boxes stacked in a corner, bin bags that were half full, clothes splayed everywhere.

'I've got markers and labels in here,' she added, lifting the box.

Fatti was leaning on her elbows and attempting to sit up.

'Hi,' she said to Farah.

Farah smiled at her and wedged her way past Mum, setting the box down at Fatti's feet.

'Still not feeling great then?' she asked.

Mae looked at Bubblee. She knew she'd had a talk with Farah and maybe it had worked because at least she wasn't behaving like a bit of a cow. On the one hand, Mae couldn't wait to leave all this drama behind her and start actually living her life; on the other hand, she knew this was also her life, and she wouldn't be around to

51

tell them all to get a grip and sort it out.

'No, I'm fine, really,' said Fatti, looking as though she might throw up there and then. 'I'm just . . . for a second . . . ' and she lay back down, covering her eyes with her arms again. 'Just a few seconds.'

Then their dad appeared.

'All right, Pops?' said Mae. 'We needed more people in my room.'

He gave Mae a faint smile. His lack of ability to get her jokes now filled her with an affection that doubled because she wouldn't witness it as often.

'What is wrong with Fatti?' he asked.

'I'm fine, really,' she replied without moving.

'Father of mine,' said Mae, patting him on the arm. 'Have you forgotten when your dear wife was pregnant with her children?'

'Tst,' said her mum. 'Don't talk about such things with your abba.'

Her dad looked at her mum and smiled, but she wasn't meeting his gaze.

'What's for lunch, Jay's amma?' he asked her.

'Dal, porota, rice, fish curry, chicken curry, meat curry and potato curry,' she replied, looking determinedly at Fatti.

These people, seriously. But Mae didn't want to think about what drama was unfolding in her parents' lives because they were old enough to sort it out between them.

'All right, all right,' said Mae, clapping her hands. 'Can my lovely parents leave us to the packing since I'm leaving in under twenty-four hours and Bubblee's erasing my identity by binning all the clothes I like. Thanks!'

With which she pushed her parents out of the door and looked at all her sisters. Bubblee was shaking her head with a smile and even Farah managed to laugh.

'Don't speak like that to people when you get to uni,' came Fatti's voice. 'You'll never make friends.'

Mae emptied out the bin bag that Bubblee had filled and said: 'I'll make the ones worth keeping, thanks. Plus, you can't choose your family but at least I'll get to choose my mates.'

The sisters got to work as Mae passed the clothes she'd be taking to Farah, who put them in a box and labelled them. They spent the next hour or so in relative silence, Fatti excusing herself in a rush to use the bathroom, and occasional conversations revolving around how petite Mae's clothes were, which didn't mean they should be worn in public.

'Whatevs,' she'd reply.

'Books,' said Bubblee, picking up a stack from Mae's shelf, and one that seemed to have fallen behind the rest of them. 'Which ones are you taking?'

'Oh, wait.'

Mae leapt up and took them from Bubblee's hands, putting them back.

'What's wrong with you?' said Bubblee, still holding the one that had fallen.

She looked at it. *The Myth of Choice: Female Sexuality and Getting it Right.*

'What kind of book is this?' said Bubblee.

'Nothing, leave it,' replied Mae, snatching it

from her. 'Just, I'll sort out the books last.'

Bubblee raised her eyebrows and turned back to Sellotape a box shut. Mae felt the colour in her cheeks rise. She didn't even know why it mattered what books she did and didn't read. Some things just interested her more. She didn't have to justify anything, but that didn't mean her family wouldn't always try and make her.

She and her sisters looked up when they heard their mum's raised voice. Mae scampered towards the door and opened it to get a better listen.

'Mum never raises her voice,' said Farah, also leaning in closer.

'Don't eavesdrop,' added Fatti.

'You lie back down, preggers,' retorted Mae.

'What are they saying?' whispered Farah.

'Shhh.'

Mae crept to the top of the stairs, leaning over the bannister for better earshot.

'Calm down, calm down, Jay's amma,' she heard her dad say.

Silence. Then there was clattering in the kitchen. Mae waited for more but nothing else came. She walked back into the bedroom to her sisters' expectant faces.

'Useless. They stopped as soon as I got to the stairs. Apart from Dad telling Mum to calm down, I got nothing.'

'How odd,' said Bubblee. 'Although hardly shocking, a man telling a woman to calm down.'

Mae smiled fondly at her sister. There was something to be said for people who were annoying all the time, because at least they were

54

consistent. Their mum appeared at the door again, this time with some kind of drink concoction for Fatti. She went and handed the cloudy, dishwater-type stuff to her eldest and then sat on the bed.

'Thanks, Amma,' said Fatti, barely touching the mixture with her lips before running to the bathroom.

'Poor girl,' said their mum, looking after her.

Farah, Bubblee and Mae looked at their mother who seemed to have made herself quite comfortable.

'Don't worry,' she added, looking at Farah who'd already begun folding clothes again and looking resolutely at the floor. 'Your time will come somehow.'

Mae wanted to shake her head. Her mum still didn't get that Farah didn't want vague platitudes, she needed concrete solutions. Fatti came back in and sat on the bed, closing her eyes. She picked the glass up again.

'Now,' said their mum, 'are you and Mustafa having the sex?'

Fatti spewed out bits of the cloudy drink, covering her top with it.

'*Amma*,' exclaimed Farah.

'Zi, you can't get a baby without the sex.'

'Oh, my actual God,' said Mae.

'Mae, you leave the room. You are too young for this talk. Bubblee, you too.'

'Mum,' they both exclaimed.

'I'm in my thirties,' said Bubblee.

'You are still unmarried.'

'This is why I'm going off to uni. At least there

I'll be treated like an adult,' said Mae.

'Only if you act like it,' said Bubblee.

'No one has to leave the room,' said Farah, 'because we're no longer having this discussion.'

Their mum looked unimpressed. 'You are just like your abba. He never talks about things either.'

'Listen, I've been to the doctor again . . . '

Farah looked at everyone. Mae noticed her voice waver. 'He started going on about IVF and surrogacy and God knows what, but I've gone for more tests. Perhaps something will be different this time.'

'Oh, Faru,' said Fatti. 'Things might change.'

Farah smiled. 'Well, let's not get our hopes up.'

The evenness of her voice suggested to Mae that Farah's hopes were already sky high.

'Make your prayers and Allah knows best, but don't worry about the results. The answer is so simple,' said their mum. 'Fatti, you have this child now and give the next one to Faru, just like your amma gave you to me. Finish story.'

'Bloomin' 'eck,' said Mae. 'Talk about pass the baby parcel.'

Farah paused. 'Sorry, Amma, but there's no way I'd put a baby through what you put Fatti through.'

Their mum looked at all of them, confused. 'What did I put her through? I loved her more than any of you.'

Fatti's face looked flushed as she stared at her hands.

'Knew it,' said Mae.

'Of course you did, Amma,' replied Fatti, taking her mum's hand.

'No,' interrupted Farah. 'No way.'

'Fatti,' said their mum, looking at her. 'You will give her your next baby, won't you?'

'It's not like she's giving me her old winter coat, Amma,' said Farah, glancing at Fatti.

There was silence. Everyone's eyes rested on Fatti, whose gaze was still firmly on her beautiful hands. She looked up.

'Anyway,' said Farah. 'Like Fatti said, the doctor might have some good news.'

More silence. Mae wasn't keen on silences.

'You girls think I am a bad mother,' said their mum. She was looking around at all of them as if in accusation. 'You have your what's-happening group and talk about these things, I know.'

'WhatsApp,' corrected Mae.

'Of course not,' said Fatti, looking horrified.

Bubblee chose to carry on filling the bin bags.

'I see you,' continued their mum, looking at Mae, 'always on the phone, messaging and laughing. When I ask who you are speaking to you say it is your sisters.'

Maybe Mum was having a late-life crisis? She looked around at all of them.

'What do you talk about?' she asked.

'Nothing,' replied Farah. 'Just . . . stuff. Like sisters do.'

'Yes, you are lucky,' said their mum. 'So many of you. Ask me. I am alone.'

More silence. It wasn't like their mum to talk about feelings. Thank God Fatti was there, who insisted that she wasn't alone.

'But you don't put me in your group,' their mum replied.

Mae glanced at Bubblee from the corner of her eye. Bubblee looked at Farah.

'Look,' exclaimed Mae, lifting up a floral summer dress. 'Remember when Fatti and Farah got me this to try and make me dress more like a *lady.*'

Mae needn't have bothered to try and change the subject.

'Jay's amma!' came their dad's voice.

'Your abba and me are going for a walk.' Their mum sounded exasperated at the very thought as she got up. 'I would rather stay here and sit with you, but . . . ' She sighed and looked at Farah. 'Remember, as long as you are having the se — '

'God, no, Amma,' the girls exclaimed in unison.

Their mum got up, gave them all another look, and left the room.

'What the hell just happened there?' said Bubblee.

Farah and Mae shuddered. The sooner Mae got out of this house, the better it'd be for her brain and self-awareness. To be told to leave the room at the mention of sex! She looked at Bubblee.

'Bubs,' she said, laughing, 'looks like you and me aren't so different.' She threw her cargo pants at her sister.

'Do you think Mum's okay?' said Fatti.

'She's probably just having a bad day,' said Bubblee. 'Unless you want to add her to our WhatsApp group?'

'Well, no, but . . . '

'The problem with Mum,' said Mae, 'is that her youngest is leaving the nest and she doesn't know what she'll do without me. Obvs.'

Bubblee rolled her eyes.

'Or maybe she's really sad,' said Farah, sealing another box. 'Maybe she does feel alone.'

'But she has Dad,' said Fatti.

Farah raised her eyebrows. 'I love Dad, but it's not as if her needs come first. I mean, I know something about that,' she added pointedly.

'Trouble in paradise, eh?' said Mae.

Fatti shot her a look. Farah pushed the box to one side.

'It's as if you're expected to be a mind-reader,' said Farah. 'One minute everything is fine and happy and the next . . . ' She shook her head. 'And it's always about them. Why is it that when women have problems we manage to go about things just the same, get on with it, but men? When they have problems the whole house comes to a standstill. Everything's about what *they* want. What *they* need.'

Bubblee was nodding, vehemently, while Mae was considering it all as if it were marginally interesting.

'Since the accident, it's always about Mustafa,' added Farah.

Fatti cleared her throat. 'Did you want to start taking these boxes downstairs?' she said to Mae.

'I know, I know,' continued Farah, ignoring Fatti. 'His life changed, but so did mine and all because of him.'

Mae saw Fatti shifting uncomfortably. She and

Mustafa might not have become close since realizing they were brother and sister, but she never did like talking about him behind his back.

'This is why marriage as an institution is so flawed,' said Bubblee.

'Here we go,' said Mae.

'You're bound to one another into this state and there's this focus on *compromise* and having to make allowances, but why?'

Farah sighed. 'Because it's adult life.'

'Says who?'

Farah looked at Bubblee as if she were crazy. 'The *world*?'

'The *old* world,' corrected Bubblee.

'I'm so glad Mum left when she did,' said Fatti. 'Bubblee would've given her a heart attack with all this anti-marriage talk.'

'Women needed men back then,' said Bubblee. 'But we don't need them for money any more. We can make that ourselves.'

'And what about babies?' asked Farah, the colour in her cheeks rising. 'Where do we go for those?'

Silence ensued again as Farah looked away and the others glanced at one another. After a few awkward moments, Mae said: 'One of your sisters, obvs.'

She jabbed her thumb towards Fatti. 'Just like we got her.'

They all paused. Fatti laughed, so did Bubblee, and before they knew it they were all laughing. After a few minutes Farah shook her head.

'Still needed a man, though.' Farah stared at

Bubblee. 'Are you really okay with being alone for the rest of your life? Really?'

'Better than being with someone and still feeling alone,' she replied.

Mae wondered what it was like to think of such big questions in life. She looked at each of her sisters and knew that whatever questions they were asking each other, or themselves, they weren't her type of questions. They heard the front door close, then footsteps come up the stairs. Jay poked his head in, said hello, and went into his little room to sleep for the rest of the day since he'd been doing deliveries all night.

'Although things could be worse,' said Bubblee when he left. 'A person could be married to someone like Jay.'

Mae laughed as they spent the next few hours finishing up the packing, her heart fluttering at the idea of all the possibilities opening up in front of her.

★ ★ ★

The following day there were tears. Bubblee had to dab the corners of her eyes in case someone saw. She remembered when she was going to university and how different it had been. How she had to fight with her parents, especially her mum, in order to follow her now ambiguous dream. Was it even worth it? As she watched Mae get into her car and wind down her window Bubblee realized that she was the most alone out of everyone. If she had actually craved some kind of love, she might've tried to find it. But she

61

never did. The idea of going back to London simply filled her with dread, the way staying at home in her prime years used to fill her younger self with fear. The only person worth going back for was her friend Sasha, and she was actually moving ahead in her career as an artist. Sasha, she heard and saw with her own eyes, actually had talent. Bubblee felt the familiar twinge of envy. It used to be a rampant jealousy that drove her to stay up late at night, working on her own sculptures. Bubblee wouldn't sleep for days, believing that she had created something extraordinary in the end. But no one seemed to see it that way. Her self-belief couldn't withstand the constancy of other people's indifference. *Indifference is worse than hating something.* Now, here she was, back at home and she wasn't sure to which place she really belonged. Things had changed yet she felt weirdly unchangeable, as though she was set in stone — a misshapen sculpture. There was irony.

'Love you, losers,' said Mae, as she waved from the window and drove down the road. Farah, Fatti, Ash, Mustafa, Jay, Bubblee and her parents all waved until Mae turned the corner and was out of view. Fatti blew her nose into a tissue that Ash handed her.

'She's going to be fine,' he said.

'I know that, but what about *me*?' she exclaimed. 'My little baby.'

'That's why we're getting a new one,' Ash replied, winking and putting his hand on her stomach.

Their dad cleared his throat and looked away.

62

Bubblee had to shake her head at how ridiculous he and all Asian people seemed to be at any display of affection. Perhaps this had scarred her? Perhaps that's why she focused so much on her work and creating something, that she didn't even think about the fact that she was alone until now? Maybe things would've been different if someone had fallen in love with her. Even then, she felt unmoved. Assigning blame to her parents didn't make her feel much better so she decided to stop.

'What time are you leaving tomorrow?' Farah asked Bubblee as they walked back into the house.

Their dad sighed. 'All my daughters are leaving. Stay a little longer,' he said to Bubblee.

Their mum shot him a look.

'Abba, she has work to get back to,' replied Farah. 'It's a shame we can't keep you longer.'

Bubblee wasn't sure whether Farah was being honest or if she felt bad for the way she'd spoken about her work the other day. She decided to give her the benefit of the doubt.

'Hmm,' replied Bubblee.

'You should stay,' added Fatti. 'I could do with some help getting to the toilet bowl.'

'Great.' Bubblee collapsed on the sofa. 'Time well spent for me.'

Mustafa got up. 'I think I'm going to go home.'

Bubblee's mum said they couldn't leave without having dinner.

'No, Farah, you just stay here if you want,' he said.

'You're going to get a bus?' said Farah.

He shifted on his feet. It seemed as though he still hadn't quite got the hang of not being allowed to drive.

'Bubblee will drive you home,' offered their mum.

Bubblee refused to move. Why should she be lumbered with this task?

'Don't worry. I'll get the bus.'

Everyone paused and looked at Bubblee. Their look was so obvious: *Uncaring, Bubblee.*

'The bus comes every two hours,' exclaimed their mum. 'Especially at this time.'

He looked sheepish and Bubblee would almost have felt sorry for him if he weren't being such an inconvenience. She gave as audible a sigh as possible, got up and grabbed her car keys.

'Sorry,' he said as he buckled himself into the seat of her car.

He looked at the back seat of her Fiat, surveying the mess.

'It's fine,' she said. 'As long as you don't comment on the junk.'

'I was just thinking how different twins can be. If Farah saw this she'd be cleaning it up before she drove anyone anywhere.'

Bubblee simply nodded as she set out onto the main road. She didn't often find herself alone with her brother-in-law and now that she did she wasn't quite sure what to say to him.

'How's your . . . ' She glanced at him, flicking her head.

'Brain?' he said, smiling.

She smiled back. 'Yes.'

'It has its moments. Medicine's keeping things in check but it's medicine, you know?' He paused. 'It makes me . . . '

'Yeah, Farah's mentioned.'

'Oh, she has?'

'When I've asked how you're doing.'

He didn't have to know that Farah had complained to Bubblee over the past few years about his increasingly erratic moods. Bubblee wasn't callous.

'I didn't think you ever asked how I was,' Mustafa said with a smile.

'Once in a blue moon,' Bubblee replied.

Their mutual indifference had never really been acknowledged out loud — Mustafa's comment was the closest they'd ever come to it.

'Which is probably more than you ever ask about me,' she added. 'So there we have it.'

'I ask about you.'

He said it so matter-of-factly that it surprised Bubblee.

'Well. Good to know. Maybe the meds are making you a concerned brother-in-law as well as keeping you alive,' Bubblee added.

'Maybe.'

He looked out of the window and they spent the rest of the journey in silence as Bubblee pulled up in front of the house.

'Thanks,' he said.

He walked inside and Bubblee thought she saw him lean his back against the door as he closed it behind him. She waited a few moments until his figure moved and he was out of sight.

When she got back home, Bubblee said: 'He seems to not feel great a lot of the time.'

'Is he okay?' Ash asked Farah.

'He's fine,' she replied, not quite meeting his eye.

It didn't seem as though Farah wanted to tell anyone else about his mood swings. Bubblee felt a sense of solidarity with her sister. Ash paused and then glanced at their parents. 'That's good. I just thought maybe he's still not quite over the accident.'

'Honey,' said Fatti. 'That was a few years ago now.'

'Well, some things change people. Not that I knew him before the accident, but . . . anyway. I'm glad he's fine.'

Farah gave a tight smile. Bubblee, Fatti and Farah's phones buzzed simultaneously.

Mae: I'm freeeeeeeeee

Mae: Crap got stoppd by po-po 4 lukin @ fone. Told em I ws runnin away 4rm opresiv brown fam. Hahaha. Msg l8r xxxx

They were all smiling as Bubblee looked up. 'She thinks she had it bad?'

'I know,' said Farah.

The sisters laughed as their mum asked: 'What is so funny?'

'Just Mae being Mae,' said Bubblee.

'How is she going to get through uni?' added Farah.

Fatti put her phone away — she looked pale

and sickly. Nothing like the way she had appeared a week ago. 'She's going to be just fine. I know it.'

'Fats is right,' said Bubblee. 'She's going to outshine us all.'

Mae's gaping absence rendered everyone silent for a moment.

'So, tell me, how does this what's-happening work?' asked their mum.

Sometimes Bubblee forgot how little her mum knew of the world and how little she tried to rectify it. How could her mum (just about) use an iPad but think an android phone was too complicated? It would be Bubblee's worst nightmare for her life to become her home, and for that home to become an impassable bubble. And even worse would be their mum, carrying on, trying to encroach on their private group.

'WhatsApp, Amma,' corrected Fatti again, getting paler by the minute.

'Do you want to go home?' asked Ash.

'I'm so sorry,' replied Fatti, looking at everyone. 'The nausea just won't . . . '

She wasn't able to make the end of the sentence before leaping up to run to the bathroom, Ash following her.

'My poor daughter,' said her mum. 'But she has a good husband.'

Bubblee thought she saw Farah bristle. Perhaps she was imagining things?

'You girls never answer me,' said their mum. 'I will learn to use this WhatsUp myself.'

'Firstly, you'd need a phone that was made this century,' replied Bubblee.

'Hmm?' Her mum looked confused. 'Can I use my iPad?'

'Well, yes, but . . . ' Bubblee couldn't be bothered to finish explaining. 'Don't worry, Farah will get you a new phone when I leave.'

Her mouth went dry as she said this; her stomach twisted in an all-too-familiar knot of anxiety. It felt like an overreaction but she'd begun to have a physical reaction to going back to London.

'Or maybe I will just stay.'

Farah frowned. 'What about work?'

Bubblee moved uneasily on the sofa. There was nothing for it. She had to tell her family the truth.

'Actually . . . well, in all honesty I resigned.'

'What?' said Farah.

Fatti and Ash walked into the room, Ash supporting Fatti as he said they were going to go home so she could rest.

'Sorry,' said Fatti.

'Stop apologizing, honey,' said Ash. 'They understand.'

They both left.

Farah had hardly taken her eyes off Bubblee. 'But your work is your life.'

This didn't make Bubblee's stomach settle very well.

'Bubblee,' said their dad, leaning forward. 'You don't have your job?'

'Why didn't you tell us?' asked their mum with a look that was far too much like satisfaction.

'Because of that look,' Bubblee mumbled.

'What?' said her mum.

'Because there was already enough going on here, wasn't there?'

'What about your flat where you were living?' asked Farah.

Bubblee paused. 'I've given it up. Couldn't afford to stay without the job.'

'Oh,' replied Farah.

'So then you must stay,' said her dad, hardly watering down his smile or his pleasure.

Her mum cleared her throat. 'Yes,' she said, apparently unsure. 'Maybe one week? Two?'

This was different. Normally her mum would've been ecstatic at the idea of Bubblee staying home for as long as possible — moving back home, in fact.

'You don't sound that pleased, Amma?' said Bubblee, a smile on her lips.

Wasn't that just the way? There was a time her mum would've begged her to stay home and now it was Bubblee who was the beggar. How could she afford to live in London without a job? What was she meant to do with her life?

'Of course she is pleased,' said her dad, rubbing his hands together. 'We both are.'

Their mum played with the edge of her paisley-patterned sari. 'Your abba likes to answer for me.'

Farah and Bubblee looked at their dad. He shifted his gaze to the carpet before looking up and smiling at Bubblee.

'One daughter gone and another is back.'

'Not permanently,' said Bubblee, leaning forward. 'It's just until I sort out what I want to do. I won't be here for ever. Anyway, I can stay with Sasha in London as long as I need when I decide to get back.'

He just met this with another smile. There were parents in the world who'd have been steeped in disappointment at their child leaving a job; asking why they left, pushing for future plans and giving lectures on responsibility and motivation. But no, Bubblee's mum felt the only important thing to say was: 'Maybe now you will have time to find a husband and settle down at last.'

Bubblee gave an exasperated sigh. 'No, Mum. I have not given up one dream just to follow yours.'

She felt her face flush, her heart beat faster. Why couldn't her mum be a friend to her the way she seemed to be to Fatti? Why did she never understand things? It shouldn't matter how different a bunch of sisters were, their mum should be able to have a relationship with each of them, irrespective of differences of opinion or beliefs.

'So what are you going to do?' said their mum.

'Jay's amma,' her dad interrupted, putting out his hand as if to tell her to wait a moment.

'You ask her then,' she replied.

He cleared his throat, his voice much softer. 'Bubblee — what are you going to do?'

There was a pause as Bubblee looked at her parents in pure hopelessness. *What was she going to do?*

'Why don't we have some dinner?' said Farah. 'Abba, Amma, let's talk about this later, okay?'

In that moment Bubblee's heart swelled with a

gratitude for Farah that she couldn't remember having felt for a while.

As Farah and her mum went into the kitchen she heard their muffled conversation, while her dad just kept giving her encouraging smiles.

'I'm okay, Abba,' said Bubblee.

'Don't worry, don't worry.'

Her dad was very good at vague affirmations, at least.

Dinner was a quiet affair. Her mum made some allusions to weddings and decided to cite as many women as possible from their community who'd got married recently to 'very good men'.

'Jay's abba, shall we go to bed?' asked their mum after they'd cleaned up, had tea and settled in the living room again.

Their dad was watching the news, eyes glued to the television.

'Hmm? Yes, I'm coming.'

'Fancy watching a film, or are you going home?' Bubblee asked Farah.

Farah hesitated. 'Actually, I've just messaged Mus to say I might stay over here tonight.'

'Farah, you shouldn't leave your husband alone like this,' said their mum.

'No,' added Bubblee. 'Grown men never know how to look after themselves.'

'Bubblee, when you are married you will see,' said their mum.

Bubblee simply sighed and pretended to read something on her phone. It was actually the job vacancy at her gallery that she was looking at. At first it was a tab she opened every day. Now it remained open and she refreshed it every time she picked her phone up.

'He's fine,' replied Farah. 'He's already in bed, anyway. I suppose he's tired.'

'Jay's abba, do you hear that? Bed.'

He looked up for a second. 'I will be up.'

Their mum paused, giving him not quite so pleasant a look, before leaving the room and walking up the stairs.

It was half an hour later when their mum's voice came booming from upstairs, calling for their dad. He sighed, switched off the television and looked at Farah and Bubblee.

'Goodnight, my girls.'

Before leaving the room, he turned around and said: 'Farah, one night here is enough, yes?'

With a smile, he turned back and walked towards his waiting wife. Bubblee raised her eyebrows at Farah.

'It just never stops annoying me,' said Bubblee. 'The backwardness of this place.'

Farah shrugged. 'You can't change people's views when they get to that age.'

Bubblee paused. 'But you were in the kitchen with Mum, trying to change her views on my getting married anyway, weren't you?'

Farah stood up and adjusted the cushion from the sofa their dad had just vacated. She looked around the room for other things to fix.

'Mum's Mum,' she replied before her eyes settled on Bubblee. 'That's a big decision you made. Leaving work.'

'It made itself.'

Farah turned the sofa her dad had been sitting

on away from the television and opposite Bubblee. 'You didn't tell me, any of us.'

'In the grand scheme of things it's not important, is it, Farah?' Bubblee knew this could lead into another silent argument, leaving things unsaid while feelings brimmed.

'You're still angry about what I said that day, aren't you?'

'What do you think?'

Farah crossed her legs at the ankle, looking so composed Bubblee thought that no matter what happened, Farah would never fall apart.

'Bubs, I didn't have enough sympathy in me for both of us. I'm sorry.'

She looked earnest.

'Yet I managed to have some for you,' replied Bubblee.

Bubblee felt like a miser; an emotional Scrooge. Never had she really considered her lack of compassion, not until this moment when she was recounting how she had managed to give some to her sister who was unable to conceive a baby. Perhaps she was always too engrossed in her work and becoming an artist. The two shouldn't be mutually exclusive but compassion also required the time to listen and she had very little of that when she was in London.

'You know that feeling that you were made to do something?' said Farah.

Bubblee raised her eyebrows.

'Sorry, yes, you do. I feel as though my life's somehow incomplete, that there's this gaping hole that can only be filled with a baby.'

'Are you sure it's just the baby?' said Bubblee.

'I know you said you felt like this before the accident, but since then it just seems . . . like you've become obsessed in a way.'

Bubblee could see Farah retreat; an invisible barrier appeared. But she couldn't stop now — she had to say it or what was the point?

'In a way that feels . . . not wholly present.'

'What are you saying?'

'Just that you'd never have let Mustafa go home alone like that before, or stay the night here.'

'So? Why is everyone making such a big deal of this?'

Bubblee quietly sighed. 'Okay, it doesn't matter.'

Her own refrain surprised her.

'I guess you think you also failed at creating something,' said Farah.

'Created plenty — just nothing worth anyone actually seeing,' said Bubblee wryly.

'You might find something else?'

'Will you do the same if you can't have a baby?'

They both fell silent and heard muffled voices come from their parents' bedroom. Farah looked at Bubblee.

'I always had this idea that I could give this baby a life that was different to ours.'

'It was . . . *is* a bit challenging sometimes. They're on another planet,' replied Bubblee.

'I know, bless them. I never really felt like I had much choice when I was growing up — and I'm not blaming you or anything at all, I wish I could've been as daring as you, but . . . it sort of felt like I couldn't really think about what I wanted because I was always trying to be the good one, lessen the upset that . . . '

'That I caused?'

Farah gave her an apologetic look. 'I suppose there's no other way to say it, but I promise there's no resentment there. But maybe I want a baby for that reason too: to fulfil a part of life that never quite . . . you know.'

Bubblee did know. A baby could be like a second chance. She'd never thought about it that way — a baby always seemed to her an obstacle in the face of her own chances.

'Hmm,' she simply replied. 'A second chance.'

The two sisters sat like that for a while, with Bubblee wondering about second chances and where, if anywhere, she was to find hers.

Mae: Im here losers! V weird nt hvin mum & dad to eavsdrop on bt its time 2 party!!!!

Fatti: Don't go crazy, please. I already have one child making me ill xoxoxoxoxo

Farah: Are you sure you packed enough jumpers? What did you have for dinner? We miss you Xx

Bubblee: Actually we're enjoying the quiet. Be good. But not too good Xxx

5

Farah had already had the scan and it was time for the results. She walked into the doctor's surgery, heart practically in her throat as she was called into his room. He swivelled in his chair and as soon as she saw his face she knew.

'I'm afraid there's been no improvement, and actually it's got worse.'

There was a way to deliver the news. Farah hadn't realized how much hope she had of the result being different until that hope was crushed. Not only that, but the situation had got *worse*.

'Now, are you very stressed?'

What a question! Of course she was stressed. She couldn't have a baby.

'No more than usual,' she mumbled.

What was she going to do? How was life ever going to work out? It all felt too helpless, too hopeless.

'And have you and your husband had sex since our last appointment?'

She felt her face flush. 'We've been busy.'

He tapped his pen on the table. 'Well, the chances of conceiving are very slim, but they're nil if you don't have sex.'

Farah wanted to cry. It was ridiculous. She knew this, Mustafa knew this, even her *mum* had told her this, and yet he just didn't ever seem to be in the mood.

'Have you given counselling some thought?'

'Sorry? No. Maybe.'

'Now surrogacy is still an option. It can be very successful if done through the right channels. Here are a few websites you should look at to help get your head around how it works and what it'd involve.'

'I've already said we can't afford it.'

'I understand, and that's something you'd need to work on, but the chances of actually getting a baby at the end of it are higher than with IVF.'

Farah drank in the word *chance*. Had she been too quick to dismiss the idea? She could always get two jobs to help save money, and her parents might be able to help them. It was just the idea of not actually carrying the baby that made her stop short.

'It would be *your* baby, with your genes,' he said, as if reading her thoughts. 'I know the concept isn't very easy to grasp, but it's a scientific feat and worth exploring, in my opinion.

I've given you the websites, so think about it and speak to your husband, of course.'

★   ★   ★

Farah's mind buzzed. It would be their baby. But she wouldn't carry it. Mae would call her crazy, but Farah couldn't help but look at Fatti and envy her the sickness she was going through. Well, perhaps not to the same extent, but she wanted to know the feeling of growing something inside her and that connection that comes because of it. Farah picked up her phone and dialled Fatti's number.

'Hello?' came her muffled voice.

'Are you in bed?'

There was a pause. 'That obvious? What's going on?'

Farah wondered why she'd even called Fatti — to ask her what it feels like to have a baby inside her and whether that was reason enough to reject the idea of surrogacy? Then she heard sniffling.

'Are you okay?' she asked.

'Yeah, yeah, I'm fine.' But Fatti's voice sounded nasal and thick.

'Do you have a cold?'

A few moments passed before she replied: 'No.' Her voice cracked. 'Don't worry, I'm fine, I'm sorry, I'm just . . . '

'What's wrong?' asked Farah, getting ready to jump in her car and see her sister. She'd taken a late doctor's appointment and had finished work for the day.

'No, it's fine, really.' Fatti seemed to be gathering herself before she cried out: 'I can't say this to you.'

'Say *what* to me?'

Farah thought she heard Fatti sob. She waited, confused and unsure of what to do or say.

'It's just so . . . so . . . ' Hiccup. 'So *awful*.'

'What is?' exclaimed Farah.

The sobs began again.

'The baby,' Fatti cried. 'I know I shouldn't say this to you of all people. I know. *I'm* the one who's awful.'

Fatti paused, perhaps waiting for Farah to say something, but she had no words. Certainly no sympathy.

'It's just that I'm *always* feeling sick. I wake up all through the night. The other day I didn't even make it to the bathroom and threw up on Ash's slippers.' She took a deep breath. 'I'm sorry. I'm grateful, really. Honestly, I am. You don't need to hear this.'

'No, it's fine,' replied Farah. 'Listen, I should go. I'm actually driving.'

Farah got into her car and started the engine.

'Okay, of course. Hang on, why did you call?' asked Fatti.

'Oh, nothing. Just wanted to see what you were up to.'

'I'm sorry, I shouldn't have come out with all of that. Not when yo — '

'I really should get off the phone,' interrupted Farah.

'Okay, I'll speak to you later, then?'

'Yeah, fine. Bye.'

Farah put the phone down and rested her head on the steering wheel of the car. A sense of panic rose in her chest — she had to wind down the window for some fresh air as she switched the engine off.

'Pull yourself together,' she said to herself. 'Just pull yourself together.'

It was so much easier said than done.

It would be your baby, with your genes.

The doctor was right, of course. Pregnancy was the beginning but it wasn't the end. Holding a baby in your arms, tending to it, watching it grow, its features morphing in and out of recognition. The way it would reflect some of her, some of Mustafa and something new altogether was all still possible. This time when she switched the engine on again there was an urgency. She sped down the street all the way home to tell her husband. They *would* have a baby. It *would* be theirs. It's just that someone else would carry it.

★　★　★

When she walked into the house Mustafa was fixing the light bulb in a lamp.

'Oh,' she said, watching him with his tools sprawled all around him. 'You're home.'

'Finished the day early so I came home and started this. I've fixed the bathroom tap too,' he said. 'It was driving me crazy. Do you know where my screwdriver with the green handle is?' He was looking around for it.

'No,' she replied.

'Oh, here it is,' he said, bringing it up and looking at it. 'It was right there. I must be going blind.'

He laughed at his own observation. She wondered how the things that had needed fixing around the house for the past three months were only just occurring to Mustafa. He looked up at her with such child-like satisfaction she decided not to point this out to him. Plus, she needed him on side, and his mood hadn't been this positive for a while. When she looked into the kitchen she saw that all the dishes and plates had been taken out of the cupboard.

'What's going on there?' she asked.

'Hmm?' Mustafa glanced into the kitchen before returning to his light bulb. 'Hinges on the cupboards were loose.'

Farah wondered whether there were any other hinges loose as she stared at her husband. But she must stop all this negativity and appreciate that today was the day he felt like being productive.

'I went to the doctor,' she said.

He looked up and paused, screwdriver in hand. 'Why didn't you tell me?'

Farah went and sat on the floor next to him, moving his tool box to one side and taking the screwdriver from his hand.

'I suppose I just needed to think.'

'What did he say? Is there — '

'No,' she replied.

He took her hand and stroked it. Farah reached for her purse and brought out the piece of paper with the websites that the doctor had given her.

'What's this?' he asked, taking the paper from her.

'He mentioned surrogacy again,' she said. She held her breath as she stared at Mustafa, scrutinizing the paper. 'It's really the only other viable option. You know, if we want a child with our genes. I know we couldn't really adopt — not after seeing what Fatti went through. And anyway, it wouldn't be the sa — '

'This is it,' exclaimed Mustafa.

Farah was momentarily taken aback by his

outburst. He waved the paper, beaming at her.

'This is the answer,' he added.

Farah paused. It wasn't the reaction she'd been expecting.

'But last time I mentioned it you weren't keen,' she said.

'What did I know?' he said.

He was looking at the paper and got his phone out to google one of the websites. Skimming past the words, he looked up and said: 'There's nothing else to think about, is there?'

'What about the cost?'

'I'll do overtime. I'll stack shelves at night. I'll . . . I'll do *anything* to have this baby.'

'Do you . . . are you sure?'

She leaned in to him, looking at his face for signs of something, though she wasn't sure what. Farah should've been happy — it was exactly what she wanted to hear — but there was something unsettling about his enthusiasm. He hadn't even paused to think any of it through. Words were spilling out of him without really considering the consequences of surrogacy.

'Yes.' He grabbed Farah's arms, pressing them and looking into her eyes. 'Let's start our family. Whatever it takes.'

'You're okay now — with another woman potentially carrying our baby?'

Perhaps he'd misheard and didn't really get what she was talking about.

'We should get a nursery sorted. This flat is so small but maybe the storage room? They have a sale on paint at Cary's in town.'

Mustafa had already stood up, looking around

the flat as if he were about to start decorating the nursery now.

'Whoa,' she said, laughing as she stood up after him. 'You were so against it before and now you're talking about discounted paint?'

'Forget what I said,' he replied, waving his hand around.

'It was only a few weeks ago.'

He stepped towards her, grabbing her arms again. 'Farah — let's make a family and be happy.'

She had to stop always seeing the negative in things. She missed seeing her glass as half full. Farah should be taking this moment and appreciating Mustafa's excitement. Even if the excitement seemed to come out of the blue. He bounded up the stairs and then back down again.

'I mean, the storage room is packed but we can work that out. Maybe store some stuff at your parents'?'

Farah laughed again. 'Okay, calm down there. We need to save up first — surrogacy is expensive and then there's the question of finding someone to actually do it. I mean, I don't even know where to begin. We should have a proper look at those websites — do our research, speak to people, really know what we're getting into.'

Mustafa seemed distracted. 'Hmm? Oh, yeah, but that stuff will sort itself out.'

'Money growing on trees now, is it?'

She smiled, half teasing him, but how exactly did he think it'd sort itself out?

'What will we name the baby?' he said, ignoring her. 'Do you want a boy or a girl? I don't care. As long as it's healthy and we get to raise it and be, you know . . . complete.'

She looked at him for a moment. 'I was beginning to think that you didn't even want a baby any more. That you just wanted it to be us.'

'Oh, what? No. No. Why would you think that? When did I ever suggest that?'

She wanted to bring up the night after Mae's party, but why spoil the moment? She realized that though there were limits to happiness, there was no reason to be the one to apply them. Questions slipped in her mind about the practicalities Mustafa was so keen to ignore, but she wanted to get caught up in his enthusiasm. It was so similar to the type of passion he used to have; Mustafa was once again familiar to her. Farah tried to shake the constant need to rationalize things out of her head. She looked into Mustafa's eyes as he kissed her.

'We're having a baby then?' she asked.

He nodded, cupping her face. 'We're having a baby.'

That night Farah and Mustafa had sex. She rested her head on his chest, savouring the closeness of his body, not caring that he left the work he'd started downstairs unfinished. Every time doubt flitted through her head, she trapped it and pushed it to the back of her mind. *Just look at us right now.* Sometimes things do work themselves out. It was all about accepting the bad in order for the good to come to the surface.

When Farah woke up the following morning she groped around for Mustafa, ready to cuddle up to him, but he wasn't there. She listened out for him around the house but only heard the faint chirping of birds outside, the rustling of trees, the tick-tock of the clock on the wall. It was seven o'clock in the morning. Perhaps he'd left a little early for work. She found herself wide awake so began getting ready for work too. When she went downstairs she picked up the mail that had come through the letterbox and her heart sank as she looked at the bills. Farah stuffed them in her bag and made her way to her job.

She arrived at the optician's, made herself some coffee, and took a deep breath before opening the dreaded envelopes. Electricity bill, water bill, TV licence up for renewal — maybe they could go without a television for a while? — phone bills, Internet, heating. It seemed never-ending. She went to check her bank account online and wondered where all the money had gone. The rent payment had gone through, leaving her barely in credit, so she looked into her and Mustafa's joint account. She breathed a sigh of relief and saw they had just about enough to pay this month's bills, but she would have to start looking into getting a second job to save for a surrogate. This could take years, though. What would her family say and how would they react? Would her parents even understand the whole concept? Then there was the task of finding the right woman to carry their baby. She tried not to think of it too much because every time she did she imagined this stranger's face and it took something away from Farah. She was already jealous of someone she hadn't met. A sense of despair washed over her. How impossible the apparently possible could seem. Yesterday, in the euphoria of Mustafa's excitement, she had managed to push these worries to the back of her mind — now that she was sitting at her desk, there was no excitement, only hurdle after hurdle. Why did things always seem to be that extra bit harder for her? Maybe she could ask her boss for a raise? She had been in the job for three years and had never taken a day off sick, was always on time and notably efficient when compared to the last receptionist. But when she broached it with her boss, she merely gave Farah a tight smile and went through all the trials of running a small business, the costs and liabilities.

'Let's see in three months' time, shall we?' she added, before going back into her office where a client was waiting, and suggesting that Farah get back to the job for which she wanted a raise.

Farah's blood ran to her face in indignation. She'd have walked out if she could afford it, or if she knew she could find somewhere else. She spent the rest of the day slamming filing cabinets and saying as little to her boss as she could.

Bubblee: Mum and Dad don't seem to be on speaking terms and I need to get out of the house. Shall we have lunch in the park? I'll bring home-made sandwiches.

Farah was grateful for Bubblee being around. She'd grown so used to her living in London and leading a life so different and unrelated from her own but it suddenly felt as though she had the sister she used to know back again. There, at least, was comfort.

⋆ ⋆ ⋆

'What's wrong with you?' asked Bubblee as soon as she saw Farah sitting on the park bench. The trees, which overarched Farah, were turning a golden colour, the sunlight streaming through the gaps, Farah's hair falling over her face, her ankles crossed. If it weren't for Farah's brow that was knitted in concentration, she'd have looked angelic.

She was bent over low, on her phone, reading something rather intently. Farah looked up and squinted at Bubblee, the sun in her eyes.

'Nothing.'

Farah tucked her phone in her bag. She was getting worse at hiding how she was feeling, but at least this made things easier for Bubblee. When Farah didn't speak, Bubblee handed her a sandwich.

'So? Have you heard from the doctor?' she asked.

Farah nodded.

'And?'

Farah paused. She then shook her head.

'Right. Sorry.'

Such a feeble word: *sorry*. It seemed so inadequate. But it was all Bubblee had. Farah picked off a bit of crust and lay it neatly on top of the foil on her lap.

'We're considering our options,' said Farah.

'Adoption?'

Farah shook her head, looking at the crust.

'Surely not IVF again? Not after last time,' said Bubblee.

'No, but it's good to know you'd have supported it.'

Bubblee leaned forward and turned towards Farah. 'Can't support anything that would make you go through that again. So? What's this other option?'

Farah looked Bubblee in the eye and straightened her back. 'We've decided on a surrogate.'

Bubblee's first inclination was to laugh. *A surrogate.* Then when Farah's face remained even and resolute, Bubblee knew it was no joke.

'A surrogate?' she asked.

'Yes.'

Bubblee took a bite out of her sandwich. She might not know the ins and outs of costings when it came to these things but she knew it wouldn't be cheap. It seemed such an extravagance. How would they afford it and *why?* And this was all aside from the cost of then actually bringing up a baby. The desperation to pursue having one made no sense to Bubblee. She looked at Farah again. Her features seemed to have lit up.

'And Mustafa's happy about it?' she asked.

Farah nodded. 'Really happy. The most excited I've seen him in a while.'

Clouds had gathered in an instant, blocking out the sun; the white light lined the grey tufts, floating in the sky. What an odd practice surrogacy was: to have someone else's sperm and egg in your body, creating a life to which you have no relation, and feeling it grow inside you. If there was anything about having a baby that fascinated Bubblee it was the process of actually being pregnant; watching your body shift and change, making room for another human. It would almost be like having an out-of-body experience about something that was happening inside your body. If she really thought about it, perhaps it was quite empowering: one woman helping another.

'No opinions to give?' asked Farah.

'Plenty,' replied Bubblee.

'Well, I don't need to hear them, along with everything else.'

'What 'everything else'?'

Farah sighed and put her egg mayonnaise sandwich down. 'It's the money,' she said. 'We don't have any, and surrogates aren't cheap. And then, look at this,' she said, putting her phone screen in front of Bubblee.

Bubblee barely managed to catch what was on there when Farah continued: 'The IVF, legal advice and all the tests that me and Mustafa would need to take would end up costing around fifteen thousand pounds — and that's not including payment to the surrogate. Whoever that will be.'

Farah went on listing all the obstacles: freezing sperm and eggs, finding an actual surrogate, the things that could go wrong. Even Bubblee could see how it'd look quite hopeless. But then, it still seemed more likely for Farah to have a baby than for Bubblee to ever achieve her dream of being a renowned artist. There was no talent needed for having a baby; chance was enough for that. And, in this case, the right amount of money.

'It was never going to be easy,' she offered.

'Yes, thanks, Bubs.'

They ate their sandwiches in silence before Farah had to get back to her job and Bubblee to figure out what she would do with the rest of her day. In London she had barely had time to pick up the phone and speak to her family, whereas now she had nothing but time, and no other option *but* to speak to her family. Still, she could walk around the village without feeling as though she had to get back to her work; without that anxiety rising in her chest. The feeling that failure was imminent had never really left her, but was subsiding now because she *had* failed. Perhaps she was beginning to accept it.

★   ★   ★

The entire afternoon Farah thought of nothing else but how they'd manage to have this surrogacy. She had to look over her shoulder constantly to make sure her boss didn't see the websites she was looking at. On her drive home she decided she and Mustafa would have to sit down and really think about how they'd manage it all. Maybe a timeline to see how long they'd need to save the money to get the process started. Then they'd have to speak to her parents and ask if they could loan them some money. She opened the front door to get into the house and heard Mustafa clattering around in the living room. He was home early. When she went inside, she realized why. Farah couldn't believe her eyes.

'What the hell is all this?' she said, glaring at what seemed to be dozens of shopping bags from Mothercare.

'Surprise,' he said, a bag in one hand and a Babygro in the other. 'I started work early so I could go to the shops before they closed.'

'That's *pink*,' she remarked, looking at the item of clothing.

'I know. Look at it.'

Mustafa turned it around and put it against his chest. The wording on it read: *World's Best Dad*. His eyes rested on Farah's, his grin irrepressible.

'But . . . what if it's a boy?'

She was so confused. Of all the questions she had, this one seemed to need the most explanation.

'Oh. Yeah, but it doesn't matter, does it? Fatti might have a girl and we can give it to her if ours is a boy.'

She was lost for words. What the *hell* was wrong with her husband?

'Fatti's already pregnant,' she exclaimed, her voice rising a few notes as she pushed through all the shopping. 'That Babygro won't even fit Fatti's baby by the time we know what we're having.'

This realization seemed to dawn on Mustafa, whose face fell. 'Oh, yeah.'

She stared at all the bags before picking one at random and emptying it out. More Babygros. Another bag: booties, shorts, two jumpers and a puffer jacket. One more bag, full of toys for toddlers.

'I mean . . . ' She shook her head in dismay. 'What *is* all this, Mustafa?'

'I was excited,' he replied, lowering his voice so that she barely heard him.

Farah put her head in her hands. 'Tell me you have the receipts?'

'Yeah, yeah.'

He began rummaging through the bags.

'We don't even have a surrogate yet,' said Farah. 'Did you use our joint account for this?'

He looked up. His silence said it all.

'You have *got* to be joking. We barely have enough to pay this month's bills and you go and spend hundreds of pounds on clothes for a baby we may not even have?'

'Of course we'll have it.'

His smile returned. He looked like a schoolboy in a sweet shop and it made Farah even angrier.

'*How?* Do you know what it costs? Have you actually bothered to look at those websites properly? Well, I did. Tens of thousands of pounds, that's what it'll cost. And it's not even straightforward. What if the eggs and sperm don't take? What if six cycles later it doesn't work?'

'You've got to be positive.'

She scoffed. 'No, I've got to be an adult

because there has to be one responsible parent in this relationship.'

She knew she was being the worst version of herself — angry, condescending, the nagging wife to a bewildered husband — but what else was she meant to do? Why did Mustafa think this was okay? He had gone into a shop and picked up all these things, with no regard for the sex of the baby, the lack of money in their bank account, the fact that they hadn't even *begun* looking for a surrogate, and now she had to explain to him why it was wrong. It was just typical — after all that they'd lost, he still had no idea how to look after money.

'It's not a big deal . . . here. The receipt.'

She snatched it from him and looked at the total amount. 'You're just unbelievable,' she said. 'Here I am, agonizing over getting another job and what to do and you're spending money we don't have.'

She couldn't look at his face any longer — the way his eyes drooped and his face sagged in disappointment just made her angrier. She left the room, slamming the door behind her. Of all the challenges they had facing them, she really wished that Mustafa being an unreliable husband and father wasn't one of them.

Mae: Mum cald today like 10X. Bubs u liv ther now cant u make sure evrythings ok?? Fats how u doin? Ive joind 5 societies this wk inc. an Islamic 1!! Mum ws well plsd abt that. L8r!! Xxxx

Fatti: Feeling okay. Bubs came over and made me soup.

Bubblee: We know when Fatti says 'okay' she means 'awful'.

Farah stared at her phone that night and couldn't bring herself to respond. She'd say something tomorrow — something light, so no one really knew she was ready to either kill her husband or throw him out of the house, at the very least. To think that just yesterday they'd made love after such a long time. So many problems; which one was she meant to begin to solve?

6

The following morning Farah woke up to an empty bed again. This time when she went downstairs Mustafa was at the kitchen table with his head in his hands. She was about to stride past him, refusing to give in to sympathy, when he looked up. It was the eyes. He looked so pained she couldn't quite keep up her level of anger.

'I'll return the stuff today,' he said.

She merely nodded, then made herself some tea, and managed to make some for him too.

'I'm sorry, I wasn't thinking,' he added when she put the mug in front of him. 'I just got so excited.'

'Okay.'

She had once loved this man so much she hardly ever spoke to Bubblee because of how her sister had treated her husband. Farah remembered the comfort of being looked after by him; the knowledge that she'd always be taken care of. It was only now that she wondered if she loved the man, or how he made her feel. What was the difference? Was safety synonymous with love? She didn't know, and she couldn't work it out either, even if she wanted to. And she certainly didn't want to. She shook the thoughts from her head.

'Will you be home on time tonight?' she asked.

'I'm going to try and get some extra hours,' Mustafa replied.

She took a sip of her tea. What if Bubblee had been right all along? What if Farah had married the wrong man and it took becoming bankrupt and barren to realize? Why did these thoughts keep coming to Farah? She watched Mustafa to remind herself of that love she'd once felt for him, but he looked so different from the man she had known — and not the way he looked physically, but the way he sat now, his shoulders hunched over; the way he walked without purpose any more; how little he now laughed and made her laugh.

'That's a good idea, babe,' she replied and put her hand over his.

★　★　★

The next few days were strategy. Farah hadn't managed a pay rise but had talked her boss into giving her some overtime. It wasn't much, but it was a start. Farah also saw that the local doctor's surgery needed a Saturday receptionist. She didn't think twice before applying. When she told Mustafa he simply nodded and said: 'Great.' His voice suggested it was anything but. Farah didn't have time to think about this, though. She also tried to forget how annoyed she felt at Mustafa for his lack of enthusiasm. There was either too much, or too little. Moderation had never been his forte but lately it was as if he didn't know the meaning of the word.

That Sunday she went to her parents' for lunch as Fatti and Ash were also going. Mustafa

96

said he was tired and he'd rather stay at home, so she went alone.

'She's a soldier,' came Ash's voice amidst laughter from inside as Farah opened the front door.

'Fatti, you should've stayed at home, I would've brought you food,' said their mum.

'No, I needed to get out of the house and see real people.'

'I've forbidden her to go into the office,' said Ash. 'The driving school can manage itself.'

How easily Fatti had settled into Ash's life. He had his business and Fatti worked with him — never thinking that she might be spending too much time with the person she was married to, that it might be unhealthy. It wasn't as if Fatti gave up her life for it — she'd still do some hand modelling. Farah wondered whether Fatti's hands would swell as her pregnancy progressed, and she realized she was rather too pleased at the thought of it. Ash's voice was mirthful, but as Farah went inside she saw that he was looking at Fatti with concern. Bubblee was the first to see Farah.

'Where's Mustafa?' asked her dad when he looked up.

Farah said that he had stayed at home because he was doing some DIY. She kept the details vague — you only got caught out in lies when you were specific about them. Fatti looked pale and was slumped on the sofa next to Ash.

'Have you lost weight?' asked Farah.

Fatti merely shrugged.

'That'd be a yes,' added Bubblee. 'Look at

how loose her trousers are.'

'She basically doesn't eat,' said Ash. 'The other day I made some chicken and I had to take it into the garden and eat it because of the smell.'

'Oh, God. Don't say chicken,' said Fatti, closing her eyes.

Their mum looked at Fatti, worried. 'My poor daughter. She doesn't even want Primula cheese any more.'

'Gosh,' said Farah. 'You'll be the envy of all pregnant women and mums.'

Farah tried to laugh when she said it. She thought she'd succeeded in making it sound light.

'Nothing to envy here,' replied Ash.

Their mum got up and told Farah to help her in the kitchen.

'Don't mind Ashraf,' she said. 'Some husbands are very protective of their wives.'

What was that supposed to mean? That Mustafa was no longer protective of Farah? Could it be that he had fleeting thoughts about her just as she did about him? But most importantly, was it obvious to everyone around them? The humiliation of failure is so much greater when it has witnesses.

'Just because my husband decides to stay at home and do some DIY doesn't mean he doesn't care about me,' snapped Farah.

Her mum turned around, spatula in hand, looking surprised. Farah didn't know what to do about the look so took the spatula from her mum and checked on the rice.

'You are not the only one with a husband,' replied her mum, looking away.

Oh, God. Mae did say something about Mum and Dad not getting along. What could be the matter?

'Is everything okay?' asked Farah, out of courtesy more than concern. Her parents had been married for over forty years, and even though it was an arranged marriage — as they all were in those days — they never struck her as unhappy. Her mum had the final say and her dad was usually more than happy to go along with it. Now her mum hesitated.

'Yes, yes. You tell me. What did the doctor say?'

Perhaps Farah should've made a family announcement. She'd have to have this conversation again with Fatti and Mae — although Mae was too busy living her life and at least her mum could pass the information on to her dad. She took a deep breath before explaining that she and Mustafa were going to try surrogacy. Farah braced herself for her mum's discontent. It just wasn't the done thing, especially in the Asian community. Why, it was like your husband sleeping with another woman! Or, at least, him leaving his seed in another woman, which was practically the same thing.

Her mum's face contorted in confusion. '*How?*' she asked, adjusting the sari on her head.

Farah tried to explain what the procedure involved.

'Hai Allah,' exclaimed her mum, looking at her. 'What is this? Zi, this is not how Allah

99

intended things. What will people say? Think of the talk.'

'People aren't living my life,' replied Farah.

'I don't understand why you don't just ask Fatti to have a baby for you.'

Farah raised her eyebrows.

'Okay, okay. She is not in the best health to have another baby.'

'And especially when it's for someone else,' added Farah.

Plus, it felt like too much joy for Fatti. Farah hated herself for even thinking it but what can you do about thoughts? They flit in and out of the mind, unbidden.

'But it is Fatti. She will do anything for her family,' replied their mum.

'Anyway,' said Farah, feeling flustered, embarrassed at her own ungracious thoughts. 'It's not something Mustafa and I want to do. It's . . . *weird*.'

'But your husband having a baby with another woman is normal?'

Farah took a deep breath. 'It won't be *another woman's*. It'll be mine. Think of the woman as the oven. The ingredients are both of ours.'

Her mum ignored the curry that was now at boiling point so Farah lowered the heat on the hob. Her eyes bore into Farah's and she wondered what her mum was thinking. Turning away, Farah watched as her mum got out some turmeric and added it to the curry. She stirred the pot slowly, as if in deep thought, before putting the lid on. After a few minutes' silence, she spoke.

'When I couldn't have a baby I would stay up all night, offering prayers and supplications that God would help me. It took so long until your kala had Fatti for me, but I saw he had answered my prayers. And then you four came along too. So much happiness in our home. And a boy too. What a special blessing.'

Farah sighed deeply. How Jay, in all his absence whenever the family was together, and presence in his little room upstairs, was a blessing, she didn't understand. All that sisterly affection she had once had for him was gone. She'd never thought it'd be possible. Life and the events that unfolded could constantly surprise a person.

'Maybe this is God giving you an opportunity,' her mum finally said.

'Really?'

'It is a very strange thing to do,' she said. 'But I know what it is like to want a baby, Faru.'

'But it's so . . . untraditional. People will talk. Especially in Bangladesh when they find out.' Farah considered out loud.

Perhaps Farah should be worried about what people would say. But there was so much else to worry her, she couldn't add that to the list as well.

Her mum nodded. 'Yes. They will talk. But we don't have to announce what is happening. We will think about all of that later. If you start worrying about that now, then you will never do it.'

Farah went and hugged her mum, who held her tight. How easily she'd accepted the idea of surrogacy and what a relief it was to know that Farah was perhaps actually doing the right thing. She didn't think she could've come up against another hurdle in the process. Farah wanted Bubblee to understand her need for a baby, but who could know it better than their mum who'd adopted Fatti, believing she'd never have children of her own, and then gave birth to the rest of them? Farah suddenly felt hopeful.

'In the meantime you don't speak to anyone, apart from your sisters, about it. Not even your abba. He is an old man and he is set in his old ways.'

Farah nodded.

'And one last thing. You mustn't have a strange woman to have your baby for you. You must find someone who doesn't run away with it.'

'That's what legal contracts are for,' replied Farah.

Her mum shook her head. 'You think contracts can help when a woman has an idea in her head? No, no. You must ask someone you know and trust.'

'Are you going to have it for me, Amma?' said Farah, suppressing a smile.

Her mum closed her eyes and pursed her lips at Farah. She then went about the kitchen, adding more salt to the curry. After a few minutes of this she stopped and looked Farah straight in the eye.

'You should ask Bubblee.'

Farah laughed out so loudly her dad shouted: 'What is so funny?'

'You don't mind,' her mum shouted back with rather more force than necessary.

'*Bubblee?*' exclaimed Farah, keeping her voice as low as possible. 'Amma, Bubblee would rather go to Bangladesh, marry someone from the village and spend the rest of her life as a housewife than carry someone else's baby.'

'Who is *someone else?* You are sisters. This is what sisters must do for each other.'

Even Farah felt that this level of expectation was rather high.

'No, Amma. That's insane.'

'What is the harm in asking?'

Farah paused, ignoring the rice for so long that her mum eventually took the turner from her.

'She'd never do it,' said Farah, almost to herself, staring at the stove.

That's when Fatti came in and started looking through the kitchen drawers.

'I need a safety pin,' she moaned, pulling at the waist of her trousers. 'They nearly fell off.'

'Oh, look at this,' exclaimed their mum, putting her hand in the gap. She ordered Fatti to take her trousers off so she could sew in the waist for her. Without thinking, Fatti started taking the trousers off in the kitchen.

'Maybe you want to go upstairs?' suggested Farah.

'Hmm?' answered Fatti, looking up.

'See?' said Bubblee who'd followed Fatti into the kitchen. 'Now you're pregnant, Mum has even more excuse to fawn over you. Nice legs.'

Their mum merely looked at Fatti in

103

sympathy. 'Doesn't matter, doesn't matter. No one will see. Just close the kitchen door.'

Farah noticed that Fatti's legs hadn't been shaved for a while.

'Go and get Fatti your pyjama bottoms,' their mum ordered Bubblee.

Bubblee sighed and left the kitchen to do as she was told as Fatti sat on a stool and put her head between her knees. Farah watched her suffering sister and bent over her, asking if she wanted any water.

'Plain toast, maybe?' she offered.

'Ohhh, God,' Fatti moaned and dashed out of the kitchen, thighs wobbling, not caring that she had to run past her husband and dad without her trousers on, and straight into the toilet.

'At least you won't have to go through that,' said their mum now that they were alone again.

'No.' Farah shook her head, thinking about it.

'First, think how much money you would save. Second, how much better to keep this in the family.'

There was no denying that it'd save them money they didn't have. But was *that* even ethical — not paying a surrogate just because she's your sister? No, Farah would have to pay her for doing something like that — it wasn't as if Bubblee had any kind of income right now. This would be her job. She couldn't believe she was even having these thoughts. It was out of the question. Wasn't it? Her mum was still talking, but she didn't really hear what she was saying.

'A job,' murmured Farah.

'Yes!' exclaimed her mum. 'It is a sister's job

104

to do things for the other.'

Farah let her mum talk, without interruption, lost in her own thoughts about what exactly one sister is meant to do for another — what is the line that should never be crossed? Bubblee came in, holding up her pyjama bottoms for Fatti.

But then, perhaps with sisters, there should be no line.

★ ★ ★

It didn't matter that Mustafa was asleep when Farah got home — she had to talk to him. Because he'd never buy the idea of Bubblee carrying their baby and that would put an end to the whole thing for her.

'Hmm?' he shrugged her off and carried on sleeping.

'*Wake up*,' she said.

It took more than a few tries before Mustafa finally managed to prise his eyes open.

'Have you drugged yourself to sleep or something?' said Farah.

But it was no use — Mustafa's eyes closed almost as soon as they'd opened. Farah didn't sleep properly the entire night.

★ ★ ★

'You were knocked out yesterday,' she said the following morning when Mustafa came down the stairs. 'I tried to wake you.'

'Did you?' he mumbled.

He sat down as Farah got up and put the

kettle on. She glanced at him staring at the table, his bathrobe open.

'Yes. A few times,' she said.

'Oh.'

She wanted to ask if he was okay but she needed to get this conversation out of the way. When she told him what her mum had suggested she expected more from him than a blank look.

'Well?' she asked when he didn't say anything.

'Bubblee?'

'Yes. Bubblee. *Our* Bubblee. My twin, whose idea of hell is anything domestic-orientated and having babies is one of them.' Farah shook her head, expecting Mustafa to get in on the joke. 'Can you believe Mum suggested it?'

He held the mug of tea in his hand and looked into it. 'Sure.'

'*Sure?*' replied Farah, bending her head so he'd look at her.

He nodded.

'You obviously need more sleep.'

'I don't need more sleep, I need you to stop talking to me,' he snapped.

Farah leaned back. Her instinct was to shout at him — get into yet another argument about this being *their* family and decisions being joint, but as soon as she was about to start she felt devoid of energy. How many times were they to go through the same thing?

'Sorry,' he muttered, not looking at her.

'*Sure,*' she said.

With that, she left the room and the house, not telling Mustafa where she was going. She hardly knew herself. Farah just got in the car and started driving. They were going around in circles: talk, argue, make up. Perhaps Mustafa needed to go to the doctor's and talk about the pills he was taking. They had known there were going to be side effects, his moods being one of them, but lately it had been getting worse. Yes, she'd tell him to set up an appointment. She had to remind herself that the man who snapped at her wasn't her husband. Farah found herself driving towards her mum and dad's house again, almost without thinking. When she opened the front door with her key she realized that she wanted to see Bubblee.

'Hey, didn't get enough of us last night?' called out Bubblee from the top of the stairs. 'Mum and Dad are out.'

Farah went up the stairs and into Bubblee's room where she was wrapped in a towel, clearly just out of the shower. Bubblee began changing and Farah noticed her perfectly flat stomach, feeling a jolt of realization at what she was about to ask. But she knew what the answer would be — so what was the harm? Bubblee would say no, they'd get over it, and Farah could start a search for a surrogate to whom she wasn't related.

'Guess what?' said Farah, faux laughing as she sat on the edge of the bed. She could see signs of Bubblee emerging in the room. Her books stacked in a corner. A few choice paintings leaning against the wall, waiting to be put up. Was Bubblee making this home again?

'What?' said Bubblee, turning around as she buttoned up her checked shirt.

'Mum went and suggested that *you* be my surrogate.'

Farah laughed again. She sounded a bit delirious. Bubblee stared at her, her eyebrows knit together as her fingers held on to the last shirt button. Farah laughed again. She had become a mad hatter.

'I know. Crazy, right?'

Bubblee didn't move.

'I told her she was insane. As if you, of all people, would want to do something like that. She went on about sisters sacrificing things for each other, but I told her there was sacrifice and then there was *surrogacy*.' Farah waited for a reaction. Nothing. 'She started going on about us saving money — not that we wouldn't pay you — and how at least we could trust you and it'd be in the family.' Farah's mouth felt dry and she suddenly needed to drink a lot of water. 'Mum said how you have time now for other things, and I tried to explain that you'd soon find something that you love as much as making sculptures. We couldn't possibly tie you down like that. It's a crazy idea.'

Bubblee's frown looked as though it was threatening a long-term stay.

'Me?' said Bubblee.

Farah nodded, rolling her eyes in exaggeration. She probably looked possessed.

'Pregnant? With your baby?'

Farah nodded again. 'Don't worry about it. I just thought it was funny.'

Bubblee wasn't laughing though. She was barely even smiling.

'That is crazy,' she said, almost in a whisper.

Farah couldn't help but find her heart heave at these words; tears came to her eyes, but she continued to try and laugh.

'I know, I know.'

It couldn't be helped. The tears fell down her cheeks as Bubblee went and sat next to her.

'Oh, Faar.'

'I'm *fine*. It's a silly idea. We'll get someone. I'd never expect you to . . . it's really absurd. You have a life!'

Bubblee gave a weak smile. Farah leaned her head against Bubblee's shoulder. She got a faint waft of coconut and tried to let the smell calm her. It was lavender she needed. Lavender and a willing womb.

'I don't even know why I'm crying,' said Farah, sitting up straight.

'Mustafa wouldn't exactly be happy about me carrying the baby, anyway,' offered Bubblee.

'Oh, no. He was fine about it, actually. He was excited,' Farah lied.

He *was* excited about the surrogacy at least, despite it having gone downhill after the Mothercare debacle.

'Excited?' said Bubblee incredulously.

Farah nodded vehemently. They both sat in silence for a while before Farah stood up.

'I just came over to see if you wanted to have lunch or something? Mustafa's still a bit under the weather.'

'He's been under the weather quite a bit lately, hasn't he?' added Bubblee.

Farah ignored her comment as they both went

down the stairs to the kitchen. Bubblee was filling the silence with inane talk about the latest documentary she'd seen on Netflix. Farah smiled and nodded when she thought it was appropriate but hardly heard two words Bubblee said. As they both sat, taking bites out of their cheese sandwiches, Bubblee seemed to have run out of programmes to talk about.

'Read anything interesting lately?' she asked.

'Just surrogacy websites.'

Bubblee dusted the crumbs from her mouth. 'Did you watch Mae's YouTube video about starting uni?'

'No,' replied Farah.

'It was pretty funny.'

Farah gave a non-committal smile.

'Well, I'd better get back — see how Mustafa's doing,' she said, standing. 'Up to anything good now?'

Bubblee took both their plates, not quite meeting Farah's gaze. 'Not sure. Maybe I'll . . . I don't know. Perhaps I'll learn to play the guitar or something.'

'But you don't own a guitar,' said Farah, eyebrows twitching in confusion.

'Yeah, I know, I was just . . . you know. I mean, I could do anything, couldn't I?'

Farah looked straight into Bubblee's eyes. 'You really could.'

⋆ ⋆ ⋆

Play the guitar? Bubblee shook her head at herself as she washed the dishes. She looked around the kitchen, searching for something to do. For a moment she even considered organizing her mum's Tupperware before realizing that that would be a new depth to her despair. Instead, she went to her room and opened up her laptop to look at pictures she'd taken of some sculptures she had in progress. She then took out her phone and went through her Instagram account. Not many people liked the pieces she'd put up. Why had she never paid attention to that before? Just then her phone rang. It was Farah.

'Did you forg — '

'The thing is,' interrupted Farah urgently, 'if I don't ask for the things I want — the *one* thing I want — from the person who might make it that much easier for me, then what's the point?'

'What?' muttered Bubblee. Her heart had lurched somewhere into her stomach.

'I can't be indecisive about *this* of all things.'

'Faar, listen . . . ' Bubblee's mouth had gone dry. She wanted to hang up the phone; close her ears; just look through all the artwork she'd created in the past ten years.

'Please, Bubs. I want you to be my child's surrogate mum.'

Was this how Fatti's nausea felt?

'There,' added Farah. 'I said it. That's all I wanted.'

'Listen, Faar,' said Bubblee, trying to keep her voice firm, but sympathetic. 'There is a lot I'd do for you. You know that. I realize I've not been the most present sister in the past, but when there's an emergency, I'm there, aren't I?'

Silence.

'But this? Come on. Even you know how . . . *ridiculous* this is. Does Mum even know what surrogacy is? Doesn't she have, like, religious opinions about it?' Bubblee shook her head. 'She probably doesn't care, does she? It's fine for her to pick and choose when it comes to having a baby. Mum won't care about any opinion but her own. She pretended Fatti was her biological child for most of her life and that wasn't exactly religious of her. She always sees things in black and white — '

'What's so wrong with being black and white, anyway? Don't you think it's progressive of her to even suggest it?'

Bubblee paused. She couldn't deny that much. It was quite extraordinary that their mother would agree to such a thing. But then her mum knew the desperation of wanting babies, the lengths that a person could go to in order to be a mother.

'Maybe. Yes, fine. But that's not the point.'

'What's the point then? What is the point of me and my life?'

'Farah,' said Bubblee, taken aback.

She could hear the tremor in her sister's voice, but her words frightened Bubblee.

'You are *not* the sum of the children you have,' said Bubblee.

'No? Then what am I?'

'You're a *person*.'

Bubblee heard what she thought was a scoff from Farah.

'A person? You don't know. You don't understand.'

'No, I don't. I'm sorry, but I just don't.'

Silence. There seemed to be no bridge to understanding here. Loving your sister didn't mean knowing and understanding them. The thought depressed Bubblee, and she never took herself for a sentimentalist.

'Listen, I've got a little money saved that I won't be spending because I'm staying with Mum and Dad. I'll lend it to you. You can have it.'

Bubblee realized that this made it seem as if she'd be at her parents' longer than anticipated, but it was the only thing she could offer.

'It's not your money I want, Bubs. What I want is for you to carry my and Mustafa's child. It's what I *need*.' Farah paused and let out a sigh. 'The rest . . . it's up to you.'

Bubblee put the phone down, hardly able to say goodbye. She sat there and stared at a spot on the table for what felt like hours, until her parents returned home. She gave nothing away to them, but noticed her mum glancing at her every so often. Did she know what Farah had asked of her? Why did she always want Bubblee to do the very things she hated? Why did her own mother not know her? And as for her sister? She'd been blinded by desperation and now it was Bubblee who had to be the one to disappoint.

Mae: Errrrr. Im the I whos meant 2b 2 bz for you losers. Where is evry1?

113

Anyway whatevs. Goin to party nw. Freedoooooooom.

Mae: Nt doom. Better nt jinx uni. L8ers! Xxxx

Fatti: My clothes are getting too loose for me. Never thought I'd see the day. Ash isn't happy. Be good at the party xxx

Bubblee waited to see if Farah would respond. She didn't have the ability to make light jokes or any kind of comment to Mae. She stared at the screen for ages, just to see if the words *Farah is typing* . . . would come up. But nothing did. Eventually, she put her phone away. She tried to do some reading before bed, but ended up just looking at the pictures of her sculptures again. She went onto her gallery's website and saw that her job vacancy had been filled. Another hopeful with probably a lot more talent than her had taken her place.

It was only ten o'clock but Bubblee decided she might as well go to sleep. She checked her phone one last time, but it was only a few more exchanges between Mae and Fatti. Bubblee closed her eyes and waited for sleep to take over.

7

Bubblee didn't sleep. And if Farah had anything to do with it, she wouldn't sleep for the rest of her life. Not with the seismic guilt weighing down on her. When she woke up the following morning she felt a surge of anger towards her twin sister. *What the hell was she thinking?* On a basic level of propriety, you don't just ask someone to carry your baby for them. And on a personal level, when you know exactly how a person feels about babies and such things, you *definitely* don't ask them. Bubblee banged around the room before going down the stairs and clattering around the kitchen, making coffee.

'Tst, Bubblee, you will break my mugs,' exclaimed her mum.

Her mum looked in an especially foul mood. Her eyebrows were knitted together as she shouted out to Bubblee's dad, who was upstairs, asking what he wanted for breakfast.

'For God's sake, Amma. As if he can't make his own breakfast.'

'This is why you're not married,' her mum snapped back.

'Yeah, well, thanks but I'm not sure what type of person wants to get married for their ability to make fried eggs and toast.'

They both ended up banging plates on the kitchen counters, bumping into each other without apologizing before Bubblee's dad came into the kitchen.

'What is all this banging?' he asked nervously.

'You go back inside,' her mum exclaimed to him.

'*Amma*,' said Bubblee.

Her dad merely cleared his throat and left.

'That was a bit harsh,' she said to her mum.

Just then Bubblee's phone buzzed. It took her a few moments to pluck up the courage to look at it, in case it was Farah. It was just Fatti on their group chat. Bubblee realized that her mum was peering over her shoulder.

'You girls are always chat-chat-chatting on that. What about your amma?'

Bubblee turned to her, mostly so she could hide the messages from her mum. Not that there was anything wrong with what was on there, just that it felt like a private space for them, without parental interference.

'What about you, Amma?' She picked up her coffee, readying herself to leave and lock herself in her room.

'Only Fatti tells me how our little Mae is. Even when she is so sick, poor child.'

Bubblee thought it was just typical that the one who was married and the most settled should be the go-between for the sisters and parents. It used to be Farah's job. Bubblee wondered how she must feel about that. Not happy, she imagined.

'Right, well. I'd better go and . . . ' What was Bubblee going to do exactly?

She mumbled something about sorting through

116

her emails and walked as quickly as possible past her mum, up the stairs, and into the sanctuary of a room that wasn't really hers.

Bubblee instinctively took out her phone and tapped her finger on Fatti's name to call her.

'You're not busy throwing up or anything, are you?' asked Bubblee.

'We're out buying baby stuff, but I'm lying on the bed in the home department while Ash looks at cots.'

'Ever heard of online shopping?'

Fatti groaned before Bubblee heard her speak to, presumably, one of the sales assistants. 'Oh, I'm sorry. I just felt a bit faint. Really? Thank you so much. That's really nice of you.'

'Why don't you get under the duvet while you're at it?'

'I felt bad because I'm always ill and we're not getting to do any of the stuff that Ash was so excited about us doing together. You should see him checking the dimensions of the cot.'

'Bit much,' said Bubblee.

'Maybe. But he says he made mistakes in his first marriage with his son and so I suppose he's trying to make up for that somehow. It's nice, actually, watching him take over and just get things done. I can't go to a shop without needing to lie down or throwing up. Hopefully it'll get better once I'm past the three-month mark.'

'Is it awful?' Bubblee asked.

'Well, it's not great.'

Bubblee took a sip of her coffee, thinking about Farah's phone call and whether she should tell Fatti. Not that Bubblee was considering it.

117

But even so, what was it like to be pregnant?

'People who have babies are crazy,' said Bubblee.

'No, they just want a family,' replied Fatti. 'Would you believe I have to go and get some trousers and skirts in a smaller size? Nothing fits me any more.'

'Will you do it again?' asked Bubblee. 'I mean, have another baby?'

'Let me get through this one first. Have you spoken to Farah, by the way? I want to call her and see how she's doing but whenever we speak on the phone there's this awkwardness. It makes me feel bad for having the baby.'

'Don't let her make you feel guilty about your happiness,' said Bubblee, accidentally sloshing her coffee on the carpet. 'We're not all here to please Farah, you know. There are other people in this family who need things. She's probably at home, cleaning, going about her business without a thought for how she makes the rest of us feel when she asks things like . . . like me being a surrogate for her and Mustafa's baby.'

There was a pause before Fatti said: 'Oh. Right. Really?'

'You don't sound very surprised.'

'I *am* surprised.'

Bubblee managed to have an incredulous look, even though Fatti couldn't see her. 'You were always a really bad liar. Farah's told you?'

Fatti paused again. 'No, I'm not exactly the person she'd speak to about it. It was Mum, actually.'

'Oh, *of course*,' said Bubblee, spilling more

118

coffee on the carpet. 'For God's sake.'

She bent down to wipe the carpet with a tissue before her mum had more to complain about.

'Calm down,' said Fatti.

'Fatti — *Mum* is the one who suggested it to Farah. Doesn't it just piss you off that she knows her daughters so little that she'd ask this of me?'

She sat down on the edge of her bed, shaking her head.

'You should try and understand her a little,' said Fatti.

'As much as she tries to understand me?'

Fatti remained quiet on the other end of the phone.

'Right,' said Bubblee after a while. 'I see. Always playing devil's advocate. I just can't believe that Mum would . . . you know.'

'It'd save them some money, I suppose. And of course they trust you.'

'Yeah, I've heard that,' mumbled Bubblee.

'I see Ash. I'd better go.'

'Hmm.'

'Listen,' added Fatti. 'If you want to talk about it or anything. You know, ask me questions or whatever. You can just call me.'

Bubblee nodded. 'Thanks. But I couldn't do it. It's insane.'

'*Let's get you home, shall we?*' Bubblee heard Ash say in the background.

'It's a big decision,' said Fatti.

Bubblee scoffed — anything anyone said about the size of the decision was making an understatement.

'You actually think I should *do* it?'

It was the first time Bubblee felt like hanging up on Fatti. She was meant to be the reasonable one. And she was one to talk — it wasn't as if she'd been turning cartwheels when Mum had suggested she have a second baby for Farah to adopt.

'I think some things are too important not to consider, at least.'

'Like you considered having a baby for Farah?'

There was a pause. 'Just one second,' Bubblee heard Fatti say to Ash. 'Of course I considered it. I went home that night and thought about it, but I knew it wasn't possible. Plus, I know Ash, there's no way he'd give away a baby of his. He feels guilty enough that he can't be around his son all the time.'

Bubblee took a deep breath. Who knew what went on in people's heads sometimes? 'I know it's a big ask. And maybe it's unfortunate that neither Mae nor I could be the ones Farah could ask, but things happen for a reason.'

Bubblee barely hid her scoff. People who said things like that were just too afraid to admit that they had failed at something. Whatever it might be.

'And just imagine,' added Fatti. 'You could change a life by bringing another life into the world.'

⋆ ⋆ ⋆

Bubblee had to get away. The weight of this question looming over her gave her claustrophobia every time she saw her mum, even heard her

120

voice in the house. It just reminded her of the idea that she'd put in Farah's head. And that was nothing compared to freezing on the spot every time she thought she heard a key in the front door, thinking it was Farah. But it seemed that Farah was avoiding Bubblee too, much to Bubblee's relief.

'I'm going back to London for a bit,' she announced the following evening to her parents.

Bubblee's mum's eyes bore into her own. Did she know that Bubblee knew she was the one who'd suggested her as a surrogate? Did Fatti throw up that information along with everything else she was throwing up?

'Why?' her mum asked, eyes squinting.

Bubblee pretended she was reading some messages on her phone, trying to be offhand. 'I've got lots of my stuff there still and I'm going to see some friends. Maybe look for another job.'

'Job?'

This time her dad leaned forward in his armchair, blinking at her. He scratched his black hair.

'Yes. I think it's time for me to look for something I might do.'

'But what?' he asked, glancing at his wife who hadn't taken her eyes off Bubblee.

'Leave your family again for London?' said her mum.

Resolution gripped Bubblee. It always did when faced with opposition.

'I'm not leaving anyone. I'm simply living my life. Last time I checked, that's not a crime. Although it's hard to know with this family.'

Her dad leaned back and shook his head. 'Always so dramatic.'

Ha! Little did he know what was going on.

'Let her go, Jay's amma.'

Bubblee's mum shot him a look, which had him lower his eyes at his paper again.

'Bubblee, you should listen to your amma.'

'No, thanks,' she said, standing up. 'I'd rather listen to myself.'

The following morning Bubblee, having packed some of her things, got into her car to make her way back to London.

⋆ ⋆ ⋆

'Well, look what the cat dragged in,' exclaimed Sasha, rushing out to meet Bubblee. 'Bubble, bubble, toil and trouble.'

They embraced as Bubblee looked at her friend and said: 'I've only just realized that you actually sound like Mae.'

Sasha smiled her wide, toothy grin and put her hands on her hips. 'Excellent. She's my favourite.'

'She's a pain,' said Bubblee as they both walked into Sasha's flat. 'Is it me or has the flat got smaller?'

'The flat's got smaller,' said Sasha.

She took Bubblee's bag and dumped it on the floor, eyeing her up and down.

'My, haven't you grown.'

'Shut up,' said Bubblee, smiling.

'Wyvernage has changed you.'

They both sat down.

'So?' said Sasha. 'How's the quaint village life?'

Bubblee filled Sasha in on her time at home — minus the surrogacy conversation. It was a bit too soon for that. Sasha asked about her family: how was Mae doing at uni? Was Mustafa still a drip? How's Fatti's pregnancy coming along? Bubblee felt the release of all the tension that came from being at home. This was home. With Sasha and this flat and all the familiarity that came along with it. How nice it was to be able to talk about her family with someone who knew them but wasn't a part of them. Bubblee had space here to be who she was, to relax and not have to defend the right to her own views every five minutes.

'You know Kyle?' said Sasha. 'Remember? The pretentious one who thinks he's Kandinsky?'

'Oh, yes. The American.'

'Exactly. Just landed an expo in the space Queen Bee Alice runs.'

'Really?' said Bubblee, shifting on the sofa. 'So, are we eating in or out?'

'*In*, of course. We're impoverished artistes.'

Sasha flung back her red curls, dramatically, but winced as she gripped her neck.

'Ouch,' she said.

Bubblee laughed. '*Old* artistes, clearly.'

'You might be old. I'm just paying the dues of art's physical work.'

Bubblee got up and walked around the flat as Sasha babbled on and got snacks and drinks from the kitchen. She looked at the intense line drawings made by Sasha, finished pieces stacked against the wall.

'People have actually bought them,' said Sasha. 'Can you believe it?'

'I can,' Bubblee said in a barely audible voice. 'I'm just going to use the bathroom. Freshen up.'

As she walked down the hall she ended up going past Sasha's bathroom and into her studio, down a short flight of stairs. As soon as she stepped into the room, she felt an almost overwhelming sense of nostalgia and loss; the envy of something that was never quite hers. The drawings dotted around the walls; the easel in the middle of the room with Sasha's work-in-progress; the papers and pencils in pots and scattered around the room — they all felt as though they belonged in a home she'd never lived in, like looking in on a dream about her, but not actually hers. It all looked so alive — as if the things in the room had a beginning with an indefinable end. Despair set in.

'Bubbles?'

'Oh.' Bubblee started as she turned around to see Sasha standing at the doorway, her eyebrows slightly creased.

'Look at all this,' said Bubblee, looking around the room again.

Sasha gave a small smile.

'I hardly recognize it,' Bubblee added. 'You're really getting there, aren't you?'

Sasha leaned against the door frame and crossed her arms, giving a small shrug. 'It'll do for now. It's slow, but yes, it's progress.'

Sasha linked arms with Bubblee as they walked back into the living room where she had laid the table out. They both sat down as Sasha looked at Bubblee.

'Right. Spill.'

Bubblee took a sip of her coffee.

'I've been having a break,' said Bubblee.

'Yeah, a pretty long one. I still don't get why you quit the gallery.'

'It depressed me. Being around art and not being included in it.'

'Bubs, these things take time. And you know, you always overthought all your pieces.'

'So you're a critic now, too?'

Bubblee didn't mean to sound harsh, but there was a bitterness to her voice that she couldn't hide.

'No, arsehole, I'm your friend,' said Sasha, gripping her hand.

Bubblee returned her friend's squeeze.

'Anyway, you're back now,' said Sasha, raising her cup of coffee to her friend. Was Bubblee back? 'A fresh start, new beginnings, etcetera, etcetera. Here's to finding your mojo.' Sasha leaned forward. 'To finding your *art*.'

Bubblee raised her cup of coffee too, her heart plummeting at the very idea.

★ ★ ★

A box room was not the ideal place to find anything. Even though Bubblee hadn't brought a lot with her, she still didn't have space to swing one of her sculptures. When Bubblee left the flat she'd get herself a cup of coffee from a local café and walk around the familiar streets. One day she got the Tube to the National Portrait Gallery to have a look at the latest exhibitions; she sat and had lunch while reading a book near St Martin's Lane. She took in the bustle of the place — the different people of all ages and colours — and smiled to herself, feeling lost in a crowd, yet as if she belonged. For a minute Bubblee felt as if she were twenty-one again, just finished university and with the world at her fingertips. But she wasn't twenty-one. The world was the same — she was not. It wasn't the fact that she was older — one's thirties were far more dignified than one's twenties, and God knows she was looking forward to what her forties would bring — it was what that age meant now. Surely you were the sum of your accomplishments, and what had she actually accomplished? Wyvernage had felt too small for her when she was growing up; now she felt too small for London. This was the place of vast opportunities; of chance encounters and unlikely friendships; of political talk and social activism; of art and culture. Yet all of this meant nothing to Bubblee now that she had no real purpose in her life. What was the point of having all these things available on the outside when it was her inside that lacked focus?

It took Bubblee a week before she dug out one of her sculptures from the cubbyhole where Sasha had let her store some things. She stared at it for an hour while Sasha was working in her studio. Bubblee frowned at the deformed arm of a woman, who was sitting cross-legged, meditating on a piece of turd. *What had Bubblee been thinking when she made this?* At the time she remembered feeling as if she'd created something ironic, symbolizing the state of our times. Now she saw that it was trying too hard to be poignant.

'This is, quite literally, a piece of turd,' she mumbled.

'Don't be so harsh on yourself,' said Sasha, who'd walked into the room.

Her hair was tied up in a messy bun and it didn't look as though she'd yet washed her face, even though it was twelve o'clock in the afternoon. Sasha poured herself a glass of water.

'It wasn't your best work,' she added. 'You were just beginning, though.'

'Did I ever actually make it past beginner's stage?'

Sasha took her hair out, running her fingers through it to untangle the mass.

'Life crisis still going on then?' said Sasha.

Bubblee threw a pen at her. Sasha didn't flinch, but simply picked the pen up and threw it back at Bubblee. She caught the pen and hesitated for a moment.

'That and my sister's asked me to be a surrogate for her baby.'

Sasha choked on her water. '*Excuse me?*' She wiped her mouth and looked at Bubblee. '*You?* A surrogate?'

'Me. A surrogate.'

Sasha walked over to the table where Bubblee was sitting. 'God. Your family like their high expectations, don't they?'

Bubblee stared at her woman on a turd. 'It's

not an expectation. Just a request.'

'A pretty big one,' said Sasha.

'Some people call it desperation. Being hopeful even. Maybe.'

'Look at you, all measured in response.'

Bubblee gave a short laugh. 'Yeah, well, I had my fair share of ranting at bedroom walls.'

'Awkward though, eh. No wonder you've come running back to London. And I'm so glad you have,' Sasha said, grabbing Bubblee's arm. 'I've emailed you some websites, by the way, for temp work, to help you get by. You're going to need a job pretty soon. My place is open to you though, for as long as you need it. Don't worry about that.'

Bubblee's heart sank at the idea of a job in an office. She felt claustrophobic just thinking about the routine of a nine-to-five. And what exactly lay beyond that?

'How depressing,' she said.

'Capitalism at its finest, my friend,' Sasha replied.

That night, when Bubblee went to bed, she replayed the conversation with Sasha in her head. Her best friend hadn't even discussed the possibility of Bubblee being a surrogate — she just sent her some links to websites for temp work. A *temp?* Bubblee tossed and turned until she couldn't take it any longer. She marched into Sasha's room and switched the light on. Sasha squinted as she lifted her head from her pillow.

'You didn't even ask me what I wanted to do,' said Bubblee.

'Huh?' said Sasha.

128

'If I *wanted* to be a surrogate.'

Sasha rubbed her eyes. 'I thought we both already knew the answer to that question.'

Bubblee felt agitated and confused. She knew, it wasn't as if she wanted to be a surrogate — no way! But the fact that Sasha dismissed it without another thought made Bubblee wonder whether there was something inherently wrong with the idea of her being one. Was she incapable of it or something? Just as she was incapable of being an artist? Her words and feelings were in knots and she didn't know how to untangle either to get to the bottom of whatever it was that was happening.

'That's not the point,' said Bubblee.

'What is then?'

'Is there something intrinsically ridiculous about me doing something for another person?'

'When it's carrying a baby, yeah.' Sasha sat up and patted the bed for Bubblee to sit next to her.

Bubblee simply crossed her arms.

'Don't take this the wrong way, Bubbles, because you know I love you, but it's not like your life is about other people. Neither of our lives are. We're selfish cows and we don't apologize for it, because, well, that's the price of following your dream.'

'I'm selfish?' said Bubblee.

She stared at the flooring. *Selfish?* What appeared selfish to others always seemed to Bubblee the logical thing to do. What was so selfish about following your dreams? Why wouldn't you? And if there were things like family stopping you, surely they were the selfish ones?

'Worst word for me to use, because it implies something negative, but that's how others see it, I'm sure. We'll go into the way women are taught language that maintains our patriarchy when I'm not ready to drop off back to sleep.' Sasha took a deep breath. 'It's called knowing your mind and going for it, Bubbles. Some people call it selfish. We call it living.'

Bubblee walked up to Sasha and sat on her bed. The beating of her heart seemed to slow down. Her friend was right, of course.

'Or making sculptures in your case,' added Sasha.

That was when Bubblee realized that she no longer knew what she was living for.

'But I can't, can I?' said Bubblee. 'You know as well as I do that's not going to work out for me.'

Sasha's silence spoke volumes. She was being a supportive friend, urging Bubblee to follow her dreams, but she couldn't lie about the fact that Bubblee didn't have the talent.

'You'll find something.'

'Really? What?'

'These things take time,' said Sasha.

'And what am I meant to do in the meanwhile? Sit around and wait for inspiration?'

'You're going to be a surrogate because you don't know what else to do with your life? Put your body through that? And what about the emotional toll it'd take on you?'

'No, I'm not,' said Bubblee, shaking her head. 'Of course I'm not going to do it. Although, I wouldn't need to worry about the emotional toll because it's not as if I'm about to go all maternal. I don't see why I'd desire to have a baby just because one was growing inside me.'

'People call them hormones.'

'It's a state of mind,' replied Bubblee.

'I'm sure that's what they teach people at medical school.'

Bubblee stared at the white bed sheet as she felt Sasha's eyes on her.

'Do you want children?' asked Bubblee.

Sasha nodded, without even pausing. 'Yes. One day. Not now. Plus, I'm dating Reuben and I don't think he's really father material.'

'Reuben?'

Sasha nodded again. 'He's hot and clever, so he'll do for now.'

'Would you ever be a surrogate for someone?'

Sasha scratched her brow. 'Why do you keep talking about this surrogacy when you say you don't want to do it?'

'I don't,' replied Bubblee.

'Every time I mention something against it you come in and defend it.'

'I'm being devil's advocate.'

Bubblee turned to look at Sasha, who'd raised her eyebrows.

'Because you always seek to understand the other side of the argument, don't you?'

Bubblee stood up to leave but paused. She wasn't sure why. This discussion felt unfinished even though she wanted it to end.

'Maybe Wyvernage really *has* changed you,' said Sasha, smiling.

'Shut up.'

'*Or* there's the flip side to things.'

'What's that then?' asked Bubblee, folding her arms around her again.

'On a philosophical level, one might consider growing a baby one's very own act of artistry. Besides — '

'Oh, my God, do you really have more to say?' interrupted Bubblee.

'Always. *Besides*, maybe it's not about you changing, but you changing things for others in little Wyvernage.'

★ ★ ★

It had been over a month since Mae had left for university and she hadn't come home for a visit. Bubblee assumed she'd been coerced into it by Fatti who'd insisted that their parents missed her, when it was really Fatti who wanted to see her. Of course, Mae could never refuse Fatti. When Fatti messaged Bubblee that she should come home too she'd initially said no. But a whole week of going through websites, looking for a job as a temp, attending three interviews at one of which she was offered a job — consisting of database entry — she felt that perhaps Fatti had a point.

'When will you be back?' asked Sasha, as they said their goodbyes on the doorstep.

Bubblee gave her a long, hard look. 'When you get a bigger room for me.'

Sasha laughed, grabbing her into a tight hug. 'You'll figure things out.'

Bubblee considered her friend and felt a surge

of pride and envy that she had such talent and knew exactly what to do with it. With that thought, Bubblee made her way back home.

★ ★ ★

As soon as Bubblee opened the door she heard Mae's voice: 'Can someone tell me what's happened to Fatti?'

She walked in to see everyone gathered in the living room, Mae having dropped her bag on the floor as Fatti was hugging her.

'Why are you . . . like, *thin?* Are you sure you're having a baby?'

'Our new woman of the world's returned then?' said Bubblee.

Mae gave her a big smile before hugging her. Bubblee glanced at Farah. This was the first time she'd seen her since the surrogate conversation. They exchanged awkward hellos. Bubblee could tell when Farah was attempting to be normal; her voice was always raised a decibel, and her smile remained fixed.

'Decent journey?' Farah asked Bubblee.

'Yeah. Fine. How're things?'

'Fine, thanks. You?'

'Good. London was great.' Bubblee found herself mirroring Farah's fixed smile. 'Where's Mustafa?' she asked.

'Doing some overtime at the stables,' replied Farah.

Mae looked at them both. 'What's wrong with you two?'

'Never mind them,' said their mum. 'Look at

what you've done to your beautiful hair,' she exclaimed. 'How will a boy marry you when you look like a boy yourself?'

Their mum tugged at the short, feathered strands on Mae's head. Their dad didn't look very happy either, but Bubblee thought it suited Mae's little face. She didn't look like an Asian clone. She looked womanly and in command.

'A new cut to go with your new life,' said Bubblee. 'Good.'

'Ow. Easy, Amma,' said Mae to their mum who was pulling at her hair again, as if she could make it grow if she did that enough. 'Also, I'm like a *foetus* in comparison to Bubblee. Bug her about marriage.' Mae took a deep breath as she mumbled to Bubblee: 'Haven't been here five seconds and she's already started.'

Bubblee put her arm around her little sister. 'Yep. Welcome to my world.'

★   ★   ★

Once the family had had dinner the girls began to clear up. Ash also got up to help before their mum exclaimed: 'Men don't do housework. Sit, sit. Fatti, you rest as well.'

'Actually, can I . . . I just need to lie down for a bit.'

With which Fatti trudged up the stairs into what everyone now thought of as Bubblee's room. Mae followed Fatti up the stairs before Bubblee realized that it was just her and Farah in the kitchen.

'How was Sasha?' Farah asked.

'Good.'

The dishes clanged in the sink as Farah ran the tap to wash up. Bubblee stood next to her to dry.

'How are you?' asked Bubblee.

'Not pregnant.'

Bubblee shook her head. 'You're getting to be as bad as Mum.'

'Sorry. I was planning to let the conversation be about you and Mae tonight.'

'You should've tried harder.'

Farah turned off the tap and was about to say something — Bubblee thought she saw tears in her eyes — when Mae walked in to switch the kettle on. She began rifling through the fridge.

'Typical. Now I'm not here there aren't any fresh mint leaves.' She took out a peppermint teabag and put it in a mug. 'Why are you both wearing those faces? It's like coming back into a time warp. I mean, it's not like I thought you'd all have changed or anything, but God.' The kettle boiled as she turned to pour the water into the mug. 'The only thing that's different now is that Fatti's thin and looks like death warmed up. Not that I'd say that to her.'

Mae went on in this vein for a rather long time before Fatti came in.

'What are you doing here?' exclaimed Mae.

'By the time you took her tea up she'd have gone into labour,' said Bubblee.

'Don't worry. I'll just sit at the table and listen to you guys talk. I miss this.'

Fatti rested her head on the table as Mae put the mug down, bending in front of her.

135

'You're a bit yellow, Fats.'

'Thanks.'

'Let's talk later,' Bubblee said to Farah.

'Talk about what?' asked Mae.

'I'd have thought now you're at uni, your hearing would be less family orientated,' said Bubblee.

'Leave her alone,' mumbled Fatti, her head still on the table, as she rubbed Mae's hand.

Bubblee could feel Mae's eyes bore into hers before she glanced between her and Farah. 'Something's going on.'

It didn't help that the colour in Farah's cheeks seemed to rise and that she turned towards the sink again, opening the tap.

'Nothing's going on,' said Bubblee, also turning around.

'Fine. None of my business, anyway,' said Mae. 'It's one of the reasons I'm so happy about being at uni — it means I don't have to worry about everything that goes on here.'

Bubblee and Farah carried on washing and drying the dishes as Fatti managed to take a sip of the tea before collapsing her head on the table again. Mae was still talking when they heard a gasp escape from Farah.

'Fazzle,' said Mae, taking her hands out of her pockets. 'Are you crying?'

'No,' she replied, shaking her head violently, her voice thick. 'I'm fine.'

Fatti sat up.

'Turn around,' said Mae.

'Leave her.' Bubblee turned to Farah and saw her tears dropping into the sink. 'It's going to be okay,' she whispered to her.

Farah nodded as another hiccup of a cry escaped her.

'Look at her,' exclaimed Mae. 'She's not okay.'

'Shut up, Mae,' said Bubblee.

'She's not!'

Mae turned off the tap and grabbed the dish that Farah had been washing, throwing it in the sink. Farah looked at the ground, her face contorted as if holding back a barrage of tears.

'Faar, tell us — what's happened?' said Fatti, scraping back her chair, but clearly unable to move.

'Will everyone just be quiet,' said Bubblee, wiping her brow.

'I'm s-s-sor-ry.' Farah covered her face with her hands.

Bubblee grabbed her arm and guided her to the chair opposite Fatti. She knelt in front of her sister, grabbing her hands.

'I'm f-f-fine. I'll b-be fine.'

Farah took deep breaths and closed her eyes. Bubblee looked at the lines of worry that now seemed to be etched in Farah's brow.

'But what the hell happened in the first place?' exclaimed Mae.

'God, you're annoying,' said Bubblee. 'Just *wait* a minute.'

Bubblee looked back at Farah. Her poor twin's face appeared to be in such pain that Bubblee felt a pang of empathy she'd not felt in years . . . or ever, maybe. Did she really have the happiness of her sister in her own hands? And if

137

so, what was she waiting to do with it? Then she had this feeling — it almost felt like elation. *Purpose.* A certainty brimmed to the surface of her mind that she also hadn't felt in a long time. 'Okay.' She paused. 'Let's do it.'

Farah gulped back another hiccup as she opened her eyes. Bubblee nodded at her.

'Do what?' asked Mae.

'*Mae,* let her finish,' said Fatti.

'I think I want to do it,' added Bubblee.

'Why does it sound like they're about to run off into the sunset together?' interjected Mae.

Farah looked at Bubblee, her brow creasing into a frown of incomprehension. 'W-what?'

Bubblee rubbed her forehead. 'Yeah. *Yes.*'

'See?' said Mae to Fatti.

Bubblee had to admit, with her kneeling in front of Farah, it did look as if she was proposing to her sister, though in this case, it was accepting a proposal.

'But you . . . no.' Farah wiped her tears away, her voice coming out with a little more conviction. 'I should never have asked. I'm not trying to guilt-trip you into anything.' Farah's voice broke. 'I just . . . I never know when I might burst into tears nowadays.'

'It's not about you, Faar. Well, not *just* about you. This is about me. Maybe.' She paused, because it did sound absurd when Sasha said it, yet it captured something in Bubblee: *One might consider growing a baby one's very own act of artistry.* But it's the only way she could understand it herself. 'Perhaps it's just another way of creating something. You know?'

138

Another tear trickled down Farah's cheek.

'Something that means something, if not to me, then to someone else. Someone I do love.'

Farah searched in Bubblee's eyes.

'Are you sure?' said Farah.

Bubblee paused. No, she wasn't, but who said that was a bad thing? Of course she had doubts. Of course she was scared, but being scared about something didn't mean it was wrong. It usually meant that you were finally shaking things up, making a change, doing something worthwhile. It was the same feeling she had when she left home for the first time, when she decided to study art history, when she moved into a studio flat all alone once she'd finished university.

Bubblee nodded. Farah flung her arms around her, and to everyone's consternation, Bubblee's eyes filled with tears. Fatti grabbed Mae's hand, a huge smile spreading across her face.

'Am I the only one who doesn't know what's going on here?' said Mae.

Bubblee laughed as she tore herself away from Farah and wiped her tears. 'Someone ought to tell her.'

'Tell me *what?*'

Bubblee stood up and glanced at Farah whose tears had transformed into ones of joy.

'Farah's having a baby,' said Bubblee.

'Oh, my God. You're joking! It's finally happened? You're preggers too?' Mae flung her arms around Farah, already talking about her and Fatti's kids being besties.

'No, not quite,' said Bubblee.

'I'm not pregnant,' added Farah.

Mae stood back. 'Okay, now I'm confused again.'

'*I'm* having her baby for her,' said Bubblee.

Mae looked around the room at her sisters' faces. Fatti was smiling, which gave her otherwise ghostly face a look of being alive, at least.

'*You What?*'

Bubblee had to laugh at her sister's look of incomprehension.

'She's agreed to be my surrogate,' said Farah, looking at Bubblee.

Mae scrunched up her nose. 'What?' She looked at all her sisters. 'Like, carry the baby inside you for nine months and then give birth to it?'

Farah nodded.

'So she'll be injected with your eggs and Muzza's, you know . . . *swimmers?*'

Bubblee's face sobered up at this, but she nodded as well.

'So let me get this straight.' Mae put her hands out, as if she were about to break into some kind of mime. '*Our* Bubs is offering to push a baby out of her own body for someone else?'

'Not just anyone else, Mae. My sister,' said Bubblee.

'And you knew about this?' Mae asked, looking at Fatti.

Fatti gave a faint smile.

'How?' Farah asked Fatti.

'Mum,' she replied.

Farah shook her head. 'Of course.'

Mae suppressed a smile. She looked at the ground as a laugh escaped her.

'What is so funny?' asked Bubblee, folding her arms.

Did the idea of her doing something for another person really seem that strange? So strange that it was comic? Her face flushed as she stared at Mae. Her little sister looked up at her, unable to control the laughter.

'I'm sorry, I'm sorry,' she said, putting her hand out, then over her mouth. 'It's just . . . It's just, and correct me if I'm wrong here, but, Bubsy, being the good Muslim girl and all — or rather the antisocial, bra-burning, man-hating creature that you are — '

'I don't hate men,' interrupted Bubblee. 'Or burn bras. Are you really learning anything at university?'

'Loads! Anyway, doesn't that mean that you're still a . . . ' Mae raised her eyebrows. 'You know.'

Bubblee felt her face flush even harder as Fatti looked between her and Farah.

'Oh,' came Fatti's faint voice.

'We hadn't thought of that,' said Farah, looking at Bubblee.

Mae clapped her hands together as she doubled over in laughter. Even Fatti looked as though she was trying not to laugh.

'This is just too good,' exclaimed Mae, waving her hands at her sisters, still looking at the ground. 'You're going to be the Virgin Bubblee.'

With which Mae lost control again, and howled with laughter.

'What is going on in here?' said their mum

who'd appeared at the door. 'Fatti, why aren't you in bed?' she exclaimed.

'And you knew about this, Amma?' said Mae, grabbing on to her mum and looking at her in awe. 'That's well progressive of you.'

Her mum looked confused as Ash also walked in.

'I thought I heard Amma shout out your name. Honey, you should be in bed,' he said to Fatti.

'I really wish you'd appreciate me knowing when I need to go to bed,' she retorted.

Their mum looked around the kitchen: at Fatti bent over the table, propping herself up by sheer force of will; Farah sitting down and looking at Bubblee in adoration and concern; Bubblee, red in the face, looking defensive but resolute; and Mae, as usual, enjoying the show. She looked at Farah and Bubblee again as her mouth spread into a smile. Mother's instinct. She knew what was happening.

'The party has moved to the kitchen,' came their dad's voice as he peered over his wife's shoulder.

She didn't move to let him in. Mae cleared her throat now that their dad had arrived.

'Who's going to tell him?' she said.

'Jay's abba. I need to speak with you.'

With that, their mum marched their dad out of the room. The girls and Ash waited until they heard their dad exclaim: 'What?' Fatti looked at Ash and nodded. Bubblee supposed they shared everything with each other. She couldn't help but feel a touch of resentment that Ash should know about the sisters' private lives.

'Well,' said Ash. 'Congratulations are in order. For everyone.'

He smiled as he put his hand on Fatti's shoulder, and she took it in hers.

'Only,' he added. 'Shouldn't someone let the father-to-be know?'

Bubblee looked at Farah. 'Oh, yes.' Was this really happening? Had she actually just agreed to carry her sister's baby? She really did feel that the path beyond her, that only yesterday had looked so much like wilderness, was approaching a clearing. Just then her dad barged in, their mum in tow. He looked wildly around the room, his jet-black hair tousled as if he'd just woken up.

'What is this your amma is telling me?'

Farah seemed to stand up straighter as Bubblee folded her arms.

'No,' he said, before anyone had the chance to reply. 'No. I forbid it.'

'You don't forbid anything,' interjected their mum.

'Jay's amma,' he replied, turning to her. 'Have you thought what our families would say? This is not halal.'

'Oh, look,' said Bubblee. 'Sorry to say it, Abba, but it's hardly surprising that it's a man who has a problem with this.'

He put out his hand. 'I let you girls do many things.'

They all scoffed — they clearly had differing views of their history.

'But this is too much,' he added.

143

Ash cleared his throat. Bubblee was sure her parents had only just realized that their other son-in-law was still in the house, and this was bringing even more shame to the family.

'No,' repeated their dad.

There was a pause.

'I'm sorry, Abba, but it's happening,' said Farah.

'It is,' added Bubblee.

Their dad looked around the room again, perhaps for someone, anyone, to take his side. But he was outnumbered. He stalked out of the room and up the stairs as they heard the bedroom door slam behind him. Their mum closed her eyes and sighed.

'You wait a few days for him to calm down,' she said.

Farah nodded. Bubblee was used to storms, and for once she was in agreement with her mum — they would have to ride this one out. Even more unexpectedly Bubblee turned to Farah and said the words she never thought would escape her today. Or ever. And yet once she'd said them out loud she knew it was what she wanted to do. 'I suppose you should tell Mustafa I'm having your baby.'

'Yes,' said Farah, her smile reappearing, standing up and looking around at everyone. 'This will *finally* change everything.'

Mae: Wondr if Bubs snoring'll be worse wen shes preggers.

Bubblee: Shut up.

Fatti: I am so happy. Even though I did just throw up.

Farah. I love you guys xxx

8

It was more than Farah could've asked for. Even apathy wouldn't have bothered her but Mustafa smiled in relief. He hugged his wife and whispered in her ear: 'That's great.'

Farah felt the coming together of the random strands of her life, and she had Bubblee to thank for it. In fact, she had her whole family to thank for it. Mum was lending some money (their dad would hear about it later), as were Ash and Fatti. Even Jay said he'd contribute. It'd take them ages to pay them all back but no one cared about it in that moment because Farah was so happy. Everyone seemed to be at peace and content with life. Apart from her dad who was bound to have some trouble processing the information, and, quite literally, the ins and outs of how surrogacy worked.

The following morning Farah had woken up feeling happy, and for a moment she'd forgotten why. Then a panic washed over her as she grabbed her phone.

**Farah: You haven't changed your mind
have you, Bubs?**

Bubblee: No. I'm not the fickle sister.

Farah: So, you're still having my baby?

Bubblee: Yes xx

It felt like joy all over again. Farah turned over and put her arms around Mustafa, pushing her face into the back of his neck that smelt of soap and the lingering smell of hay, which seemed to have seeped into his very pores. She inhaled the scent as she fell back into a contented sleep. When she woke again, Mustafa had already gone. She got out of bed too, stretching her arms, savouring this new peaceful feeling, looking forward to going downstairs and for them to finally start planning their family together.

★ ★ ★

The technicalities of having a surrogate mother for their baby wasn't as joyous. Particularly when their dad was involved in the conversation and Mae wasn't there to make light of it. He gave Farah a reserved salam when she entered the house the following day after work — so unlike how he'd ever spoken to her before.

'You are not doing the right thing,' he added before she went to go and see Bubblee in her room.

'But I am doing it,' she replied. 'I'm sorry, Abba, but there's no other way.'

'Just *think*. What about your sister? Bubblee isn't even married and she will have another man's baby?'

He looked more desperate than angry today. Farah wondered if she was being selfish — but it was Bubblee's decision. She wasn't being forced. Her mum leaned forward as though she was explaining something to a child.

'Better to have this than a strange woman carrying their baby.'

He shook his head. 'Didn't you ask Fatti to have a baby for her? Isn't that better?' he added, looking at Farah.

'Tst, forget that,' replied her mum. 'These girls have their own ideas. Anyway, maybe when Bubblee feels the love that comes with carrying something in you for nine months she will want one also. And *then* she will get married. We just won't tell her husband what she did, because then no one will marry her.' Her mum leaned back with a look of apprehension. 'Damaged goods.'

Her dad nodded. Farah had to shake her head. There was her thinking that her mum was finally catching up with the times and really it seemed to be an emotionally manipulative tactic. Sometimes she wondered whether her parents really knew their children, or whether they were too busy trying to make them fit into a Bengali's ideal of them. Although, perhaps her mum had a point. Maybe carrying a baby would give the kick that Bubblee's maternal instinct needed.

Farah's mum seemed to be lost in thought. 'But there will be signs,' she said.

Her dad nodded again.

'Jay's abba. What if she now never gets married?' said her mum.

'That is what I am saying. And how to explain to people that Farah is having a baby but that

148

it . . . ' He lowered his voice, as if he was saying something rude. 'That it is growing in Bubblee.'

'Abba,' said Farah. 'Things are moving forward. People are doing things differently now. We have more options. Shouldn't we take them?'

He simply put his head in his hands. Farah gave her mum an apologetic smile, leaving her to him as she went up to Bubblee's room. When she knocked on the door she entered to see Bubblee organizing everything. The wardrobe was open and her clothes were neatly hung or stacked. Since that morning the fear that Bubblee would change her mind kept washing over her, but she knew, looking at the room, that this was her own anxiety and she'd have to learn to stop being so cynical. Good things could happen. They *were* happening.

'Mum and Dad are now worried you'll never get married,' said Farah as she sat on the bed.

Bubblee nodded as she hung a jacket in the wardrobe. 'Excellent.'

'Aren't you worried?' asked Farah.

Bubblee shook her head. 'Giving birth? Yes. Not getting married? No.'

Farah looked at her twin, in awe of her emotional independence, the sheer lack of need she had for anyone. Or anything. Bubblee paused and looked at her tidy wardrobe, her things in order.

'You're really here now,' said Farah.

She nodded. 'I really am.'

★　★　★

The next few weeks consisted of doctor's appointments. Mustafa asked if he should come to any but Farah insisted that he needn't take time off work.

'So, what's my purpose then?' he asked as he turned towards her in bed one evening.

'When we need your best swimmers.'

He gave a faint smile.

'Do you feel used?' Farah said, laughing. When he didn't answer she put her arm around him. 'I'm only joking.'

'Oh, yeah, I know you are, babe,' he replied.

He squeezed her hand and turned his back to her. If he had let go of her hand she might've been worried, but he was probably just tired.

Bubblee's physical health had to be assessed, of course; whether she could actually carry the baby, and what seemed to irk her more than anything else, constant questioning about her emotional health.

'I mean, yes, I made this decision on a whim because why not have someone else's baby? Do they not realize that people who decide to do this actually do think it through?' she said in the car on the way back from their fourth appointment.

'They're just doing their job,' said Farah.

'It's so patronizing,' replied Bubblee. 'As if I don't know my own mind. I'm a grown woman.'

'You know they have to be sure that you're sure.'

Farah's heart turned a somersault every time a question was asked, as if Bubblee would turn to her and say: *I'm sorry, I can't.* But she'd never seemed so resolute. Well, she had; when she'd been creating her artwork. Farah felt a pang of sympathy for her sister. And what's more, she felt pangs of guilt that she had never really tried to understand Bubblee's needs or passion. It seemed easier to comprehend now that Bubblee was fulfilling Farah's.

'Well, I am sure. And it seems my uterus is too since it's perfectly healthy.'

Farah gripped the steering wheel a little harder. But she wasn't going to compare their uteruses now.

'Don't forget to take the pills they gave you,' said Farah. 'To suppress your menstrual cycle.'

Bubblee checked her bag to make sure she had them.

Farah was *not* going to be ungrateful — she was going to go back to being the Farah she used to be.

★   ★   ★

Farah dropped Bubblee home and went in to work.

'Everything okay?' asked her boss. 'You've had quite a few doctor's appointments.'

Farah wasn't sure what to make of her feelings sometimes. She was bursting with joy whenever she was with her family, but the minute the idea of telling someone on the outside came, she was filled with a shame as if she'd failed an exam.

'Yes, thanks,' said Farah.

Her boss gave her an unsure look and was about to walk back into the office when Farah burst out with: 'I'm having a baby.'

151

Her boss paused. Farah noticed a brief look of inconvenience pass over her boss's face.

'Oh, congratulations,' she said, coming closer to give her a rather awkward hug.

There'd never been any call for such proximity before and Farah felt it odd to put her arms around someone she'd known for so long, but actually knew very little about.

'Thanks — though I'm not actually pregnant yet,' said Farah, and for a moment she wondered whether she'd jinxed it all just by saying it out loud to someone who wasn't her family.

'Oh?'

Her boss stepped away, brushing down her jacket as if the hug had been a mistake. Farah shook her head. 'No, I mean, I'm not having the baby at all. Well, I'm having the baby, it's just that I'm not pregnant with it. Come to think of it, nor is my sister yet . . . '

Why was she babbling? Her boss's eyes were contracting and widening with every word that came out of Farah's mouth. Farah took a deep breath.

'Sorry. My head's all over the place. From the beginning.' She tried to untangle her thoughts. 'I'm having a baby, but my sister's going to be the surrogate. She's not pregnant yet, we've just been going for all the tests. There are about a million.'

Farah laughed nervously and waited for a reaction. When none came she went and sat behind her desk.

'Gosh,' her boss finally said. 'That's a brave move.'

Farah simply smiled. Then she thought about it and paused. 'Why?'

'I meant your sister. To do that for another person is extraordinary. Especially when you think of the possible repercussions.'

Farah didn't ask what these might be, but her boss volunteered them anyway.

'Coming from someone who has three kids of her own, I can't imagine having to carry them for nine months, just to give them up.'

'Well, it won't be her child. It's my egg and my husband's sperm.'

Farah opened up the filing cabinet, just to have something to do so she didn't have to look at her boss.

'Oh, no, of course, of course I know the technicalities. It's really quite incredible. If I couldn't have my own children — there's no reason I wouldn't explore that route.' She paused in thought about it. 'But I don't think it's anything I could do for anyone — I'm not that kind!'

'Not even for your sister?'

'I don't have any,' she replied. 'Anyway, I'm just always thinking of how I'd react in a situation.' She shook her head. 'I have to remember not everyone is the same.'

'Yes, no, of course,' replied Farah, rummaging through paper in the cabinet.

'And obviously it's brave of you as well,' her boss added, buttoning up her jacket.

Farah slammed the cabinet shut. 'Not really. I'm just sitting back and watching it all unfold.'

'Exactly,' her boss replied. 'That's the bravest thing of all.'

With that her boss went into her office. Farah couldn't help feeling that it can sometimes take having a baby to learn more about a person. Including herself.

Mae: 2days the big day!!!! G'luck bubs & fazza. Fatti can u lemme kno wots goin on cos these 2 will b 2 bz gettin preggers & stuff. Ur already there so be a good sista & gimme upd8s. Cheers. Luv u guys. cant wait 2 b an aunt 2 TWO babies. Xxx

Fatti: I will, but they won't know anything for about two weeks.

Mae: Yeh yeh I kno all tht. Jus gimme the deets, k?

Fatti: Yes, Mae. Xx

The buzzing from Bubblee's phone was enough to drive her insane. She took a deep breath and had to remind herself of what her mum said to her yesterday: it was all in God's hands and she wasn't responsible for how this went. It was a decent time to think about God. She looked up at her bedroom ceiling. 'Sorry, I don't do this a lot, but if you could make this work then I promise I'll do it more often.'

She shook her head at the beating of her own heart. She didn't expect to feel this much anxiety, the fear of another failure, another purpose lost. Every time someone said how selfless she was being — her mum praising her;

even her dad recognizing what she was doing, despite the fact that he still didn't like to talk about it openly; Fatti's expression of pride whenever she looked at Bubblee — it all made her feel like a bit of a hack. Yes, she was doing this for Farah, but more than anything she knew she was doing this to prove to herself that even though she couldn't create something useful, at least she could house someone else's creation.

She lifted her shirt over her head, standing in her jeans and bra, and took a moment to look at her stomach that wasn't concave the way it used to be, but was still relatively flat. Then she took her bra off and looked at her breasts. Still perky, rather small according to her mum, but they existed and never gave her pause for thought or anxiety. Her body never had. It was a decent vessel in which she existed. Sasha always teased her for being the only woman she knew who didn't talk about being on a diet, or wanting to lose weight or gain tone — but that was mainly because Bubblee never needed to. Perhaps she'd taken it for granted her whole life. But even now, the prospect of all of this changing didn't alarm her. In fact, it excited her. She'd be able to watch how her own body changed in relation to growing another body inside her. Wasn't that fascinating? She lay her hand on her stomach.

'Don't fail me today, uterus,' she mumbled.

Without thinking, she got out her phone and took a photograph of her body. It might never be the same again, after all, and she wanted to have it as a comparison for after she'd had the baby.

Bubblee felt a rush at the idea of things changing. Now, along with the anxiety, simmered the excitement of the tide turning, and Bubblee finally having an anchor.

'You ready?'

Farah had opened her door. Bubblee grabbed her bra and put it on, along with her shirt. She wasn't sure how long Farah had been standing there.

'I never really thought about it before,' said Bubblee.

'What?'

'The way your body changes when you're pregnant.'

'I got you cocoa butter. For the stretch marks,' replied Farah.

Bubblee straightened up her shirt. 'Getting a bit ahead of things.'

'It'll work. I know it will.'

Bubblee had to take a deep breath because Farah was excited and she didn't know how each expectation weighed on Bubblee's uterus. And none of Farah's expectations compared to Bubblee's own.

'Is Mustafa waiting downstairs?' asked Bubblee.

Farah nodded. 'We've both been up since five this morning. Just saw Dad. He managed to look me in the eyes, which is good.'

Bubblee didn't care what her dad thought, but it was a pain being in the house with a man who still hadn't got over what was happening. At least he didn't pretend that his forbidding it was actually going to work any more.

156

'What if it doesn't work?' said Bubblee. 'All that money . . . '

'I know. And I know it might not, but *God*, I have such a feeling that it will. Everything in my life seems to have been building up to this moment.'

'No pressure then.'

'You know what I mean.'

'Exactly,' replied Bubblee. 'On top of that, Dad still hasn't got his head around the fact that I won't have to . . . you know, conceive the traditional way.'

Farah shook her head as she folded her arms, car keys jangling in her hand. 'Honestly. Modern science and Dad just don't get on.'

'It's more the idea of a modern immaculate conception, I'm guessing.'

Farah made a face as if she'd tasted a lemon. 'Hard luck. For you.'

Bubblee saw the conflict of sympathy in Farah's features. The type that looked and felt sorry, but wouldn't want anything to change. Because it would change everything for Farah. Sasha's words came back to Bubblee: *Some people call it selfish. We call it living.* She was pleased to find that people were all selfish in their own unique ways. You just had a harder time justifying it when the thing you were being selfish about wasn't the socially expected norm. It didn't fill her with resentment, though — Bubblee was getting on board with the idea that *living* might also mean creating life.

'Ready?' asked Farah.

Bubblee nodded. 'Ready.'

157

★ ★ ★

Small talk with her brother-in-law had never felt so arduous to Bubblee as it did in the car, on the journey to the hospital to be inseminated.

'Good weather today,' said Mustafa.

'Yeah. Blue skies,' replied Bubblee.

Farah switched on the indicator before realizing she was going the wrong way. Her phone rang and she put it on speakerphone because she didn't have her hands-free kit. It was Mae.

'Fazza and Muzza sitting in a tree,' she sang out.

'Oh, God,' said Bubblee.

'B-a-b-y-i-n-g.'

'Mae, you're on — '

But Mae was clearly enjoying her new rhyming skills too much.

'First came Bubblee then a petri dish . . . Hang on, is it a petri dish? How exactly does it work?'

'You're on speaker,' Farah and Bubblee both said.

Mustafa had his head in his hands.

'Oh! Hahahaha. Who's there?'

'Asalamoalaikum, Mae,' muttered Mustafa.

'Wasalam, bro-in-law. How are the happy trio today?'

Bubblee had to suppress a smile at how unfazed Mae always seemed to be. She almost wished she was coming to the hospital with them. At least she'd distract Mustafa for a while.

'Don't you have to be in a lecture or something?' said Bubblee.

'Where are you taking us?' said Mustafa to Farah, who'd entered a road that wasn't on the way to the hospital.

She shook her head, looking flustered.

'You were meant to go straight, just like you always have on our way to the hospital,' said Mustafa.

Bubblee cleared her throat.

'Did you want to drive?' said Farah. 'Oh, that's right, you can't.'

The noise of the car's engine seemed to increase with the silence as Farah found herself back on the main road.

'Right, well, you crazy kids,' said Mae. Bubblee had almost forgotten she was still on speakerphone. 'May your reproductive features be strong.'

Mustafa let out a groan.

'Like, seriously,' added Mae. Her voice sounded a little more sombre. 'I really hope this works. I even prayed this morning. Woke up early and everything.'

Bubblee felt like reaching down the phone and giving her little sister a hug.

'Thanks, Mae,' said Farah.

'Call me when it's done. Or whatever. Yeah?'

'Go and study,' called out Bubblee as Farah said she would and pressed the call-end button.

'Was it such a good idea your parents letting her go to university away from home?' said Mustafa. 'She's not exactly sensible like you and Fatti.'

Bubblee felt her face harden, not least because apparently she wasn't in the sensible category. This probably had to do with the fact that she was deemed to have too many opinions.

'I suppose you'd have her stay at home and cook nice meals for the men in the family?' said Bubblee.

'Come on, I'm not a caveman, but she — '

'She's more sensible than people give her credit for,' interrupted Farah.

Ugh. If only Farah had considered another sperm donor for her baby. Bubblee felt disturbed at the idea of Mustafa's genes being inside her in any way. Was it really a good idea to be a part of perpetuating such mediocrity? If so, then it was too late, because Farah was already parking outside the hospital.

★　★　★

The three of them walked down the hospital corridor and were taken into a private room.

'How are we all today?' asked the doctor, looking at her notes.

'Fine, good, yeah,' came their mumbled voices.

Bubblee's heart was pumping so fast she thought she might have a heart attack. *What was she thinking?* Having a baby when she'd a) never had sex and b) it wasn't her own? She saw Mustafa grab hold of Farah's hand. His gaze was fixed to the ground. Perhaps the hospital was bringing back memories of his accident and being in a coma.

'Right. Bubblee Amir — you are the brave lady today.'

Bubblee tried to give a smile but she wasn't sure if she succeeded.

'Mum and Dad, would you like to be in the room for this?'

The doctor got out a catheter and ultrasound and that's when they saw the small dish, which had the makings of a possible baby. Bubblee leaned forward, frowning at it.

'Is that it?' asked Mustafa, who'd managed to tear himself from staring at the grey lino.

'We hope so,' said the doctor.

Everyone left the room so Bubblee could change into her gown. She couldn't stop looking at the catheter, and if she was this sceptical about such a thin tube going into her, how would it be having a baby coming out of her? She recalled the feeling of starting university, walking into the unknown, away from her whole family, just as she had dreamed. That was the place she was going to begin to become something, and it thrilled her just as much as it filled her with fear. The same emotional mixture whirred around her now when someone knocked on the door.

The doctor was followed in by Farah.

'Mustafa's waiting outside,' she said. 'Probably the appropriate thing.'

Bubblee should hope so.

'Now, this should be painless, but given that you've never been sexually active . . . '

Bubblee sensed the strain in the doctor's voice. Was it judgement? Pity? Awe? She couldn't

161

quite guess. Probably judgement.

'You might feel some discomfort.'

Farah came up to Bubblee and held her hand. 'Thank you for doing this.'

'It's not done yet,' Bubblee replied.

Farah brushed her hand over Bubblee's hair as Bubblee closed her eyes, willing for it to be over.

It didn't hurt but no matter how thin a tube was, it was still a tube. She scrunched up her face and thought: *Well, this is it. If it works, there's no going back now.*

★ ★ ★

They came out of the room and Bubblee found it hard to meet Mustafa's eyes.

'Here, let me carry your bag,' he said, trying to take her handbag from her.

She held on to it. 'I'm fine. I'm not pregnant yet.'

He cleared his throat, looking at Farah. 'Was it . . . okay?'

She nodded as the three of them walked back to the car and Farah drove them home.

When they reached their parents' house they found Fatti inside. She was lying on the sofa.

'Well?' she exclaimed, getting up apparently too fast because she went an extra shade of pale. 'Is it done?'

Their dad nodded briefly to Mustafa, his cheeks flushed. 'Come, let me show you the garden,' he said, as they both walked out of the room.

'For God's sake,' said Bubblee. 'How long are

162

we not going to be able to speak about it in front of Abba?'

'Some things are delicate,' explained her mother. 'You girls have no shame.'

But their mum was already fussing and seating Bubblee on the sofa, bringing her extra pillows.

'I'm not pregnant yet,' she found herself having to say again.

Her mum frowned. 'Then when will you be?'

'Amma, I explained to you it'll be a few weeks before she can take a test and we find out.'

Their mum looked disappointed. Fatti grabbed Bubblee's hands and said, 'I can't wait to be pregnant with you.'

She could barely conceal her excitement as Bubblee glanced at Farah, still standing in the doorway.

'And we'll be mums together,' added Fatti, also looking at Farah.

Farah smiled and said something about making tea as she went into the kitchen, leaving Bubblee behind.

★　★　★

Bubblee wondered whether it would be less pressure to take the pregnancy test without telling anyone. It was so much easier to deal with disappointment without seeing the weight of it in other people as well. Farah would be the first to know of course, after her, whatever the outcome. Then she remembered the look on her sister's face when they came back from the hospital; this pregnancy was Farah's and Bubblee had to remind herself of that, for Farah's sake.

'I brought five different kinds. In case,' said Farah, handing Bubblee the plastic bag as she walked into the room.

'You didn't tell anyone?'

She shook her head. 'Let's do that if it's good news.'

'Even Mustafa?'

'No.' Farah seemed to hesitate. 'I don't think he'll mind. Anyway, I want to give him *good* news. Give us both — all — a reason to celebrate.'

Bubblee felt her heart somewhere in her throat; she rubbed her sweaty palms on her jeans and went into the bathroom, Farah following her. Their parents had gone out for a grocery shop, but would be back soon.

'Okay. So I suppose I'm going to pee in front of you?' said Bubblee.

'Sorry. But I can't not be here.'

Bubblee's hand shook as she took the test out. She wasn't sure whether praying to God in the bathroom was appropriate but she felt she needed it. She and Farah looked at each other as she took the now used stick and put it next to the bathroom basin.

Farah kept looking at her watch while Bubblee washed her hands, her eyes fixed on her phone.

'How long does three minutes take?' said Bubblee, drying her hands on a towel.

Bubblee noticed Farah's chest rising and falling more dramatically, as if she was about to hyperventilate. They looked at the stick again.

'Anything?' asked Farah.

Bubblee shook her head. The problem was that Farah and Mustafa couldn't afford another round of this, even though having Bubblee as a surrogate helped their financial situation. What's more, if this didn't work, Bubblee wondered whether it was a sign that she shouldn't actually be doing this. She didn't even believe in signs, but until recently she didn't believe in having babies for other people either, so what did she know? Bubblee's heart was thudding so hard she wondered whether it echoed in the bathroom. Farah looked at the stick again. This time her eyebrows contracted and Bubblee looked at the stick too as Farah picked it up.

'Oh, my God,' Farah whispered.

'Is it . . . '

This was it: the moment of truth. Farah's eyes were filled with tears and a look of pain seemed to cross her face. No. Bubblee shook her head and realized that she wasn't relieved. A wave of disappointment crashed over her as she stared at her sister.

'Oh, Faar.'

Bubblee sat back down on the toilet, staring at her sister, her brain flitting around with ways they might be able to try again. Farah broke into a smile. What? Why was she smiling?

'We're having a baby,' whispered Farah, her face contorted in disbelief and, Bubblee realized, happiness.

'But you — '

She snatched the stick from her sister and saw the two lines. Positive.

'Oh, my God.'

The disappointment turned to something else, and it was unprecedented, even for Bubblee, as she flung her arms around her sister. Just then they heard the front door open and their parents walk in, accompanied by the rustling of shopping bags. Farah ran from the bathroom, halfway down the stairs as Bubblee heard her exclaim:

'Amma. Abba. I'm having a baby!'

9

There were a lot of emotions from outside forces, but Farah couldn't even begin to process any of those. She recalled the look in Bubblee's eyes when they were waiting for the result and experienced a fleeting panic. Whether it was doubt she saw in Bubblee's look, or a wisp of doubt Farah felt in herself, she wasn't sure. For the first time in what felt like decades, her and Bubblee's emotions seemed to be indistinguishable.

She couldn't wait until Mustafa got home from work that evening and called him, after realizing that she'd told her parents about the baby before she'd told its father.

'It's happening,' she said, barely able to suppress her smile and laughter.

'What?' he asked, sounding distracted.

What else did he think it could be?

'Our baby. We're having a *baby*.'

There was a pause and Farah thought she felt her heart skip a beat as well, because however much she tried to shrug off the idea, she never quite knew how her husband would react to things.

'A baby? A baby?' came his voice. 'We're having a baby!'

She heard something clang on the floor as he carried on repeating what she already knew.

'When? How?'

Farah shook her head. 'Well, you know *how*.'

'A catheter and a petri dish,' called out Bubblee.

Farah hadn't realized she'd been listening, but she heard her footsteps fade as Mustafa's voice had quietened.

'You didn't tell me she was about to take a pregnancy test,' he said.

'Oh, well . . . I wanted to give you good news.'

There was a pause.

'It's bad enough that she's carrying our baby, but even she knew we were having one before the actual father.'

His twinge of jealousy surprised Farah. She turned her back to Bubblee's bedroom door and lowered her voice.

'No,' she said.

Another pause.

'Well, yes,' she added, 'but that couldn't be helped.'

Farah tried to recall a time when Mustafa had sounded so cagey about Bubblee, or any of her sisters, and remembered his little jabs at Mae. What had they ever done but been supportive the entire time he'd been in hospital and in a coma? Farah chose to ignore the multiple jabs that Bubblee would deal out to Mustafa when he'd take them with a laugh or ignore them entirely. That was before the accident though, and before Bubblee decided to make a sacrifice to help them have a family.

'I'd better get back to work,' he said.

'You're not serious.'

'I'm doing overtime tonight too. The loans

aren't going to pay themselves back. You celebrate.'

With that he put the phone down. Farah stared at the screen in disbelief. She was in half a mind to call him back. Or better yet, go to the stables and flood him with exactly why his behaviour was so bad, but her mum was calling out for her to come downstairs and she had to get back to work as well.

As her mum hugged her she felt the anger fizzle out. Her dad stared at her and cleared his throat.

'It's going to be okay, Abba,' said Farah. 'People might talk but . . . I *need* this. And if it was wrong then it wouldn't have worked, would it?'

When he didn't respond she added: 'Aren't you glad you're going to have another grand-child?'

She saw the flicker of a smile appear. 'I am happy about that, Zi. Yes. But — '

'So let's just leave it at that?' offered Farah.

He paused before patting her head and giving her a kiss.

'Is the father of the baby happy?' said Bubblee, eating a bag of crisps.

'Should you be eating those?' asked Farah.

'No. This is not going to happen. You won't police my eating habits. It's your baby, but it's my body, okay?'

Their dad cleared his throat again and mumbled something about needing some milk as he left the house, even though they'd just done a grocery shop. Their mum watched him walk out of the door.

'It's going to be a long nine months,' said Bubblee.

'We need to book a doctor's appointment,' said Farah.

She was already on the phone to do that as her mum sat down and stared at the carpet. When Farah had arranged a day with the surgery and hung up she said: 'I suppose Abba's worried about announcing this to the family?'

Her mum looked up with a slight shake of her head as she picked up the house phone and dialled a number.

'Fatti. You are going to become an aunt.'

Farah and Bubblee both heard her shouting down the phone and laughed.

'No, no, you must stay home,' their mum said to her.

They noticed her dab at her eyes before she put the phone down.

'Amma,' said Farah. 'Tears of joy. Thank you.'

Their mum looked towards the door where their dad had left and stood up. 'Tell Mae or she will cry that no one tells her anything.'

With that, Farah had to go back to work and leave the carrier of her baby behind. She began making mental notes of all the things she had to do — she knew there were a million tasks to complete but couldn't think of them, her mind and heart were in such a flurry. What could she do for Bubblee over the next nine months to make things comfortable for her? How was she going to spend more time with her sister, just so she could be near her unborn child when she had full-time work, as well as a new Saturday job? Then she thought of her husband. But she was always thinking of Mustafa and his moods. Her brain was packed with incidents between them and she was, quite frankly, bored of it. Here was happiness, growing inside Bubblee's belly, and she wasn't about to let Mustafa spoil it. She wasn't about to let anyone spoil it.

★ ★ ★

There'd been so many messages being pinged back and forth, Farah had to put her phone on silent and in the drawer. *Must not get overexcited.* A few minutes later she opened the drawer, read the new messages, and closed the drawer again, unable to wipe the smile from her face. After a few hours she checked the phone again and there weren't any new messages. It wasn't the right time to tell her boss because Farah wanted to go to the doctor first and ensure Bubblee had a scan to make sure it was all real, not a figment of her imagination.

When she got home the place was empty. She switched on the lights, trying to bring life back to the house but it felt too quiet. Her footsteps were loud, the rustling of her skirt increased in the silence of the home. The rest of the day at work had been unremarkable and a few times she'd even forgotten about the good news that was going to change her life. It seemed to Farah that the further away she was from Bubblee the more it all felt like a dream — as if the happiness was happening elsewhere and she could only feel it when she was there. Is this how the next nine months would be? Her emotions were almost becoming as erratic as Mustafa's and so she busied herself, making some dinner and eating it alone, wondering what Bubblee was doing.

Mustafa didn't come home until nine o'clock that evening. She'd been standing in the box room, wondering how it could be the nursery. It was so small — what would happen when the baby got older, where would it sleep? But one step at a time. That's what her parents had always said to her and she knew that overthinking things wasn't going to help anyone. Each hurdle must be passed when they came to it. For now, having a healthy baby born to them was the most important one.

'Hi.'

Farah didn't turn around. 'Hello.'

'What are you doing in here?' he asked.

His voice sounded repentant, but how many times was she meant to accommodate his moods? When would she stop having to walk around on eggshells? She thought of their baby, though, and perhaps she should've told him about the test they were about to take.

'Do you really think this could be the nursery? Like you suggested before? We need to think of somewhere to put the baby.'

He came to stand beside her. She could smell the manure and sweat on him as she shuffled a little away under the guise of making room for him.

172

'Yes. Definitely. I could put extra shelves up.'

'Hmm,' she said.

'Don't sound so excited about it,' he replied.

She turned to look at him. 'What?'

'I never said anything about you not being able to have a baby, but you can't even pretend to appreciate me putting up shelves.'

What? Her face must've shown her confusion. Why was he constantly leaping from one thought to the next without any indication? More to the point — did he resent Farah for not being able to have a baby? She had no words, just a look of disgust on her face as she left the room, went into their bedroom and slammed the door behind her. It didn't take him ten minutes before he came inside to apologize. She was pacing the room in quiet fury, wondering how she was meant to calm down. In that instant she was glad she wasn't carrying their baby because this kind of stress wasn't what it needed. No one needed this.

'I'm sorry,' he said, coming up to her, taking her hands.

She wanted to snatch them away from him, turn around and tell him to leave and to sleep on the sofa.

'I don't know what's got into me,' he added. 'It's like I can't help it. One minute I'm fine and the next minute someone will say or do something and it just . . . switches.'

She felt her hands relax a little in his.

'I'm not the person I used to be,' he said. 'Am I?'

He seemed to implore Farah, looking into her

eyes, wanting her to reject the very idea. But she couldn't.

'None of us are,' she said.

'Because of me,' he replied.

The tone alarmed her. 'No, no, not at all.'

'Really?'

'Of course.'

But perhaps Mustafa was right. Maybe he had changed her — all this angst and erratic behaviour of his, not being able to get back to the way they were before his accident, her lack of trust in him, his dependency on her — having to drive him around. Farah tried to sweep these thoughts out of her brain. She sat on the edge of their bed and he sat with her.

'Who am I, Farah?' he asked.

She had to calm the beating of her heart. The earnest way he looked at her, as if she could provide the answer, and the question itself filled her with something like dread.

'You're *you*,' she said, trying to smile, as if the question was silly and not a cause for alarm. 'My husband.'

She took his hand and put it to her chest. 'The father of our baby.'

He nodded as if that almost answered his question. 'Right, yeah. Of course.'

Then he stood up and said he was going to take a shower.

'Do you want me to get some dinner ready for you?'

'No, I'm not hungry. I think I'll just go straight to sleep.'

She nodded, swallowing hard as she tried to

smile. 'And congratulations again.'

For a moment he looked unsure before he also smiled and said: 'Yeah. Congratulations to us.'

★ ★ ★

The doctor's appointment confirmed it. This time Farah told Mustafa exactly what was happening, giving him minute-by-minute updates via WhatsApp. She almost told him to come to the appointment with them but then realized this would require time off work and they couldn't afford to do that right now. She didn't want him to feel guilty for not being able to be there. She spent a lot of time now considering his feelings and trying to ensure there wasn't a repeat of last time. Farah wasn't sure she could deal with him asking her again: *Who am I?* It still alarmed her when she thought about it, but there were baby things to organize and so she pushed it to the back of her mind, promising herself that perhaps she'd try to talk to him about it when there wasn't so much going on.

'Congratulations,' said the doctor, smiling. 'It's always nice to hear the success stories.'

'What can I expect?' said Bubblee, leaning forward.

'Every woman reacts differently, but nausea and vomiting are very common. I'd suggest avoiding any stress or strenuous exercise and to just enjoy this time.'

Farah wished the doctor would look at her too.

'We intend to,' said Farah. 'What about diet?

175

She's been eating a lot of crisps lately.'

Bubblee shot Farah a look as the doctor laughed.

'Well, I can't condone eating junk food, but when a craving hits . . . '

As Farah drove Bubblee home, she said, 'It's so annoying you living with Mum and Dad. I want to be around you and know what you're doing. When I'm away from you it's like it's not happening.'

'Oh, it's happening,' said Bubblee, putting her hand on her as-of-yet flat stomach.

'How are you feeling?'

'Weirdly fine. No nausea or anything. Is that a sign there's something wrong?'

Farah flashed her a look; the tone of concern in Bubblee's voice felt uncharacteristic. 'It's all healthy so far.'

She took a deep breath. So many things could go wrong but Farah was going to focus on the things that had gone right.

'Otherwise you're okay?'

Bubblee looked at her and smiled. 'Yeah. I think so. I mean . . . '

'What?'

'I don't think it's hit me yet. I know it's happening but even that appointment — it's like I'm looking at everything from the outside.'

Farah suddenly felt so fond of her twin sister that she wanted to hug her. 'I suppose that's normal.'

'What if it doesn't hit me until I go into labour and then I just freak out?'

'Don't be silly.'

'Or one day I forget I'm having your baby and eat prawns or shellfish or something?' said Bubblee.

'I really do wish we had an extra room so you could stay.'

The idea of staying with her parents flashed through Farah's mind and for a moment she resented that she had to take her husband into account.

'We could try and make it work at mine?' she said to Bubblee.

'But you just said you don't have any room. Anyway, it's fine at Mum and Dad's. Kind of.'

'Mustafa can borrow their blow-up bed and sleep in our living room and we can share. So if you need water, or get up to throw up or whatever, I'm there.'

Bubblee seemed to hesitate. Was Farah being too pushy?

'Yes, I'm sure he'll love that,' replied Bubblee.

'He'll love whatever makes this better for everyone.'

Bubblee put her hand on her stomach again and Farah felt a stab of envy.

'Why don't you ask him first?'

'Yes, of course. I'll ask him.'

⋆ ⋆ ⋆

Farah shouldn't have been surprised at his openness to the idea because by now she knew that she never could tell what Mustafa might say or do.

'Are you sure you don't mind sleeping on a

mattress in the living room? Hardly great for you.'

Though Farah had to admit his comfort only occurred to her when she spoke to him about it that evening.

'No, it's fine. It'll be great having Bubblee around.'

Farah felt her eyebrows contract in confusion. Since when would it be great having the sister who most disliked him around? But she didn't want him to change her mind and so she let Bubblee know the good news.

'Oh, really?' she said down the phone. 'Okay, fine. Maybe just a week.'

'A *week?* You'll be pregnant for nine months.'

There was a pause. 'Let's see how it goes.'

'Yes, of course.'

Farah felt the seams of her life tightening and breathed a sigh of relief. With Bubblee around she could cook for her and make sure the baby was getting the right nutrients. She could also talk to her baby whenever she wanted. They say that playing classical music to a foetus in the womb is good for them and that's not something Bubblee would think of doing. Plus, she could monitor just how much time Bubblee spent on her phone and laptop because that couldn't be good for the baby either. Farah switched off the downstairs lights and made her way to the bedroom. Yes, things were going to get better because she was in control.

★　★　★

178

'But this makes no sense,' said Bubblee's mum.

Bubblee shrugged. She knew she had opinions about it somewhere but the guilt of seeing Farah's pained face every time the doctor had addressed Bubblee, rather than the mother of the baby, buried them. It was an extraordinary thing. She didn't realize her opinions were capable of such a thing.

'There is only one bedroom,' her mum added, putting down the shirt and the button she was sewing for Bubblee's dad.

'Mustafa's going to use the blow-up bed you have and sleep in the living room.'

Her mum put her hand to her mouth as if to prevent a gasp from escaping. 'A husband and wife sleeping separately. But this is very bad.'

'In case you've forgotten, Amma, you and dad share a bunk bed.'

Though Bubblee had to admit, it was very odd how quickly Farah suggested it and how readily Mustafa agreed. But then she didn't want to think about her sister and brother-in-law, and what went on between them in the bedroom.

'And ask me the difficulties,' replied her mum.

Bubblee looked up from her phone as her mum went back to her sewing. The front door opened and slammed shut as Jay's voice came from the passage.

'How's the baby carrier?' he asked, popping his head in.

But Jay didn't seem to care about waiting for the answer as he simply nodded and went up the stairs to go and sleep after his night shift. Their mum followed him up with food that she'd made. Maybe staying with Farah for a little while would be just the thing. Bubblee decided to go for a walk — it was a chilly day, but the sun was out and the orange and red leaves on the trees felt like a source of inspiration for something.

I'm carrying a baby. I'm carrying a baby. She thought she'd feel different, encumbered by the weight of another soul, but she didn't and it surprised her. She had been preparing for resentment and perhaps it was just around the corner, but for now, she almost felt . . . could it be? *Happy.* Something had actually worked out and she'd been the reason behind it. Perhaps it was just that it was a beautiful autumn day.

'Thanks, Sprout,' she said, looking down at her belly, catching herself in the silliness of talking to something the size of a peanut.

Her phone rang and it was Fatti.

'How's it going?' Fatti asked.

'Fine.'

'No sickness yet?'

'Not really,' replied Bubblee.

Not at all if she was honest, but she thought perhaps that would make Fatti feel worse.

'That's good,' said Fatti, sounding a little hard done by.

Fatti's nausea really must be awful if she couldn't be pleased about Bubblee's lack of it.

'How about you?' asked Bubblee.

Fatti paused.

'I wake up feeling as if I've spent the night tumbling around in a washing machine and my food's stuck in my chest. I wake up to pee every hour. I'm losing weight but my feet are really swollen and I look like I might burst into dust when I walk into the daylight.'

'Huh?'

'Like vampires. I'm so pale,' Fatti clarified.

'Oh, right.'

Bubblee caught sight of her reflection in a car window and had to admit, she had a glow about her.

'Ash is constantly worried about me and I wonder . . . '

'What?'

'Nothing, it's silly,' said Fatti.

'Why don't you let me be the judge of that.'

'I wonder whether he thinks I'm making it all up and will leave me because it's been so difficult.'

Bubblee thought she heard Fatti's voice crack.

'Yes. You're right. It's definitely silly.'

Fatti let out a laugh. 'Thanks.'

'No worries.'

'I know it's stupid and of course he loves me. It's just the hormones.'

Bubblee felt what a relief it was not being in love or in a relationship, not being tied down by worrying about another person's feelings for you. She never did understand this need people had to be in couples and share things like life. It all sounded more trouble than it was worth.

'I'm not sure there is a word for what Ash feels for you, Fats.' Bubblee recalled the way he looked at her. 'It's more than love. And no one deserves it more than you.'

Bubblee found that she didn't feel even a smidgeon of envy and it relieved her. Perhaps it was strange to others that she didn't feel jealous, but to her this was normal. She never did want what other people wanted.

'We all deserve it,' said Fatti. 'One day you'll find it too.'

Bubblee didn't bother trying to explain that she didn't want it. No one ever understood this part of her and after a while it became easier to avoid the subject.

'So I'm going to stay with Farah for a week or so,' said Bubblee.

'Oh.' Fatti paused. 'Any reason why?'

'Because it's Farah and if she doesn't have control of things she loses her mind.'

Fatti laughed again. 'Poor Farah. She does have a bit of a problem.'

'Poor me, more like. I'm only putting up with it for a week to please her, then I'm back to Mum and Dad's. Living there isn't ideal but at least I can stay in my room or go out for walks without being hounded about what I'm eating or doing. It's going to be a long week.'

When Bubblee said she'd be sharing the bed with Farah while Mustafa slept in the living room, Fatti hesitated.

'I suppose it's only a week,' she finally said. 'And that's nice of Mustafa to be so considerate.'

Bubblee contemplated this. Her lack of emotional dependency meant that she never really thought about what other people needed, or what they might be asked to sacrifice now and again.

'Hmm,' she replied. 'I guess it is considerate of him.'

'It is, and maybe try and be, you know . . . '

'What?' asked Bubblee.

'Nice to him.'

'He — '

'Bubs . . . '

'All right, all right. I'm trying all sorts of new things in life nowadays, aren't I?' Bubblee replied.

'And you'll feel all the better for it. Trust me.'

Fatti didn't get a chance to say goodbye because with that she had to hang up and run to the bathroom to throw up. Again.

⋆ ⋆ ⋆

'We're so happy you're staying,' said Mustafa, shuffling around the house. 'Oh! Farah made a roast. She said it's your favourite.'

Bubblee put her bag down and looked at the immaculate living room and a very fidgety Mustafa.

'Are you hungry?' asked Farah, who didn't seem to mind that her husband was darting around the place as if he'd had too much caffeine.

'I am actually.'

'Great!' exclaimed Mustafa.

He pulled out a chair for Bubblee as Farah went into the kitchen to bring out the food.

'How are you doing?' he asked Bubblee.

'Fine. Thanks.'

'Baby okay?'

He looked at her stomach. She nodded.

'She gets enough of that from me, Mus,' called out Farah from the kitchen.

183

She had her back to them as she stretched her arms to get out plates from the cupboards. There was something different about Mustafa. He couldn't seem to sit still. When Farah sat down she realized she'd forgotten the mashed potatoes and he jumped out of his seat. A look of alarm passed over Farah's face too. At least, that's what Bubblee thought. When they were all finally sitting down, with everything they needed at the table, there was the passing of the vegetables and pouring of drinks while they ate in silence. Bubblee couldn't help but glance between Mustafa and Farah. Their gazes both seemed to settle on her and her plate so often that she felt compelled to make sure she took double helpings of everything. The clattering of the cutlery was becoming a little much to bear.

'Nice of you to give up your side of the bed for me,' said Bubblee, looking at Mustafa.

He waved his arm about, flinging a piece of chicken across the table. Farah calmly picked it up and put it in a bit of tissue.

'Nice of you to have our baby for us,' he replied.

Bubblee glanced at Farah who was cutting her chicken into tiny pieces. The rest of the dinner was quiet and by the time they had finished, whatever had propelled Mustafa into such energy was clearly wearing off. Farah picked up the dishes as Mustafa took a sip of water. Bubblee got up, pointedly, taking the dish of leftover vegetables from under Mustafa's nose while he just sat there.

'Mustafa can wash up, can't he?' said Bubblee,

loud enough for him to hear.

'It's fine, he's had a long day at work,' replied Farah.

It's not as if Farah's day would've been easy, but that never did seem to matter. She managed to come home, cook and now she was cleaning up while Mustafa sat there, staring into space.

'Longer than yours?' said Bubblee.

'Don't, Bubs.'

Farah looked at her intently when Mustafa turned around and shook his head. 'What? Oh, yeah. I'll do the dishes.'

'You're tired,' said Farah. 'All that overtime in the stables isn't easy.'

But he'd already taken the washing-up gloves from her and gently moved her out of the way. Bubblee said she'd dry, at which there was plenty of protesting but she wasn't an invalid. She got her way as Farah put the leftovers in the fridge. Bubblee kept looking at Mustafa from the corner of her eye. She hadn't expected him to acquiesce so easily, and he didn't even seem to mind. Had he been like this before? Or maybe she never really got to see it because she'd never come here often enough. Perhaps her sister wasn't the doting little wife to his I-am-the-man-of-the-house routine. In fact, perhaps this routine didn't even exist.

'Well, that's the last of them,' said Mustafa, handing over the final plate.

He went and arranged the blow-up bed in the middle of the living room. There was barely any space between the dining table, sofa and bed, but he managed.

'I'm going to call it a night.'

There was nothing for it but for Farah and Bubblee to go to bed too. It was only nine thirty. Bubblee wondered if this was how most of Farah and Mustafa's evenings went and felt a sense of claustrophobia. It was speedily followed by gratitude that this wasn't her life; that she hadn't married someone and pretended to play house with them. The sheer routine of it made her baulk. Perhaps not all married couples were like this, but she couldn't imagine it was very different. It's not as if Fatti and Ash seemed to her to be beacons of dynamism.

'Are you sure he's okay?' asked Bubblee as Farah took her studs out of her ears.

'Yeah, he's fine.'

After a bit of chatting and some reading Farah switched off her bedside lamp. Bubblee also switched her lamp off but lay awake as she heard Farah's heavy breathing, signalling that she'd fallen asleep. Staring at the ceiling she put her hand on her stomach, tapping on it, knocking on the door of the baby's home. She felt wide awake so scrolled through her phone for a while. She opened up a tab to have a look at any new exhibitions happening at the gallery. Of course there were some. She sighed and closed the tab, putting her phone away. It already felt like a distant past and she wasn't sure whether she missed it, or whether her feeling was something else. It was now only ten forty-five. Knowing that Sasha would be awake, Bubblee got out of bed and made her way into the box room to call her. As she walked along the passage she saw the light was on in the kitchen. Bubblee crept down the corridor, just to rule out any burglars, when she saw Mustafa at the dining table, his head in his hands, his shoulders shaking. She swallowed hard. Was he crying? Surely not. She waited a moment and saw him draw breath as he wiped his eyes. Bubblee felt glued to the spot and for a moment considered turning around to go back into bed, force herself to sleep and pretend she hadn't seen a thing. She crept a few more steps. Surely a man doesn't want to be seen to cry? And then she thought of the unfairness of this and other gender-based expectations. Still, she made a little noise, taking her time so she knew he could prepare himself before she went into the living room.

'Oh, hi,' she said. 'I thought you'd be asleep.'

He'd already got out of his seat and into the kitchen for a glass of water. His back was turned to her.

'I was tossing and turning,' she added. 'Saw the light on and thought I'd . . . you know.'

He took a moment before he looked around. His wide smile and false cheer did something to Bubblee's heart. How horrible that he should be forced to put on the facade when she knew, just minutes ago, he was sobbing his heart out, all alone. For once she wondered why she had never got to know her brother-in-law. Why had she spent so many years disliking him for loving her sister? For not being good enough for Farah?

'Hope the bed's comfortable,' he said.

'Oh, yes, the bed's fine. It's me.'

'Do you want some warm milk?' he asked,

already taking a bottle out of the fridge.

Maybe she'd imagined the crying. Was hallucinating a side effect of pregnancy? He was acting far too normal. There was something about the heaviness of his steps though, the slope of his shoulders, that told her otherwise.

'All right. Thanks.'

He went about warming the milk in a pan before he sat down, placing a mug in front of her.

'Not having one?' she asked.

Mustafa shook his head. They sat in silence for a while, Bubblee staring at the milk, wondering what to say.

'Are you excited about becoming a dad?' she asked.

'I can't wait.'

He didn't quite meet her eyes as he said it.

'I never really understood the need to have children myself,' she blurted out.

It seemed far easier to talk about herself than anything else at this time.

'That's because you never do things people think you should,' he replied.

Bubblee bristled. Of course; this was why she had never tried to get to know her brother-in-law. Always judgement, never understanding.

'I happen to think most people are unimaginative bores.' She glugged down half the mug of milk. 'People just raise children because they want to perpetuate their own gene pool, or correct mistakes that they made, live through them somehow. Which is really great for the children when they're growing up. Mess them up for life.'

Bubblee felt her face burn with indignation as

Mustafa looked at the table, unmoving.

'Yeah,' he mumbled.

This, she hadn't expected. 'Sorry?'

'That sounds right. The thing about correcting mistakes.'

She took another sip of milk as they both stayed quiet for a while. When she looked up she realized that Mustafa was staring at her.

'I wish I could correct mine,' he said. 'I don't want my son or daughter growing up with a dad who cleans stables. Who lost all this money and now the family has to live in this one-bedroom flat.'

Bubblee wanted to agree with him. What kind of example would he set for the baby? But she thought of her own failures in life — and even though it wasn't as if she'd brought anyone down with her, there was no denying that she too had failed. That we all fail sometimes.

'You do honest work,' she said.

And it was true. There was no shame in the job he did. It might not pay all the bills or give him and Farah the lifestyle they were used to, but it was preferable to the kind of money he must've made in his business before he went bankrupt. At least what he did now was honourable.

Mustafa gave an incredulous laugh. 'I want my baby to aim for more than just honest work.'

'How about just wanting your baby to be happy and healthy? Health might not always be in your court, but happiness . . . that, I think, in the beginning anyway, is all yours.'

She tried to smile. It didn't always come

naturally to her, but she tried. Mustafa looked past her shoulder and she wondered whether Farah was behind her. She looked around but there was no one there.

'You never liked me. Why?' he said, looking back at her.

The question took Bubblee by surprise. Things in this family were quietly understood and never spoken about, but he seemed genuinely curious; as if ready to take notes on whatever Bubblee had to say.

'That's a question,' she said.

He gave a sad smile. 'I like that you don't deny it.'

'It's not as if you ever particularly liked me.'

'I've liked you. Farah loves you, so why wouldn't I?'

Bubblee took another sip of her milk. 'Why is it that couples begin to like the same things, just because they're a couple? That they begin to share opinions?'

'Farah and I don't like all the same things or share all opinions, but . . . when you love someone it's natural to see others the way they see them. You trust their opinion. Plus, I could never not like a person who loved Farah.'

Bubblee felt her face flush. 'Well, I suppose I'm lacking in empathy.'

'I didn't mean it like that. I was just stating a fact. Not everyone is the same.'

Bubblee tried to read whether he was being sincere or not, but there didn't seem to be anything calculating about his features, or even tone.

'I suppose I just have high expectations,' she said.

He nodded, slowly. 'They're important.'

She wanted to say that they could also drive you to insanity, into a depression at your own failures, that high expectations came at a high price and it wasn't always worth it. Instead she finished her milk. Mustafa seemed to be in a faraway place again. She stood up and put her empty mug in the sink.

'Better try and get some sleep,' she said.

'Yeah. You should.'

'Thanks for the milk.'

He was still lost in a daydream as he mumbled: 'It's okay.'

She hovered at the doorway before turning around. He wasn't even looking her way.

'Mustafa?'

'Hmm?' He looked up.

'Just so you know . . . I like you a lot more now that you've offered to sleep on a blow-up bed,' she said. 'It's commendable.'

He gave her another sad smile. 'I'm glad.'

That night, Bubblee didn't sleep properly, and she knew that it had nothing to do with being in a new bed.

★ ★ ★

The following morning, when Bubblee awoke, both Farah and Mustafa had gone to work. She came into the kitchen to find breakfast things laid out on the table with a note from Farah, telling her to eat eggs for protein and that she'd bought some decaff coffee. Bubblee screwed up the note and threw it in the bin. When she had slept she dreamed of Mustafa cleaning the stables, but the spade turned into a small fork and he started threatening everyone around him with it. His eyes were crazed and Bubblee jolted awake. She shook her head and wondered whether she should tell Farah about seeing him cry, about the conversation between them that ensued. It's not as if he said anything particularly telling, but she felt uncomfortable nonetheless. Should she ask Fatti what to do? She'd probably just worry and Fatti had enough to deal with. It'd be impossible to get anything useful out of Mae, so she called Sasha, but it went straight to voicemail. She was probably working.

That afternoon Bubblee decided to meet Farah for lunch. She even made her a sandwich.

'You didn't have to do that,' said Farah as they walked out of the optometrist's towards the park. 'What have you been up to all day?'

'Reading mainly. Looked up some antenatal classes as well.'

'Oh, don't worry about that, I've already booked them to begin after your first scan.'

Bubblee had to take a deep breath. 'Next time, do you mind asking me?'

Farah looked at her. 'It's not as if you have anything planned.'

Sometimes it was so difficult to keep calm when faced with such inconsideration.

'That's not the point,' she replied. 'Stop telling me what to eat and drink and stop booking classes for me without asking, okay?'

'Excuse me, but it is my baby. I want the best for it.'

'Or perhaps you just want to control everything?' said Bubblee.

Bubblee had a flash of realization. Imagine being married to a person who could hardly trust you to breathe on your own. Had Farah always been like this or had the events of her life led her to become this way? There had been small signs when they were little; the dolls and animals organized by alphabetical order, the tidy room, always wanting to be the teacher when they played together. Then there were greater signs: the way Farah had set out to get married, how she was always managing their brother Jay, giving money to their parents (in her wealthier days) and pretending it was from him. Was this for the family, or merely because she liked controlling everyone?

Bubblee thought Farah might turn around and walk away, her facial muscles seemed so tight.

'Someone has to,' replied Farah. 'Some people can't be left to their own devices.'

'I'm not some people.'

They walked down the path; the sky overhead was getting greyer, but it didn't look as though it'd rain. Sitting on the bench, Bubblee took out a smoothie she'd made for herself.

'It has all sorts of vitamins in it,' she explained to Farah.

Farah gave a small smile. 'I know. I'm so — '

'It's fine,' Bubblee interrupted.

Farah sighed. 'I'm so happy about this baby, but you know . . . '

Bubblee leaned forward, noticing the fine lines at the edges of Farah's eyes. She realized she must have them too and made a note to look in the mirror more often. It'd be a shame to miss the way she was ageing.

'But what?' Bubblee asked.

Farah looked at her and let out a laugh.

'What's so funny?' asked Bubblee.

'I've realized that we've had more meaningful conversations in the past three months than we have since I got married almost ten years ago.'

Bubblee rested her elbows on her knees, legs apart, swirling her smoothie around in her bottle.

'Do you have to sit like a boy?' said Farah.

Despite having read up on hormonal changes while pregnant, Bubblee was pretty sure her annoyance with Farah had nothing to do with that.

'It's amazing Mustafa doesn't sleep in the stables with you constantly going on at people,' she said, spilling some of the smoothie on the ground. 'He's not a happy man.'

Bubblee hadn't even thought about it, but once the words came out she realized how true they must be.

'You've spent one night with us and you know my husband? The man you've chosen to pretty much ignore for most of my married life?'

Farah's face had gone red and she was already getting hold of her bag. Bubblee had to roll her eyes.

'The repetition of you accusing me of ignoring him is becoming really boring, Farah.'

'Maybe your art was a blessing for us all. You've been back for three months and you think that you can read people and know them? Well, you don't know anything. You know nothing at all.'

Bubblee thought she heard a crack in Farah's voice, but it was too late to tell. Her sister was already marching away from her, down the path and back to work. How could Farah be annoyed at Bubblee when she was the one being difficult? When Bubblee was the one holding back her annoyance at Farah? Shouldn't it be Bubblee who was marching off? If she were a better person she'd follow Farah and try to pacify her, but what was the point? Because Bubblee knew that between the two of them, if there was anyone who didn't know anything right now, it was Farah.

★   ★   ★

That evening dinner was a very quiet affair. Not even Mustafa attempted to interrupt the clattering of the cutlery with questions. Bubblee noticed the way Farah pushed the steamed vegetables closer to her, but she ignored this. The problem with the flat was that there was nowhere to really go and be alone. Bubblee went to bed early and when Farah came in she pretended to be asleep.

This couldn't last. A week was far too long to stay in this place. So, the following evening, Bubblee made dinner for the three of them and said she'd go home earlier than expected.

195

'It's not really fair on you,' she offered to Mustafa. 'Not getting a decent night's sleep when your work is so physically draining anyway.'

'I'm all right,' he insisted, looking at Farah. 'Honestly, it's fine.'

She smiled at him, and this time she didn't even feel she had to force it. 'Thanks for being so nice about it. But I feel bad and, you know, I could do with my own space as well.'

'Well,' said Farah. 'There's never any stopping you, is there?'

Bubblee put her knife and fork down, pressing a tissue to her lips. 'No. There isn't.'

'Sorry that this place is so small,' said Mustafa, looking around the room as if it scared him somehow.

'It's fine for two people,' said Bubblee. 'And a baby.' She patted her stomach.

'No,' he said. 'It really isn't.'

Mae: Hows da happy fam? Ive made a nu friend — Tayyaba — shes da best. Met her @ Islamic soc. Wears hijab. Mum wil luv her. Has Bubs kild Mus yet? Bit lyk livin lyk Mormons isnt it? L8ers! Xxx

Fatti: I don't know if it's the pregnancy but, Mae, I'm finding it increasingly difficult to make out what your messages mean.

Bubblee: Yes, please learn how to spell, Mae.

Farah: Fatti, there's a buy one get one half price offer on Pregnacare. Let me know if you need more.

Bubblee supposed she'd be benefiting from this offer too. She wasn't sure whether she was grateful for Farah's consistent concern, or if she'd been wrong about her marriage with Mustafa all along. Being pregnant really was opening up new and unexpected avenues of thought.

10

Farah was livid. The day after Bubblee left, Farah banged plates in the kitchen, slammed doors, snapped at Mustafa.

'All I want to do is look after my baby growing inside her and she can't stick around for one week.'

Mustafa was still in bed when she came in, looking for her watch. She'd been rummaging through the freezer and had seen the fish curry she'd made and frozen for when Bubblee would want lunch. It reignited her anger that her care should be mistaken for control. She never seemed to do anything right. Anyway, what did Bubblee know about responsibility?

'It's fine for her,' said Farah, fastening her watch around her wrist. 'She went off to London to live her life and who had to look after the family? Not Fatti who spent all her time in her room, eating Primula cheese from a tube; not Mae, who was too young anyway; and as for Jay? Oh, no, God forbid he did anything that benefited anyone but himself.'

She turned to Mustafa. 'No, it was me, wasn't it? I had to be the grown-up and make sure Mum and Dad were okay and deal with family crises.'

Bubblee, who would hardly call home or see how they were all doing, was now lecturing Farah on how to manage things?

'It's eleven o'clock,' she said when she heard no response. 'Mustafa? *Mustafa?*'

She had to shake him before he made any movement.

'You sleep like a log.'

The problem was that Farah's own voice was beginning to annoy her, and yet she didn't know how to change it. Control? *Control?* She couldn't even control her own tone. Mustafa rubbed his eyes as he leaned over to take his medication. He groped for his glass of water, but it was empty. Farah handed him a bottle from her bag.

'There's a sale on at the DIY shop. I thought we could go and buy some paint for the box room. Start working on it — for the nursery,' she said.

Mustafa sat up and nodded. 'Sure.'

Bubblee's words came back to her: *He's not a happy man.* Farah wasn't even sure what happiness even meant any more. But why shouldn't he be happy now that they were having a baby? She knew the job at the stable wasn't exactly fulfilling, but nor was hers and at least they both *had* jobs. There was the driving he was no longer allowed to do. The business he lost, and the people he lost along with it. Who was she kidding? They'd lost all their money and he was raking manure for a living. Neither of them was happy.

'What colour do you think we should make it?' she asked.

He shrugged.

'It should be neutral, shouldn't it, because we

don't know if it's going to be a boy or a girl.'

'Yeah.'

He stayed sitting in bed, staring at the white sheet.

'Do you want to stay in bed a little longer?' she asked.

'You don't mind, do you?'

She did mind. She minded a whole lot, but perhaps sleep was the best thing for Mustafa right now. Plus, Bubblee was wrong about Farah's need to control things — she was wrong to make her feel like this persistently nagging woman, so Farah walked up to Mustafa and planted a kiss on his brow.

'No. You rest. We can go later. Or I'll pop in on my own.'

Without another word, he slunk back under the covers while Farah went to the DIY shop alone.

★ ★ ★

It was hard for Farah to stay angry with the person carrying her baby, harder still to tell herself that Bubblee was selfish. Somehow this one act of Bubblee's, carrying Farah's baby, made up for all the times she had never been there. She *had* been selfish. She wasn't any more. Farah went over to her parents' after shopping for paint to find the passage blocked by a large mattress, covered in plastic.

'What's going on?' she asked as she came into the living room.

Her mum slammed a mug of tea next to her

dad. He was too busy watching the television to notice, but Farah saw the fleeting look of disdain in her mum's eyes.

'Salam, Abba,' said Farah to her dad.

He put his hand up in a semi-wave, but didn't take his eyes off the television. 'I told your amma: why do we need a new bed? The bunk bed is now going to waste.'

His voice might have been gruff, but at least he spoke to Farah.

'It is not going to waste,' her mum retorted. 'We are giving it to your sister's twins.'

It was very odd that her mum would suddenly decide to get rid of the bunk bed that they'd refused to throw away, because if it ain't broke . . . But then they were getting old, and there was only so much climbing her dad could probably manage now, even though, it seemed to Farah, he was in perfectly good health.

'I have been saying to your abba since this morning to take the mattress upstairs.'

'Jay will do it when he comes home later,' he replied, glancing at Farah as if he hoped she wouldn't see.

She looked at her mum, bustling around, and her dad, glued to the television, and wondered if all couples eventually became this way? Is that what she had to look forward to? Or were she and Mustafa already there? Only much worse. Her dad was at least in front of the television; Mustafa couldn't seem to get out of their bed.

'Where's Bubblee?' she asked.

'Gone to see Fatti.'

'Oh.'

Why hadn't her sisters told her they were getting together?

'Poor Fatti, still so ill. I sent Bubblee with tamarind and dry mango,' said her mum.

'I just came to see how she was,' said Farah, but no one seemed to be paying attention to her, least of all her mum who was glaring at their father.

Farah left the house and was about to make a right turn towards Fatti's place when she thought: why should she go somewhere uninvited? But then Bubblee was moving around freely with Farah's baby inside her. Farah's motherly instinct induced her to make that right turn.

As soon as she entered the house she could tell they'd been talking about her. It was that look of surprise on Fatti's face, the quiet that came from the living room, the overly friendly way Fatti told her to come in.

'Not disturbing the mothers' meeting, am I?' said Farah.

Fatti was in her dressing gown, her hair up in a messy bun and dark circles under her eyes.

'Technically it's only a mothers' meeting now that you're here,' said Bubblee.

She was sitting on the sofa, feet up on the table, flicking through a magazine.

'Where's Ash?' asked Farah.

'Quality time with Asim. I told him I'd not be much fun so they should do something on their own.'

Fatti went and lay down on the sofa opposite Bubblee.

'Do you need help with anything around here?' asked Farah. 'Shall I cook something?'

Fatti shook her head. 'Ash said he'd bring back takeout.'

'And Fatti here hasn't eaten anything in about four months,' added Bubblee.

'What about you?' asked Farah.

Bubblee looked at her, raising her eyebrows, and Farah decided they didn't need another argument. She was exhausted and wanted to lie down too, only there were no more sofas for that.

'See the new bed Mum and Dad have got?' said Farah.

'Never thought I'd live to see the back of that bunk bed,' replied Bubblee, flicking past another page.

'Mum was very excited about it,' added Fatti.

Farah wasn't sure where to sit. She decided to go into the kitchen and make a cup of tea.

'Sorry,' called out Fatti, who was unable to move to make it for Farah.

Must act normal, Farah kept saying to herself as she pottered around Fatti's kitchen, searching for the teabags and sugar. They were her sisters, so why did she feel there was a coldness in the air towards her? Even from Fatti.

'I wonder how Mae's doing,' said Farah, coming back into the living room with a mug of tea in her hand.

She settled into the single sofa.

'She's made new friends,' replied Fatti. 'Some really good ones, it seems.'

Bubblee flung the magazine on the coffee

table. 'How's Mustafa?'

Farah and Fatti both looked at her as Farah paused before saying: 'In bed.' She rolled her eyes. 'That's where he spends most Sundays. Honestly, today I wanted to go and get some paint with him but it was like he couldn't even move. I told him just to stay in bed and I'd get the paint myself. Might as well. I do everything else by myself.'

Farah expected some kind of unimpressed facial expressions from Bubblee. Fatti, as usual, ignored any comments made about her biological brother. But even Bubblee didn't join in this time.

'What's he up to today?' Bubblee asked.

Farah took a sip of her tea. 'Like I said — his Sundays are all about being in bed.'

'Hmm,' was Bubblee's response.

There it was. Except was she judging him? Farah couldn't make it out. And if she was then for what reason? Laziness? Not spending time with his wife? His constant exhaustion? Farah wasn't sure if these were Bubblee's thoughts or her own.

'Why?' asked Farah, an iciness in her voice.

'Just wondering,' replied Bubblee. 'Thought maybe he'd come over with you later. To Mum and Dad's.'

'So you can avoid him?' Farah tried to say it with a laugh.

Bubblee looked at Farah, but Farah couldn't quite read her expression. 'No. Like I said, I just wondered.'

'Why don't we watch something?' said Fatti.

She switched on the television and put on Netflix. The three sisters stayed like that for the entire afternoon, hardly speaking, watching back-to-back episodes of a trashy reality show. Hours later, when they emerged from their stupor, Farah offered Bubblee a lift home.

'I brought my car,' she replied. 'But thanks.'

Farah got up and hesitated, looking at Bubblee. 'Lunch tomorrow?'

There were still seven months of Bubblee's pregnancy to go, and she was resolved that nothing, not even her own paranoia, should spoil it.

'Yeah. Okay.'

With that Farah left and went back home to her husband.

★　★　★

'The appointment's at one forty-five,' called out Farah to Mustafa as she was about to leave the house.

When she didn't hear a response she wondered again whether Mustafa should see a doctor. She knew he was working hard, but any time he was at home he'd spend it sleeping. Mustafa had done so much overtime, including working weekends, that he managed to get a day off during the week for Bubblee's first scan. The past month had gone without too many glitches. Farah carried on organizing baby things while Bubblee sat back and let her. Mustafa was too often at work to take part in much of it. Apart from today. Farah ran and opened the bedroom door.

'Did you hear me?' she asked, wrapping a scarf around her neck.

He wasn't in bed, but was sitting on the edge, staring out of the window.

'Are you okay?' she asked, looking at her watch.

She'd be late for work if she didn't leave in the next thirty seconds. He turned his head towards her.

'A baby,' he said.

She smiled at him, hand on the doorknob, one foot out of the room. 'Yes. Okay, have to go. Don't be late.'

'Farah,' he called out, just as she'd turned around.

'Do you think I'll make a good dad?'

She really was going to be late and it was bad enough she was taking an extra hour for lunch in order to go to the scan.

'Yes, of course,' she replied.

'You know you'll make a great mum,' he said.

She paused and looked at him, still in his boxer shorts. His belly was slightly protruding, the hair on his chest dark, his beard neat. She felt a rush of affection for him because he looked so much like a child in that moment. She walked up to him and held his face in her hands as he clasped on to her wrists. Farah thought his eyes looked sad. She made a mental note to speak to him; talk openly about whether he was happy, and if he wasn't what they could do to make sure he was. Maybe try to look for another job? Because today felt as though it was the beginning of something new and fresh. She felt a hopefulness for everything, even for Mustafa.

'I think we're both going to be quite good parents, actually.'

She gave him a kiss on the lips, and he held her there for a moment longer.

'I have to go. I'm getting late,' she said, giving him one last peck.

'Okay,' he replied.

'See you at the hospital.'

She waved her hand as she left the room, springing down the steps, the joy of the future swelling in her heart.

★ ★ ★

When Farah got to the hospital, Bubblee was already waiting there, a book in her hand, though she didn't look as though she was concentrating.

'Nervous?' asked Bubblee as Farah sat down.

She nodded. 'You?'

Bubblee seemed to hesitate before she nodded too. 'It's going to be fine, I know, just . . . you know.'

Farah nodded again. Anything could go wrong. She was going to be positive but a bit of realism was important too. They were both early so tried to make conversation about things other than the baby: the weather, Farah's job, how it was going at home for Bubblee with Mum and Dad. Farah kept looking at her watch.

'Mustafa's not here yet.'

'Wyvernage buses,' said Bubblee.

Fárah agreed. Perhaps she should've picked

him up, but it would've added an extra twenty minutes to her journey and she didn't want to take a longer break than necessary. The last thing she needed was to be fired for taking too much time off for all these appointments. As for Bubblee, her dad had dropped her and Farah was going to take her home since it wasn't that much of a detour between the hospital and work.

'Do you have any nausea or anything?' asked Farah.

Bubblee shook her head.

'I wonder if that's something to worry about.'

She noticed Bubblee put her hand to her stomach.

'I read online that pregnancy doesn't always give you nausea,' said Bubblee.

'But still.'

Farah wasn't sure whether she felt relieved or apprehensive at Bubblee taking an interest in her own pregnancy. Of course she would, it was her body, but Farah had to remind herself that it was her and Mustafa's baby, because without the little thing growing inside her, it felt like an easy thing to forget. She looked at her watch again and got her phone out to call Mustafa. Their appointment was due to start in five minutes.

'No answer,' she said to Bubblee.

'He's probably on his way.'

Farah was writing him a message when Bubblee said: 'How's he doing?'

'Hmm?'

'Mustafa. Work and stuff. All okay?'

It was odd. Bubblee had taken to asking this question about Mustafa every so often since

208

she'd stayed at their home. And Farah didn't even detect any irony in it.

'Yeah, fine.' Farah hesitated before she added: 'I mean, I want to have a talk with him actually.'

'About?'

'Just . . . I've been so caught up with how our life has done a U-turn since the accident — '

'Quite rightly,' Bubblee interjected.

'And then the baby. I suppose I've not really thought about how he's doing. His moods . . . well, I thought about suggesting we go to the doctor's to change his medication a while ago but I've been too busy either being annoyed at him or getting caught up with things.'

Bubblee paused before replying. 'I don't blame you. He messed things up in a big way.'

There it was, the usual Bubblee judgement.

'But,' she continued, 'maybe it's even worse for him.' Bubblee paused as she turned towards Farah. 'At the expense of sounding like Fatti — '

'Not a bad thing,' said Farah.

'I don't suppose living with the weight of knowing what you've done to your own family can be easy.'

'Has pregnancy made you sympathetic?' asked Farah, smiling at her sister.

'For a man who used to love business ventures, clearing out stables isn't exactly going to be fulfilling.'

Perhaps Bubblee was thinking of her own failed artistry. Somehow, listening to her sister have sympathy for Mustafa brought about a pang of sympathy of her own. Perhaps forgiveness was now truly rearing its head.

'Miss Amir?'

'Where is he?' said Farah, looking towards the corridor and calling him again.

They'd both got up, explaining that they were still waiting for the father of the baby.

'I'll direct him in as soon as he comes,' explained the receptionist.

Farah glanced from the door once more before closing it behind her.

'He probably missed the bus,' said Bubblee. 'And you know they don't come very regularly.'

Farah nodded. She didn't want to be angry with him. He might still make it, after all.

'How are you feeling?' the doctor asked Bubblee.

'She's not nauseous,' replied Farah.

Farah saw Bubblee take a deep breath.

'I'm not,' she added.

'All pregnancies are different. Let's check that all's okay with mother and baby, shall we?'

The doctor looked at Bubblee when she said this.

'Actually, this is the mother,' said Bubblee, putting her hand on Farah's arm.

'Oh, yes, I see, sorry. It's here in my notes. Well, I hope the mother is keeping healthy?' she offered, this time looking at Farah.

Farah tried to smile, but wasn't sure if she managed it or not.

'She's at her healthiest when people know it's her baby,' said Bubblee.

The doctor simply asked Bubblee to get on the table and to lift her top up. Farah looked towards the door again, checking her phone.

Mustafa hadn't read her messages — she could tell because the WhatsApp ticks weren't blue. Then she heard it. The beating of something that sounded as though it was coming both from within her and outside her. She turned to the screen to see a black-and-white blur.

'There's the baby, right there,' said the doctor, pointing at somewhere in the middle of the screen.

Farah leaned in and squinted.

'Where?' said Bubblee.

'Oh, my God,' whispered Farah. 'Can you see that little bit?'

Farah also pointed towards it.

'Oh,' said Bubblee, looking at the doctor as if to say: *Is that it?*

'It's a healthy heartbeat, and, let me see.' She moved the wand round a little more. 'Yep. Everything seems to be fine.'

Farah and Bubblee found themselves staring at the image. How weird that everything that Farah had wished for and prayed for was now there, right in front of her, on this tiny screen. It seemed extraordinary that, all being well, this would be a fully formed baby and she'd be holding it in her very own arms in just over six months' time. Farah would've pinched herself if she didn't think Bubblee would judge her for being dramatic.

'So, there's really life in me?' said Bubblee.

The doctor laughed. 'Yes. You could certainly put it that way.'

'Am I meant to feel emotional?' Bubblee asked the doctor, almost as if Farah wasn't there.

'Do you?' asked the doctor.

'I'm not sure. I'll have to think about it.'

'Don't worry. It's a lot to process. Women have been having babies since the beginning of time yet each one feels like a tiny miracle.'

'Tiny?' said Bubblee. 'Not that tiny.'

Farah tutted as she got her phone out and took a picture of the screen.

'He'll hate that he missed this,' she said. 'Even though it's his own fault.'

She took the picture and sent it to her husband.

Farah: It's our baby! You missed it. Where are you? I'm going to pop home to show you the real life photo xx

He still hadn't read her previous message. Farah didn't even care about going back into work. She'd start early tomorrow, or stay late, but she had to show her husband the picture.

'He's lucky we're having a baby or there's no way he'd hear the end of this,' said Farah as they got into the car after she'd called her boss to let her know she'd be a little later than expected. Farah said she'd make up for it.

'Obviously you still have to tell him off,' said Bubblee. 'So it doesn't happen again.'

'Of course.'

'But maybe not too much,' Bubblee added.

'How do you feel?' Farah asked, pulling out of the hospital car park.

'I don't know. How do you feel?'

Farah indicated left, looking into her rear-view

mirror. 'Like things are moving forward.'

'Yes. I know what you mean.'

Farah saw Bubblee gazing out of the window. Was life also moving forward for her sister because of this? And if so, how? At the end of it Farah would finally have a family, but Bubblee . . .

'Have you thought about what you might do? Afterwards?' asked Farah.

'I suppose I'll get a job. No one's going to want to employ me right now, that's for sure.'

'Shame there aren't any galleries around here. That's if you don't want to go back to London.'

Bubblee merely mumbled something incoherent as Farah pulled up in front of the house and parked the car. They got out and Farah opened the front door, calling out Mustafa's name. When there was no reply, she said: 'God, I hope he got the time right and isn't at the hospital.'

She called again: 'Mus! Are you here?'

Farah got her phone out, realizing he still hadn't checked his messages. She dialled his number again, and this time she heard it ring.

'He's left his phone at home,' she said as Bubblee looked at her.

The ringing was coming from the bedroom.

'For God's sake, just when I'm feeling forgiving towards him he goes and does something so careless,' she said as she ran, following the sound of the phone.

The bedroom door was ajar. When she opened it the room was dark, the curtains drawn, even though she'd opened them before leaving that morning. Mustafa was lying there, on top of the bed, completely oblivious to the ringing of the phone right next to him.

'You have *got* to be joking,' Farah exclaimed. 'Mus! You missed our baby's first ultrasound because you were asleep. In the middle of the day?'

She flung her phone on the bed, almost hitting him, then swept around to open the curtains. 'You'd better get up right now.'

'Do you want some tea?' Bubblee called out from the kitchen.

'No,' replied Farah as she marched up to her husband. 'I've got to get back to work.'

She shook him by the shoulders. 'Mus,' she said, as his face flopped to the side. 'Mus?'

Her heart beat faster. A pool of drool had gathered on the pillow, and Mustafa's face looked ashen.

'Mus,' she repeated, more urgently, shaking him. 'Mus, wake up.'

She leaned further into his face, staring at him as if in a dream. 'I'm here, Mus. Wake up.'

Farah fell to her knees, staring into his face, shaking him again. 'Why aren't you waking up, babe?'

Bubblee's figure appeared at the door. 'Did you want me to quickly make you something to eat? Oh,' she said, seeing the scene that lay in front of her.

'Bubs, he's not waking up.'

Farah looked up at her from the floor, her hands on Mus's face. Bubblee rushed to Farah's side.

Bubblee said something but Farah didn't catch it.

214

'What?'

Farah was shaking Mustafa again. How deeply could a person sleep? But he'd become like this lately. She just had to shake him harder, that was all. Nothing.

'Your *phone*, Farah. *Now.*'

But Farah couldn't move. Bubblee was looking wildly around the room, before reaching out on the bed and picking up Farah's phone.

'Yes, hello? We need an ambulance,' came Bubblee's voice.

'He's just asleep,' said Farah, but her voice was breaking. 'You don't need to call them. What are you doing? Mus, wake up. The ambulance will come and it'll be a waste.'

Farah felt Bubblee's hands on her arms, nudging her to the side. She saw her pick up a bottle of Mus's medicine. The cap was on the floor. The bottle empty.

'How many pills were in this, Farah?'

Farah just stared at it and blinked. She'd have to go out and pick up another prescription from the pharmacy. It was important that he take his medication on time, every day. She'd do it on the way back to work.

'No, I can't,' Bubblee said into the phone. Bubblee's fingers were on his neck. What was she doing?

'I don't know. We've just got home. I'm . . . ' She lowered her voice. 'He's on medication but there aren't any pills left in the bottle. No, I can't, but I can try. Right, okay, yes. Yes. Yes.'

Bubblee pushed Farah out of the way as she turned Mustafa's face towards her, flinging the phone on the bed. A voice came from the speaker.

'I'm here. Just remain calm and do as I've explained.'

The woman's voice was so soft and calm that Farah thought she must be very pretty. Farah looked at Bubblee, leaning over her husband, her mouth on his, her cheeks puffing out. She didn't understand any of it. What was she doing? What was happening?

'Come on, Mustafa,' muttered Bubblee.

Bubblee shook her head. Farah could feel the roughness of the carpet on the palms of her hands. She didn't realize she'd been gripping it so hard she'd pulled a bit of it out. Bubblee was doing something to his chest now, pushing her weight down onto her hands, pressing into him so that his chest concaved.

'Stop, you're hurting him,' exclaimed Farah. 'Mus, wake up. Look at what she's doing to you.'

The sound of sirens came in the distance, getting louder by the second. Bubblee's mouth was against his again. Farah noticed the way his arm had flopped down the side of the bed. His hand, drooping; the glint of his wedding band caught her eye as she reached her hand out to take his. The doorbell rang but Farah merely rubbed the ring, staring at it, the tiny scratches, then turned over his palm and traced the lines with her finger. His hand was cold, but so was hers.

'We're having a baby,' she whispered to him. 'We're having a baby.'

But then bodies barged into the room. Bright

216

colours and loud voices. Someone took hold of Farah, attempting to drag her back, but she gripped his hand.

'We're having a baby,' she said louder. 'I sent him a picture.'

'Faar, shh, it's okay.'

'Do they know we're having a baby?'

Farah looked up at Bubblee, whose face was contorted into features Farah didn't recognize. All she could feel was Mustafa's hand, the calluses on his fingers, the roughness of his skin.

'You have to let go of him and let the paramedics help,' said Bubblee.

'But he hasn't seen the scan. He hasn't seen his baby.'

Bubblee nodded. A tear fell down her face. Why was Bubblee crying? Farah felt his hand slip out of hers as she turned to the people in yellow and green uniforms.

'Where are they taking him?' Farah exclaimed.

'Look at me, Faar.' Bubblee grabbed Farah's face. 'Are you looking?'

Farah wanted to wipe the tears off Bubblee's cheeks. They didn't suit her.

'They're taking him to the hospital. We're going to go in the ambulance with them and it's going to be okay. Do you hear me?'

Farah nodded. 'He'll see the baby?' she asked.

But Bubblee simply pulled her into a hug. She smelt coconut in Bubblee's hair, the washing powder on her T-shirt, and closed her eyes as Bubblee's tears somehow mingled with her own.

★　★　★

Bubblee sat with her sister, in the hospital chair, as she stared at the grey lino. To any onlooker, the image must've been so similar to when Mustafa was in a coma.

'I'm sorry,' said the doctor to Farah and Bubblee as they stood up to meet him.

Bubblee had expressed some kind of shock, emotion, but Farah just stared at the doctor as if he was speaking a foreign language.

'Your husband was on phenytoin, yes?' he asked Farah.

'They're by his bedside. I need to get him another prescription.'

Bubblee took Farah by the elbow and told her to sit down while she spoke to the doctor.

'I'm very sorry. I know this must be a terrible shock for your family.' He paused. 'It seems to us that he overdosed on his medication.'

Bubblee put her hand to her mouth. She looked at Farah who'd caught her eye. Her face seemed to collapse just as their mum and dad, along with Fatti, rushed into the ward. Bubblee still had her hand over her mouth as she looked at Fatti and shook her head. Their mum grabbed on to Farah's arms, Farah looking up at her: 'Amma, they've got Mustafa. Why do they have him?'

Her mum looked helplessly at their father. He took Farah into his arms and just hugged her as she stared out into space.

'Phenytoin is known to induce mood swings, and even suicidal thoughts,' said the doctor. 'Did you notice anything abnormal in his behaviour of late?'

Bubblee thought back to a few weeks ago, when she saw he'd been crying. She nodded.

'Right. There'll probably be a lot of questions for your sister and family, so I think you should go and be with them for now.'

'I can't tell them,' Bubblee began.

The doctor paused and looked at her. 'No. Of course not. That's for me to do.'

He looked tired, as if he had seen this too many times. So Bubblee walked with him towards her shocked-looking parents and sister, resting in her mum's arms, to tell them that Mustafa no longer wanted to be part of the family. That he no longer wanted to be part of the world.

Mae: Im coming home.

11

They'd all taken to staring at the ground in the past twenty-four hours. Each seemed to be lost in their respective thoughts. When the doctor went over what had happened to the family, Farah looked so confused that Bubblee had to repeat what he said. But she'd looked at Bubblee too as if she didn't know what she was saying. All Farah kept repeating was that they were having a baby. Bubblee took her by the arm and went into the room where Mustafa's body lay.

'He's gone, Faru. You have to see. He's gone.'

Farah had walked up to the bed and looked at his face, before holding on to it, the realization of what had happened finally washing over her.

'No,' she said, kissing his face, sobbing into it. 'I'm sorry, Mus. I'm sorry, I'm sorry, I'm sorry.'

The rest of the family were at the door. Their mum crying, Fatti holding on to her and Jay putting his arm around her. Their dad just stood there, in shock.

Now they were home and had given Farah a sleeping pill and put her in the spare room to sleep. The rest of them were downstairs with Ash who said he'd start making phone calls to the family members. It had been agreed that there was no need to announce to the world that Mustafa had made the decision to leave it. Surely they had to process it themselves, understand it, before they could explain it to the people they knew. How could they tell them that Mustafa had come to hate his life so much that he decided to end it? It seemed so unimaginable and yet here they were, living its reality.

Bubblee opened the door to the room in which Farah was sleeping. She could make out the shape of her under the duvet and stepped in to check if she was awake. She wasn't. Bubblee walked back downstairs, returning to the rest of the family. Their mum had just got off the phone to another family member and closed her eyes as she put the receiver down.

'So many questions,' she said.

No one responded.

'That is everyone, I think,' said their dad, looking through the diary.

'How'd his mum react?' asked Bubblee.

She was in Bangladesh and wouldn't be able to come for the funeral.

'I never thought the day would come that we would have to make such a call,' replied her dad.

Jay sat silently, hands clasped together, head bowed low. Was he thinking of all the mistakes he'd made and how he was part of the problem that had led to this moment? Bubblee couldn't muster much sympathy for him. Not while her widowed sister was asleep upstairs. *Widow.* Widows were meant to be old, to have lived their life, not be young and on the verge of starting a family. Bubblee's hand went to her stomach.

'Oh, Sprout,' she whispered,

Fatti dabbed her cheeks with the palm of her hand. Mae would be home shortly. She was probably the only one who could really give Fatti any comfort — even Ash looked as though this was beyond his scope.

'Did you tell them the whole story? What he . . . did?' said Fatti, through quiet sobs.

Their dad simply shook his head. They heard keys rattle in the door and Mae walked into the living room, stopping to look at everyone. She locked eyes with Fatti and dropped her bag as she rushed to her sister and Fatti sobbed into her arms. Bubblee felt tears run down her cheeks, but no sobs escaped her. This wasn't good for the baby. None of this was good for the baby.

Bubblee made her bed in the room in which Farah slept. Mae tried to insist that she'd sleep on the floor in Farah's room because Bubblee was pregnant, but Bubblee wouldn't hear of it. She was the one who wanted to be there when Farah awoke. She was the one who had to comfort her twin.

* * *

The following day when Bubblee woke up, Farah's back was turned to her. She whispered her name, but there was no reply. Bubblee stood up and glanced over to see that Farah's eyes were wide open, staring at the wall in front of her.

'Shall I bring you some breakfast?' said Bubblee.

Nothing.

'Maybe just some tea?'

Again, nothing. They'd have to make her eat something at some point, but right now the best

222

thing was to leave her alone, so Bubblee told Farah that she'd be back a little later and went downstairs.

The day mostly consisted of organizing the funeral. Jay had left the house early to make deliveries. Their mum said he was covering his friend's shifts, but Bubblee knew he didn't want to be around anyone. Especially Bubblee — she wasn't shying away from giving him accusatory looks or avoiding his gaze completely when she had the misfortune of having to speak to him directly.

Everyone had tried to get Farah to eat something, but even Fatti hadn't managed to persuade her, coming back with a full plate of food that evening. Bubblee mentioned that she was tired and went to lie down in her bedroom. It was just as well she could use the baby as an excuse; in reality she needed to be alone with her thoughts, which mainly concerned the baby growing inside her and that image of Mustafa, sitting at his kitchen table, sobbing, while she looked on. How much worse it seemed now. Even more so because she hadn't raised the alarm the way she should have done. Why had she stayed silent about it? Why had it not occurred to her, in a more pressing way, that Mustafa had clearly needed help? And then there was the baby. What would become of it? How would they explain that its father didn't think of it when he ended his life? Bubblee felt a tear fall down her cheek again.

'I'm sorry,' she whispered to the baby.

Her door opened.

'How are you?'

It was Fatti. Bubblee sat up and nodded. She didn't trust her voice not to break if she spoke.

Fatti sat on the edge of Bubblee's bed. 'I just . . . I still can't believe it.'

She looked at Bubblee with her doleful eyes. Perhaps Fatti felt what happened with Mustafa even more keenly because he was, after all, her biological brother. Bubblee felt the weight of her own guilt and she wasn't even sure why.

'I just don't understand it,' added Fatti.

'I . . . ' began Bubblee.

'What?' asked Fatti.

'Nothing.'

'It's something,' replied Fatti.

Bubblee looked at Fatti and felt an overwhelming need to throw up. Anxiety had tied her stomach up in knots because Mustafa's image wouldn't relent, no matter how much she tried to rid herself of it. She needed to confess.

'The thing is . . . ' started Bubblee. 'I saw him crying once.'

She relayed what had happened to Fatti who looked at her, surprised.

'Shoulder-shaking crying,' said Bubblee. 'The worst thing is, Farah said that after the scan she was going to speak to Mustafa because he'd been acting strangely. She felt it was time to really move on from what happened with the accident because the baby . . . it was a fresh start.'

'Oh, God,' said Fatti, wiping her eyes. 'You never told her about him crying?'

Bubblee shook her head. 'It felt too *personal*.'

Mae came into the room and sat on the floor, hugging her knees. 'She's still asleep.'

Fatti and Bubblee both looked at their little sister, so slight and frail-looking.

'I mean, like, *who* takes their own life?'

'Keep your voice down,' said Bubblee.

'It was the medication,' added Fatti.

Mae looked incredulous. 'Yeah, I'm sure that didn't help and stuff, but it's not like his life was going great.'

Bubblee put her hand on her stomach. 'All Farah kept saying was: *We're having a baby, we're having a baby.*'

The sisters retraced every family gathering over the past few years. Mae's leaving party when he lost his temper with Farah; the way he'd sleep all the time when he wasn't working; the fact that he was no longer allowed to drive and of course his job; the loss of their home.

'I can't believe we didn't even think of it,' said Fatti. 'All that he went through and we never once supposed it'd come to this.'

'Farah went through it too,' said Bubblee. 'She didn't take an overdose.'

'Bubs,' said Fatti. 'We're not all the same. And you have to remember the medication.'

'Will that be the family line then?' said Bubblee.

'I can't even remember the last time I spoke to him,' said Mae. 'What were his last words to me?'

'For God's sake,' said Bubblee. 'He knew we were going for his baby's scan. How could he not think there was anything worth living for? His flesh and blood is literally growing inside me and he just . . . '

'I don't think thinking comes into it,' said Fatti. 'You don't have thoughts in emotional vacuums.'

Mae looked at her sister and furrowed her brows,

'I'm sorry,' said Fatti, 'but I can't deny there were times when I felt I didn't want to be here any more.'

'*Fats*,' said Mae, unfurling her legs.

Fatti leaned against the wall, pressing her back into a cushion and resting her hands on her bump.

'I'm sorry if it sounds awful or uncomfortable, and I don't feel like that any more. But growing up, always feeling out of place, I sometimes wondered whether I should just . . . end it.'

'Jeez,' said Bubblee. 'Why didn't you say?'

'I wasn't one to talk about things.'

Bubblee felt the physical weight of regret on her chest. She wished she had got Farah to talk to Mustafa sooner, that *she* had tried to talk to Mustafa.

'Anyway, instead I just ate my way through tubes of Primula cheese.'

Mae let out a laugh.

'Sorry,' she said when Bubblee and Fatti both shot her a look.

'When Farah wakes up,' said Fatti, 'we don't let the conversation go to why he didn't think about her or what he'd be doing to the family.'

Bubblee and Mae both nodded.

'Sometimes when there's darkness,' Fatti

added, 'you just never believe there'll ever be light again.'

Bubblee's mind flashed again with the thought of the baby she was carrying — would it be born into light or dark?

★ ★ ★

Farah hadn't spoken or eaten anything in three days. People were flooding in, family members and friends, paying their respects, but every now and again Bubblee would catch them whispering and she wondered if, somehow, they knew. When anyone asked what had happened, they'd all give vague answers about the medication and an epileptic attack. In all the collective emotions the family seemed to be feeling, Bubblee hadn't bargained for embarrassment to be one of them.

She frowned when her parents spoke about what to tell other people.

'All this lying . . . ' she said. 'It feels wrong.'

What she really supposed was that it felt almost disrespectful to Mustafa. As if it diminished what he'd done. That it could be hidden and disguised.

'Lower your voice, Farah will hear you,' said her dad, a sternness to his tone she'd never heard before. 'This is what we will tell people and I don't want any arguments.'

There was a finality in his statement and it didn't seem like the right time to argue, not with her mum nodding in agreement, Fatti and Mae silent, and Bubblee lost in a daze of disbelief.

'What he has done is a very big sin,' said their mum.

'Amma, I don't think that's what we should be thinking about right now,' mumbled Fatti.

This had the fortunate effect of quietening their mum. Fatti's words always weighed heavier than anyone else's. She also seemed to be the only one who remembered Bubblee was carrying Farah and Mustafa's baby. The family was going to announce the unusual pregnancy after the three-month scan, but imagine telling people now. They'd think Bubblee and Mustafa had had an affair or something, he'd got her pregnant and then either he'd killed himself or Farah had killed him. Bubblee wasn't sure what was worse: her sister being a murderer or Bubblee having an affair with Mustafa. She had to get out of the deathly din and escape to her room to be alone. Lying down on her bed, she put her hand on her stomach.

'You just have no idea what's going on, do you, Sprout?' she said to the baby. 'Or maybe you do. Maybe you're taking it all in and it's going to stay with you for the rest of your life.'

A bout of anxiety took hold of her and for the first time she was angry with Mustafa. What would Farah tell her child about its father when it got older? What would it feel like to be the daughter or son of a man who didn't love it enough to stick around? The tears that fell from her eyes were ones of sympathy for this unborn thing. She tapped her fingers on her belly.

'Don't worry, Sprout. It'll be okay.'

Mae came into the room and let out a deep

breath, closing the door behind her and resting against it.

'Man, aunties ask a lot of questions. Like, a man's dead and all you care about is why I've gone to uni, that I'm living away from home, and my haircut. I think maybe we should get Farah in here, away from the herd downstairs.'

Mae plonked herself on the floor, staring absently at her nails. 'Sometimes I just think, nah, this has to be some crazy joke or dream.' She looked at Bubblee. 'But it's not.'

Bubblee shook her head. She thought about the picture of the scan Farah had sent Mustafa, how when they checked his phone he hadn't opened it. Was he already dead when they sent him the picture of the life growing inside her? If he had opened it, if they'd been able to send it just that little bit sooner, would it have changed things?

'What's she going to do?' said Mae. 'The baby, the house, money, life. It's all just — '

'Too much,' said Bubblee.

Mae gazed at Bubblee. 'Oh, my God, you don't think she's going to top herself too?'

'Mae, for God's sake, sometimes Mus was right about you. Take things seriously now and again. And whatever you do, don't say 'top herself' to Farah.'

'I'm not an idiot,' she exclaimed.

Bubblee raised her eyebrows. She turned to her side to face Mae, feeling exhausted all of a sudden. 'Has Farah spoken to you at all?'

'Nope. Nada. You?'

'No.'

Bubblee closed her eyes, wondering whether it was the pregnancy that brought on this wave of fatigue for life. Opening her eyes again she said: 'You know she hasn't once mentioned the baby.'

Mae itched the side of her head. 'Guess that's not totally weird. She has some stuff on her mind.'

'I know but . . . it's her baby.'

Mae bounced up, off the floor, and opened the door. 'You should get some sleep, you know. Look after her baby and all that. Yourself too, I guess. Shout if you need anything.'

Bubblee couldn't keep her eyes open and drifted off into a dreamless sleep as soon as Mae left the room.

★　★　★

Farah slept. When she wasn't sleeping she stared at the ceiling, the walls, the lamp in the corner of the spare room. She looked at the carpet, the bedside table, all the inanimate objects, without a thought slipping into her mind. By contrast she avoided anyone's gaze when she was in a room with people. Family she hadn't seen in years came and hugged her, sobbing for her loss. She patted them on the back, retrieved herself from hugs, noticed their pores, the blotchy noses from blowing into tissues, unruly eyebrows, chapped lips, flushed cheeks.

'Such a young widow!'

'And no children!'

'God is great!'

He is better than people. She had a distant

thought about children. How hard she and Mustafa had tried and how much it drove them apart. Perhaps she was lucky she didn't have any. And then she thought of Bubblee and the thing she was carrying inside her. How could a child that wasn't inside Farah belong to her? Wasn't it clear that no one belonged to anyone?

'He was a very good man,' said one auntie.

They were all aunties and uncles, even the ones who weren't related.

'God took him away too soon,' said another.

Farah felt her eyebrows contract. 'God,' she mumbled.

'You mustn't blame Him for this. He is all wise and knowing.'

The auntie looked at her, her orange scarf draped over her head, her teeth slightly yellowed from God knows what, eyes narrowing. It was a consolation that there was someone who was all knowing and wise. It seemed to Farah that she knew nothing. Certainly she'd not known her husband.

When people had left and she was in the room, alone — after her sisters had opened the door to check on her and she'd pretended to be asleep — she'd lie there and think of the way she'd gripped Mustafa's hand, had stared at his wedding band, his face ashen and lifeless. He *was* a stranger.

'Mustafa,' she whispered into the dark. 'Mustafa.'

She repeated his name several times. She liked the way the hiss of the 's' was different from the rest of his name, which turned into a kind of breathless whisper; like the extinguishing of a flame. A gap of light shone into the room and a silhouette loomed at the door.

'You awake?'

It was Bubblee. Farah turned her back to her.

'Have you eaten something?' she asked.

The light disappeared and Farah thought she'd left the room, but felt the bed dip slightly as Bubblee sat on the edge, her hand on Farah's arm. She wanted to move it off her, but wasn't able to muster the energy.

'You should have something,' Bubblee said. 'You've not eaten properly in days.'

Farah wanted to scoff. It was so ridiculous to even think of things like eating, or having to go to the bathroom, or brushing her teeth. She remembered how big Mustafa's appetite used to be, and how it then dwindled over time, so that it seemed to become a function to him rather than a joy. She wondered how many other things had become a function for him. Perhaps everything?

'Faar?'

'I'm fine,' Farah replied.

'We don't have to be at the mosque until around twelve tomorrow. The men will take the body earlier.'

Farah had a flash of Mustafa sitting at the breakfast table. She was sitting opposite him, looking down at her phone. An ache opened up inside her from where the sob seemed to escape.

'Oh, Faar.'

Bubblee rubbed Farah's arm but she pushed it away. It seemed like a while before she felt Bubblee stand up.

'I'll let you sleep,' she said, as she left the room and closed the door behind her.

⋆ ⋆ ⋆

The following day came, and with it another argument.

'All I'm saying is it's weird, and sorry, but, you know, *stupid*,' said Mae.

'Don't say stupid,' their mum retorted.

She wouldn't meet Mae's eyes as Mae stared at her, hands on her hips, frowning.

'There's no better word for it, actually,' added Bubblee.

The blood had rushed to her face when their dad had mentioned it that morning. Fatti remained quiet, sitting at the table with her head in her hands.

'On top of everything else you girls want to make it harder for everyone,' said their mum.

She turned to Bubblee and Mae, pointing at Fatti. 'See how your sister sits and listens and doesn't shout, shout, shout at everything.'

'We didn't shout,' said Bubblee. 'Mae's just made a very good point. For once.'

'I'm sorry, Amma, but this is . . . I can't agree with it,' Fatti added.

Bubblee imagined that Fatti probably thought about how she'd feel if she were told she wasn't allowed to see her husband's dead body before they buried him. Their mum's eyes settled on Fatti and her features seemed to relax.

'You've always had a very soft heart,' their mum said to Fatti. 'But these are traditions and now is not the time to break them.'

'Now is exactly the time to break them,' replied Bubblee.

'Hello! Exactly,' added Mae.

They all fell silent. Their dad, Ash and Jay had gone to the mosque to make sure arrangements were proceeding smoothly. Bubblee shook her head at how the women, yet again, were confined to the home; the kitchen.

'I mean, it's the twenty-first century, for God's sake,' she exclaimed. 'And has anyone asked how Farah feels about this?'

She knew the answer to that. Farah still hadn't spoken to anyone and Bubblee had already asked her sisters if they'd managed to get anything out of her.

'Farah is a very good girl and she doesn't make trouble,' said their mum.

'Amma,' said Fatti, 'wanting to see your husband before he gets buried is not making trouble.'

Fatti's voice was so soft that their mum went and sat next to her. Bubblee noticed tears in Fatti's eyes.

'But, Fatti, you must understand these things have been happening always,' replied their mum.

'Oh, *always*. Like, we've *always* been destroying the planet so, you know, let's carry on.'

Mae popped a grape in her mouth as her mum gave her a scornful look.

'Anyway, Amma,' added Bubblee, 'you're the one who wanted me to have Farah's baby. That's not exactly traditional, is it?'

The hypocrisy was incredible. Tradition was

what suited a person for that moment in time and her mum couldn't even acknowledge it.

'How come that was okay, but this isn't?' she asked.

'That was different. She was desperate and wanted a stranger to carry the baby,' her mum said. 'I know what it is like to be desperate for a child and family — what it means to a woman.'

'Not every woman,' asserted Bubblee.

'Yes, yes, we know you are different.'

Her mum gave her a curious gaze, one that seemed at the same time to be both in awe of her and anxious.

'To be fair,' said Mae, putting another grape in her mouth, 'some men are pretty desperate for babies too, you know.'

Bubblee looked at Mae eating the grapes and felt sick at her callousness, at her being hungry at all at a time like this.

'What it means to a woman?' Bubblee repeated her mum's words. 'What about what it means to a wife to see her husband one last time?' she spat.

It was unlike her to stick up for the institution of marriage, but it was the principle of the matter. It was another right being taken away from a woman under the guise of a tradition that, no doubt, some man had cooked up.

'Bubs,' said Fatti, lowering her voice.

'When you are a wife, you will understand,' said her mum, standing up and pointing a finger at her. 'If that will ever happen with a mouth like yours.'

'I'd rather have the freedom of having a mouth

that speaks my mind, than a husband who thinks he can speak it for me.'

Fatti put her head in her hands and let out a groan. 'Come on, now isn't the time for this.'

'Yeah,' said Mae. 'I mean, bigger picture, people.'

'Speak to your abba,' exclaimed their mum to Bubblee. 'He decides all the things here.'

'Exactly,' said Bubblee, leaning in as if to try and make her mum understand. 'Don't you see how wrong that is?'

Their dad wasn't a brute. He was kind and caring, even though he had been angry about the news of the surrogacy, but you didn't have to be a brute to be a misogynist. Couldn't her family see that it was in the small ways that women were undermined as well as the big ways? Why weren't they angrier about it? Why did everyone accept the status quo in the name of *tradition?* Her mum held her gaze for a while. Did she want to say something else? Was that a look of concession? *Yes, my troublesome, independent-minded daughter, you are right. It is wrong.* A second more and her mum simply looked away and went back to checking the rice on the hob.

'What Bubblee's trying to say, Amma,' Fatti said, 'is that just because it's tradition, doesn't make it right.'

Their mum didn't respond, she just carried on with her kitchen duties, preparing food for the family for when they got home. There'd be no food at the funeral or any kind of wake, as per tradition. At least that was one Bubblee could appreciate. Fatti glanced at Bubblee. Mae looked a bit perturbed.

'No. It doesn't,' said Bubblee. 'If she wants to see her husband, she bloody well will.'

Bubblee folded her arms and stood, resolved to help her sister in this way at least. Surely it was the least they could all try to do? But when she went up to Farah's room she saw her sitting on the edge of the bed, staring at the carpet.

Farah looked up at her but didn't seem to see Bubblee. She stood and made her way down the stairs, Bubblee following behind her, not saying a word. Bubblee wanted to bring up the whole not-being-allowed-to-see-your-husband thing but it felt almost petty in that moment; watching Farah in her plain white, traditional clothes, scarf over her head; the mourning widow. Their mum, Fatti and Mae watched as the two came down the stairs. They were all ready at the door. Their mum put a hand on Farah's face, trying to look into her eyes, but Farah's gaze was averted. The five women walked to the car in silence. Bubblee drove, Farah sitting in the passenger seat. When they pulled up in front of the mosque there were hardly any people there, just their dad, Ash and Jay, standing outside, talking to the mullah.

'Put your scarves on,' said their mum to the girls.

Bubblee reluctantly took one out and covered her head with it.

'Are you ready?' Bubblee asked Farah.

Farah was staring at her hands on her lap but didn't speak. Her mum seemed to take a deep breath, a crack in her voice as she said: 'She'll have to be.'

They got out of the car and the men directed them to the women's section. She watched as a look passed between Fatti and Ash — they knew how lucky they were and Bubblee was sure that Fatti would feel guilty because of it.

'We will tell you when it's done,' said their dad.

'Abba-' began Bubblee before her dad cut her off.

'This is not the time,' he said.

He gave her a severe look. She was ready to argue with him there and then, but then she looked at Farah — she didn't even seem to know what was happening.

'It's not right,' said Bubblee, meeting his gaze. 'You know it's not right.'

She turned away with the rest of them and they left their shoes at the door and went into the women's section, the men's section separated by a curtain. They could hear the men greeting each other, offering condolences, just as the men could probably hear them. Their space was small, much smaller than the space for the men, yet there were just as many women.

'Typical,' mumbled Bubblee.

Her mum was greeting guests as they hugged her, some crying into her arms, before they went to cry into Farah's. Bubblee caught words of comfort that were whispered into her ears as well but she was looking at Farah and how vacant her gaze was.

An aunt then entered, wailing with grief.

'Who *is* that?' asked Mae.

'God knows,' replied Bubblee.

There was a lot of lamenting at Farah's fate, while Farah sat there, tears running freely down her cheeks, without a muscle moving in her face. Bubblee looked at her, the anxiety for her sister rising, along with her annoyance at other people's false anguish.

'She has to see him,' Bubblee whispered to Fatti who'd taken hold of some beads and was muttering some prayers. 'It's not healthy, her not being able to say goodbye.'

Bubblee's voice cracked and it took her by surprise. She felt a pain that somehow pressed upon her, but also a sense of urgency. Something that would somehow redeem her for her lack of doing or saying anything about Mustafa earlier to Farah.

Fatti nodded, wiping tears from her eyes. 'I know.'

Bubblee got up and sat in front of Farah. 'Faar, do you want to see Mustafa?'

Farah looked up, this time as if she barely knew who was in front of her.

'I know, Faar. I know this is difficult, but do you want to see him?'

'Mustafa,' she simply said.

'Yes. Your husband. They're going to say the funeral prayers and they're going to take him away to be buried.'

Mae came and knelt down in front of them. 'There's a gap in the curtain. I've put a chair there and dumped people's coats on it so no one can sit on it. You can see him through it, Faar.'

Bubblee often forgot to appreciate that Mae was a doer in life, always seeking solutions to problems, bouncing around, fixing things.

'Did you look?' asked Bubblee.

'N-no. I mean, if Faar can't then . . . I will — when she does.'

But the muezzin's voice, calling people to prayer, came from the speaker and women were already shuffling to stand in line, side by side. Fatti, Bubblee and Mae all stood up, waiting for Farah to do the same.

'Come on, Faar. Let's pray,' said Fatti. 'It'll help.'

Fatti took her hand, guiding her to the front of the women's congregation where everyone made room for the four sisters. For the next few minutes, their movements were all in harmony. Bubblee felt the pain that pressed upon her lighten with each prostration. She closed her eyes to try and stop the tears from falling as she regretted every time she'd scoffed at Mustafa, every time she'd spoken out of turn, and especially never pressing Farah to speak to him about how he was doing. Guilt wasn't an emotion Bubblee was accustomed to feeling and here it was, crawling through her veins.

Everyone was sitting as their heads turned to the right, then to the left, to give salaam to the angels on their shoulders. Then their hands were raised as the mullah began to say prayers for Mustafa, to grant him heaven and peace. Bubblee wondered whether the mullah knew how Mustafa had died, and whether he'd be quite so open to praying for heaven for him if he did.

'May you grant his family patience during this difficult time, especially his wife, who Mustafa loved very much.'

Bubblee felt a ripple of tension, maybe heard a few murmurs. Perhaps this mullah wasn't that traditional. They never really talked of love between husband and wife. And now that he had, Bubblee thought that the least he could do was let the wife see her husband before he was taken to be buried.

'We don't know why we are tested with certain trials, but we know that Allah is all wise and we must trust in Him and His guidance. We are not alone.'

Bubblee gripped Farah's hand and saw Fatti grip Farah's other hand as well as Mae's, who was sitting next to her. Farah lowered her head and they noticed her shoulders shaking, teardrops falling onto her top. Bubblee, Mae and Fatti looked at each other, giving a nod as the mullah finished his sermon and the congregations broke.

'Come on, Faar,' said Fatti as the three sisters took her towards the curtain.

Farah was shaking her head, wiping her tears, resisting her sisters who were looking behind them, making sure no one could see what they were doing. Mae had already pushed the coats off the chair to make room for Farah to sit so nobody suspected them.

'You need to do this,' said Fatti to Farah. 'Okay?'

But Farah continued shaking her head as they sat her down on the chair. 'Please don't.'

'He's there,' said Mae, trying to smile as she wiped her tears. 'You look first. Say goodbye, Faar. Then we can say goodbye too.'

'I don't want to,' sobbed Farah. 'I don't want to say goodbye. Please.'

Fatti had already parted the curtain a little, but Farah's head turned away. 'Please don't make me.'

Bubblee caught a glimpse of the men, surrounding the coffin. Farah wouldn't be able to see even if she did turn around. *Come on, don't block this too.*

'You'll regret it if you don't,' said Fatti in her soft voice. 'I promise you will, and we'll never forgive ourselves for not making you.'

Farah turned towards Fatti. Her eyes were red, skin blotchy from the crying; strands of hair fell out from under her scarf.

'I can't,' whispered Farah, but her hand was already on the edge of the curtain.

Bubblee noticed how she gripped its edges, as if she might fall away if she didn't. She glanced at the men's section again and the crowd seemed to be parting.

'You can,' said Mae, pulling at the curtain a little more.

Farah looked at her sisters who all had their eyes on her. She seemed to hesitate before her head moved slowly towards the gap in the curtain, just as the men parted. Bubblee looked at where Farah's gaze rested, and there was Mustafa's face, visible just above the white sheet

242

in which he was wrapped.

'Oh, Mus,' came Farah's voice. 'What did you do?'

Bubblee grabbed Farah's arm, and she wasn't sure if it was to steady her sister or herself.

'It's okay,' said Fatti, now also looking at Mustafa.

Mae covered her mouth with her hand, also staring at her brother-in-law as if she'd only just discovered what had happened to him. It was a mere few seconds before the men bent down and lifted the open coffin to carry it outside.

'No,' said Farah. 'They're taking him. They have to stop.'

Mae put her arm around Farah's shoulder. Bubblee felt as if this couldn't really be happening. Surely this was something you'd see on television or read in the paper. How could the normality of everyday living be punctuated by so much grief?

'Stop them,' said Farah to her sisters. 'Where are they taking him? You have to stop them.'

'We're here, Faar,' said Fatti.

'Mustafa,' said Farah, between sobs. 'Mustafa.'

The coffin was lifted and his face went out of view as the curtain fell back and Mustafa was taken away from them, one final time.

Bubblee: Love you, Faar. xx

Fatti: Me too, Faar xxxx Call me if you need anything. See you tomorrow. Xxxx

Mae: Me 3, Fazzle Xxxx

THREE MONTHS LATER

12

Farah had been staring at the empty side of her bed for an hour. Or maybe it was mere minutes. Time had started to play tricks on her. She was never sure when day merged into night, but she knew that it didn't matter what time of day it was — all she wanted to do was close her eyes and fall away from the waking world. She'd been sleeping on Mustafa's side of the bed, looking on at the space where he'd died, now and again touching the sheets, smoothing out the creases. The rain pelted against the windows. The day outside would be sodden and grey, without a sign of the spring that was meant to have arrived. Farah couldn't remember the last time she'd left the house. Someone had given her notice in for her at work. Probably Bubblee. The idea of having to get ready, do the mundane things in life when there was nothing but a vast chasm in front of her seemed ridiculous. There was a light knock on the door.

'I've made breakfast.'

It was Bubblee.

'Thanks,' Farah mumbled.

But she didn't turn around to look at her sister. Every time she laid eyes on Bubblee, the shock of her growing belly hit her again. It never ceased to surprise her or remind her of something inevitable. Something she really wanted to forget.

'Scrambled eggs and toast,' added Bubblee.

'Okay.'

Bubblee entered the room to open the curtains.

'No, don't,' said Farah, as if the light from outside would turn her to dust.

Even Farah had to admit that she was looking rather pale. Bubblee paused and Farah knew she was looking at her, even though she'd shielded herself with her duvet from the potential daybreak coming through.

'It's twelve o'clock in the afternoon,' said Bubblee.

'Then shouldn't you have made lunch?' mumbled Farah.

Silence.

'Would you eat it if I did?'

Farah gave a grunt by way of response.

'Exactly.'

Bubblee tugged one of the curtains to the side, but left the other as it was — presumably to stop the light from blinding Farah, not that there was any sun filtering through. A waft of fresh air came in as Bubblee also opened the window.

'It's cold,' said Farah.

'This room smells insanitary.'

Wasn't it ironic that when Farah had wanted Bubblee to live with her, Bubblee couldn't wait to get back to their parents' house (their parents, for God's sake!), but now that Farah wanted her out of her sight, Bubblee refused to leave. Farah had urged her to go, told her she didn't need her; she even shouted at her once, but Bubblee stayed, steadfast and unmoved. She didn't sleep in the bedroom with Farah, but on the blow-up bed that Mustafa had used in the living room. Farah should've felt guilty for making her pregnant sister sleep like that, but she hadn't felt anything for a while. She'd cried at the funeral, even before it, but since then it had felt as though all her tears had dried up. Once, she sat at the breakfast table when Bubblee went to the supermarket to get groceries, and Farah conjured the image of Mustafa, sitting opposite her. She watched the empty chair, forcing the memory of Mustafa drinking his tea or coffee, but all she saw was his figure and it would vanish and no emotion would come to her. No sadness, no anxiety, no fear. Perhaps she would never feel anything ever again. Even this thought didn't trouble her.

'Come down after you've showered,' said Bubblee, making her way out of the room. 'Fatti's coming over in a bit and Mae's coming down from uni too.'

Bubblee left the room, leaving the door open behind her.

With a sigh Farah heaved her body out of bed and sat on the edge for a while before dragging herself into the bathroom. She looked in the mirror above the sink and saw her sullen face, but didn't quite recognize it. Farah pulled at the skin around her neck — had it become loose just in these past few months? When she opened the cabinet and shuffled around for paracetamol she noticed that Mustafa's razors had gone. So had his shaving cream and pills. She swept out of the bathroom and looked in his drawers. Were some of his shirts missing too? His socks? She'd been wrong, she was still capable of feeling things. She swung around and marched towards the kitchen.

'Where is it?' she exclaimed.

She pretended not to notice that Bubblee seemed to have been talking to her stomach when she came in.

'Where's what?' Bubblee asked.

'His razor. His shaving cream. His shirts are missing too. What have you done?'

'Faar, calm down. I didn't think you needed to see that stuff every time you opened the bathroom cabinet. I haven't done anything with his shirts, though.'

'It's not up to you what I need or don't need to see. Give me back his razor.'

Bubblee took a deep breath.

'I've thrown it away.'

The blood rushed to Farah's face, her breathing rapid as she felt like flinging the chair at the breakfast table to one side.

'I'm sorry,' said Bubblee.

'Do *not* touch his things,' said Farah, jabbing her finger in the air. 'Do you understand? Don't touch anything of his.'

With that, Farah turned around and stamped back to her bedroom. She began opening all the drawers and her wardrobe too, looking for other things that Bubblee might've thought she didn't need to see. What did Bubblee know about what Farah needed? What did she know about losing a husband, about finding him lying on the bed, a face void of life? How could Bubblee understand being abandoned? Farah grabbed a pair of

Mustafa's socks and threw them against the dressing table, knocking down her perfume and deodorant. The anger evaporated. She heard the doorbell ring and Fatti's voice from the passage. Farah closed the bedroom door and crawled back into bed.

★   ★   ★

'Should you even be driving when you're still prone to throwing up everywhere?' said Bubblee to Fatti, ignoring the slamming of Farah's door.

Fatti's bump had turned into a mini mountain in the space of three months. Unfortunately, the time that elapsed hadn't improved her health and, therefore, the way she looked. She seemed even more tired than usual, her face almost gaunt. Bubblee missed her sister's plumpness, realizing how much it suited her. With Fatti being unable to help Ash at their driving school, Bubblee had stepped in. She thought it'd kill any creativity she might have left in her, but keeping busy and earning some much-needed money ended up being a welcome thing. They needed it to keep Farah's home running since she was in no state to work. A year ago she never would've dreamed that she'd be pregnant and organizing admin in an office in her home town, but there she was, taking phone calls, putting in dates, sprucing up the office with interesting paintings and drawings. She'd even hung one that Sasha had given her for her birthday a few years ago. It seemed to be needed in the office more than anywhere else.

'Ash dropped me, of course,' said Fatti, handing over a dish of roasted chicken. 'Just put it in the oven for another twenty minutes.'

'Farah still hasn't had breakfast,' replied Bubblee. 'Getting rid of Mustafa's things in the bathroom didn't go down too well.'

Fatti walked in and looked around the living room. 'Bubs, I said you need to leave his things until Farah's ready to sort them out herself.'

'It's been three months.'

'They were together for ever,' replied Fatti, leaning back on the chair, placing her hand under her belly before sitting down. 'It's going to be a long time before she even begins to think about moving forward.'

Bubblee's heart sank. 'So what about this?'

She pointed at her stomach, at Farah's baby growing inside her. Concern was etched in Fatti's face.

'She hardly looks at me,' said Bubblee. 'And she certainly never looks at my stomach. I know it's hard and awful, but God, Fatti. She needs to get a grip on things and soon.'

'Bubs,' said Fatti.

'Yes, I sound selfish and horrible but it's true. Who's going to be this baby's parent? Because it's certainly not going to be Mustafa.'

'*Bubblee.*'

Fatti winced and gripped her belly.

'Are you okay?' asked Bubblee.

'Baby's pushing against my ribs.' Fatti closed her eyes and took a deep breath. 'You're going to have to be patient with her.'

The doorbell rang again and it was Mae.

Bubblee went to answer it. Patience wasn't exactly one of her strong suits and how was she going to manage that on top of the way her hormones kept putting her in a rage about things?

'The prodigal daughter has arrived,' said Mae, waltzing in.

She flung her hot-pink knitted hat on the sofa and bent towards Fatti's stomach.

'Your fave aunt's here, young grasshopper.' Then she turned to Bubblee and lowered herself, talking to Bubblee's belly. 'Aren't you lucky that your fave aunt is here too?'

She looked at both her sisters. 'Isn't it totally weird that there are five people in this room right now? Freaky. Where's Faar?'

'In bed,' said Bubblee. 'Again.'

Mae checked her phone for the time. 'I'd say that's awful but this is pretty early for me too.'

Bubblee frowned. 'You were always a morning person.'

'Well, now I have a life and parties to go to. I'm very popular, you know.'

Bubblee felt a rush of envy, remembering her own uni days and that she'd never live them again.

'Ooh, eggs,' said Mae, already taking the plate from the kitchen and eating them with a fork, leaning against the counter.

'So, Mum asked me to collect her on my way here,' said Mae. 'I said I was already here. Last thing we need is our sis subjected to Mum's tears.'

'You shouldn't have lied, Mae,' said Fatti. 'I

spoke to her last night and she sounded really down.'

Mae slowed down her eating. 'Oh.'

'She's always down,' said Bubblee.

Their mum had never, after all, been particularly cheerful. Perhaps that's where Bubblee got it from? Of course. It made sense. She wondered what else she might've got from her mum.

'Bubs, ever the empathetic one,' said Mae.

'You're one to talk, lying to Mum when she just wants to be around us,' replied Fatti.

'Right, well, much as I love all this affectionate chat,' said Mae, 'what are we going to do about our sister in mourning?'

Fatti winced, but this time it seemed to be at Mae. 'I do wish you'd be a bit more . . . '

'What?' asked Mae. 'Dishonest? Oh, Fatti-rama with your drama. Okay, I'll be a bit more sensitive, but only because you're preggers.'

Bubblee related to Mae the story of her disposing of Mustafa's stuff in the bathroom.

'Well, it has only been three months,' Mae replied.

It was amazing that someone as blunt as Mae could have such reserves of empathy. Bubblee's little sister always seemed to surprise her.

'O wise one, what do you suggest?' said Bubblee. 'Because, believe me, I'm open to ideas. I'm the one living with her and carrying her baby, so I'm sure it's really easy for you to say.'

'All right, all right, point taken, Bubs. You're right, obvs. But that is Faar's baby and she'll love it.'

'How?' Bubblee asked Mae. 'And, more importantly, when? Because it's not like we have all the time in the world. I'm due in less than four months.'

'Right, yeah, another good point. Jeez, you're on fire today, aren't you?' said Mae, finishing up the scrambled eggs. 'And you make very good eggs too.' Mae walked into the living room and curled up on the sofa, looking at both sisters.

'We obviously need to distract her,' she said.

'Genius idea. Why hadn't we thought of that, Fatti?' said Bubblee, looking at her. 'Is that all we needed to do? Come on then. What are we waiting for? Oh, yeah, that's right, she never gets out of bed.'

Mae made a that's-tricky face. 'Not that this is the main issue right now, but is you helping out at Fatti and Ash's driving school paying the bills?'

'For now, but I'm not sure how long that'll last,' said Bubblee.

She refrained from telling her sisters that she didn't even have time to think of what she wanted to do with her life. Bubblee was sure that it wasn't the hormones that made her feel sorry for herself, but it was good to be able to blame them right now. Bubblee had spent a lifetime avoiding getting caught up in family dramas, and here she was, in the eye of the storm. Although there was no way she would've chosen to avoid this one. Mae clapped her hands together and shot up off the sofa.

'Okay, step one, we get her out of bed. Step two, I go and collect Mum.'

'I don't see how that's going to help,' said Bubblee.

'Step three, we go and, I don't know, take her to get her hair cut or something.'

'Yes, a new hairstyle is what she needs.'

'Well, Ms Bright Ideas,' said Mae, 'you tell us what to do then.'

Bubblee wished she had something, or *anything*, up her sleeve.

'Fine, go and take Mum to the hairdresser's and me and Fatti will get Farah out of bed and meet you there.'

★ ★ ★

It wasn't easy. Especially since it took Fatti ten minutes to stand up and another fifteen to get out the door. Bubblee hadn't yet started waddling, but it was probably imminent. Her back was sore from all the standing around she did in the kitchen nowadays and her temper was almost as bad. She also found herself needing the toilet, and rather urgently, more often than not. *Why do women do this to themselves?* She decided that carrying another's baby was the first and last act of charity she'd commit to. But there were those moments, in the evening, when she was alone and spoke to the baby. There was something comforting in thinking about what the baby might look like and the kind of things it might enjoy, growing up. She'd already decided to get its first art set as soon as he or she was ready to start holding a pen. She would be cool Aunt Bubblee.

Eventually, Fatti managed to get Farah out of bed and even laid out clothes for her. Farah took so long in the shower Fatti and Bubblee began exchanging nervous glances; she wouldn't follow in her husband's footsteps and do anything, would she? But then Farah came out in her dressing gown, her skin red from the heat of the shower, hair wrapped in a towel.

'Don't you feel better?' said Fatti.

Bubblee could tell by the look on Fatti's face that she immediately regretted making such an inane comment. *Yes, a shower's going to fix Farah being a widow with a baby on the way.*

'Mae's bringing Mum and we're meeting them at the hairdresser's,' said Bubblee.

'Hairdresser's?' Farah asked.

'You know Mum's been a bit restless lately. Bad mood,' said Bubblee. 'We thought we should take her out and do something nice for her.'

Fatti gave Bubblee a discreet thumbs-up. It wouldn't do to make this about Farah — their mum would serve as a great excuse. This way they could spend time with their mum too, all together, and she'd stop repeating the fact that she felt left out all the time. Farah picked up the grey woollen dress Fatti had taken out, fingering its knitted patterns before looking up.

'You can wear something else?' Fatti offered.

Fatti had refused to sit down on the bed because she said she'd never be able to get up again, and walked over to the wardrobe. Farah took off her robe and started changing without a word.

'Tights,' exclaimed Fatti, who seemed so

overjoyed at Farah's acquiescence that she almost forgot she was pregnant, and her body couldn't quite move as fast as her thoughts. 'Or leggings? Yes, leggings, I think. It's cold.'

She took out a pair and laid them on the bed in front of Farah. Bubblee was watching every move made by Farah, whose face was vacant, her movements almost mechanical. She almost wished that Farah would be angry again. At least it showed there was something of a person still in her. Bubblee guessed that she should be grateful for Farah's outburst earlier.

★   ★   ★

When they got to Cathy's salon Mae and their mum were already there. Mae was flicking through a magazine and Bubblee saw, with some alarm, that their mum was having a very animated conversation with Cathy. Since when did Mum become such a sociable person? As soon as they walked in Mae looked up and widened her eyes as if to say: *Thank God you're here.* She chucked the magazine to one side and got up to hug Farah.

'You're looking rather nice, sis,' she said. 'Our ma's getting all spruced up and they're kinda empty in here so I felt bad for them and booked you in for a wash, cut and blow-dry too.'

'I've just washed my hair,' said Farah.

'Look at Cathy,' whispered Mae to Farah. 'Look at her dead salon. Don't make it worse for her.'

Bubblee had to suppress a smile at just how

smooth her little sister could be. They all knew that Cathy's salon was a busy one, they were just lucky it was quiet when they went in. Cathy gave them all a wink, which none of them really knew the meaning behind and felt was rather more familiar than their acquaintance suggested necessary.

'Turns out Cathy and Mum are besties,' whispered Mae. 'They've been gabbing since the minute we got here.'

Her mum turned towards them.

'Anyway, I also have YouTube project numero cinq to begin. That's five, Amma,' said Mae when her mum looked at her. 'I'm doing stuff on the media's portrayal of femininity so well done for helping with that, ladies.'

'How is this helping?' asked Bubblee, gesturing around the salon.

Her tone might've been clipped, but she was genuinely interested.

'I'm documenting the everyday lives of women; the small and intimate ways they can come together and what those interactions mean.'

It was incredible how Mae turned into such an articulate, thinking person when it came to the work she did. Bubblee felt a rush of pride for her sister, and oddly, a hope. She wasn't sure of what, but perhaps she'd find out once she wasn't pregnant and living with her family.

'How's this all going to come together?' Bubblee asked.

Mae paused. 'I'm not sure yet. But that's the fun of it, Bubsy-baby.'

Their mum had come and hugged Farah. 'Look how thin you are getting.'

'We'll give her a cut so gorgeous it won't matter how thin or big she is,' said Cathy, aiming another little wink at their mum.

Farah went first and Cathy did most of the talking, asking her questions, commenting on the thickness of her hair, how clear her skin was. Farah fell into the conversation without too much protest, giving short answers, smiling by way of reply, closing her eyes to avoid eye contact, but keeping a face that remained, if not engaged, then at least placid. It was probably much harder to be rude to someone she didn't know very well, after all.

'Your mum's a sweetheart,' Cathy said to all of them.

The sisters looked at each other. Mae had got her phone out and was already recording. Even Farah glanced at them in the mirror as Cathy removed the towel from her head.

'Oh, Cathy,' said their mum, giggling. 'You are so nice to me.'

'She always pops in for a chat while your dad goes to do the shopping. Always has time for a cuppa with me. You're all very lucky, girls. I wish I lived closer to my mum.'

This was a very weird turn of events. Their mum and Cathy were hardly the likeliest of people to become friends. Anyway, their mum preferred home to the outside world — always had. Or maybe it's what was always expected of her.

'How is your amma?' asked their mum.

Bubblee almost let out a laugh at her using the Bengali word for mum.

'Did her knee operation go well?' she added.

'She's recovering, bless her. Dad's helping, but you know what men are like. Usually make things worse,' Cathy replied, rolling her eyes.

Their mum did the same.

'They're only good for one thing,' Cathy added with another wink.

What was happening? Mae lifted her phone to zoom in on Cathy and their mum. Bubblee wanted to take the phone from Mae but was too confused and engrossed in witnessing this interaction. Even Farah seemed to be taking in the scene around her. Their mum gave a dissatisfied noise.

'How many inches do you want off, sweetheart?'

She pulled her fingers through Farah's hair.

'Doesn't matter.' Farah shrugged.

'Three or four,' said Fatti. 'Nice short layers, I think.'

'Your sister knows what she's talking about. Not too long until you're ready to pop, is it? Another six weeks or so to go, yes?' she said, looking at Fatti's belly. 'Although these things can always happen earlier than expected. Don't worry, if your water breaks here at least it's lino and I have a mop. I always say — and I say it to your mum too, don't I? — you have to spell everything out for men.'

Mae leaned forward, a twinkle in her eye, clearly enjoying the turn the conversation had taken.

'Cathy, tell us — what kind of things do you have to spell out?' asked Mae. 'Spare us no detail, please.'

Cathy laughed and looked knowingly at their mum. 'You don't have to use your imagination — wash the dishes, pick up the towel, feed the baby. You leave a list and even that's not enough.'

Their mum was nodding as she walked over and stood behind Farah, observing the locks of hair that were falling to the floor.

'My husband is a nice man,' said their mum.

'No doubt about it,' replied Cathy.

Fatti shuffled on her seat as Farah practically had a monobrow from frowning.

'But sometimes that is not enough,' added their mum.

'Skies are clearing up, aren't they?' said Fatti, looking at Bubblee.

'Yeah. Yeah,' Bubblee said. 'Might turn out to be a nice day. We can go for a walk. Or something.'

'At least you and your husband sleep in the same bed,' said their mum.

Silence. The four girls paused and didn't even look at one another. Cathy carried on snipping at Farah's hair, unaware of the verbal impact of their mum's words.

'It's only healthy,' Cathy said, measuring both sides of Farah's cut with her hands. 'I wonder if we should put a bit of colour in it. Her hair, that is,' Cathy added with a nudge to their mum. 'Something to think about for next time, anyway.' She made a few more cuts to the ends of Farah's hair. 'I mean, we go through lulls, but a husband and wife have got to have a healthy sex life.'

Oh, God. Mae leaned back, unsure of what to do with her phone, but carried on recording.

'Double bed hasn't helped?' asked Cathy.

Bubblee wanted to put her hands over her ears but this wasn't becoming of a modern, enlightened woman. Their mum shook her head.

'He sleeps so far on one end and me on the other.'

'Would anyone like some coffee?' Bubblee said, getting up and ready to dash out of the salon under the guise of needing caffeine. She noticed that Farah didn't even flinch at the idea that Bubblee would consume caffeine in her state. Perhaps Farah did stiffen a little. Or maybe Bubblee was imagining her sister actually caring.

'Oh, Cathy,' said their mum.

What Bubblee didn't understand was why their mum was even entertaining such a conversation? Why was she not embarrassed and scolding this *stranger* for her obscene talk? Although, of course, it wasn't obscene.

'It has been a very long time since I've had the sex.'

Mae dropped her phone and it went skidding across the lino, stopping right at their mum's feet. Farah seemed to choke on her own saliva as she coughed and Bubblee and Fatti were apparently glued to the spot.

'Tell me. Your husband likes it?' said their mum.

Did she not know her daughters were there? And since when had their mum, this little

Bengali woman, become desperate for *the sex?* Cathy laughed.

'He doesn't complain, let me tell you that. But it's completely natural for their libido to die down in old age. Some men want more, some want less. But you know what the problem is? No one ever thinks about what women want.'

Their mum let out an almost evangelical sound of agreement. Mae scrambled to get her phone and seemed to hesitate as to whether she should carry on recording or stop.

'Turn that off,' said Bubblee to Mae.

Mae simply waved her hand at Bubblee, the other hand still holding her phone, recording the scene that was unfolding before them.

'Women want the sex,' exclaimed their mum. 'I want the sex!'

'Oh, my God,' whispered Fatti, who looked as though she might give birth there and then. 'Bubs . . . what's happening?'

'They do,' said Cathy, waving her scissors in the air. 'They really do. And you need to tell your husband that.'

'I have tried!'

Their mum gripped the back of Farah's chair and almost shook it. Cathy sighed and looked at the sisters.

'Well, girls, what advice do you give your mum? Your dad's a lovely man, but I don't think he's a very good listener.'

Where the hell had Cathy even come from? Who was she and why did she know so much about their family?

'I know, I know. It's not a comfortable

264

conversation to have. They're your parents, after all. I wouldn't like to have this talk with mine, but we're adults, aren't we?'

She looked at both Fatti and Bubblee's expanding bellies.

'You are really a brave one,' said Cathy, looking at Bubblee. 'To have someone else's baby when you're still a virgin. So your mum tells me.'

Bubblee had to sit back down. She felt faint and nauseous, and wondered whether the stress of this conversation would put both her and Fatti into early labour. Their mum looked at the floor, her face flushed a little. Bubblee's eyes locked with Farah's.

'I think waiting until after marriage is a commendable thing to do, but God, you can have some shockers,' said Cathy.

Their mum looked up and nodded. 'Shocker,' she said. 'When I got married I didn't even know how babies were made.'

'It was a different time,' said Cathy. 'But now you girls have all kinds of knowledge at your disposal, don't you? You can't watch a television programme without a sex scene nowadays. Even good Muslim girls like yourselves will know a whole lot more than your mum's, and even my mum's, generation.'

'So much time it took me to get used to it,' said their mum. 'It's very painful first few times. And now? I am so old but I like it and want it and my husband pretends he is too tired, or looks at me as if I am . . . dirty and shouldn't want such things. God made me like this.'

'Madonna complex,' said Cathy knowingly.

Their mum looked confused. Bubblee knew she was probably thinking of the singer Madonna. Bubblee put her head in her hands. This conversation couldn't be happening. This was meant to be about Farah and the world had gone topsy-turvy.

'Is that short enough, love?' said Cathy, looking at Farah in the mirror.

Farah nodded, hardly looking at the cut she'd been given. Cathy got the hairdryer out and began blow-drying Farah's hair, pulling at it with her bristled brush, while shouting over the noise.

'Nonsense, too old! You tell your mum, girls. She's a fine-looking woman.'

Normally, Bubblee would have gone into the fact that it wouldn't matter if she were fine-looking or below average; needs shouldn't be aesthetically based. This was part of the problem of being a woman. But this theory of course wasn't the pressing matter at hand. The most important thing was to put a stop to this conversation.

'My daughters don't even include me in their phone talk.'

Cathy looked confused. 'You mean WhatsApp group?' She tutted at the four sisters. 'Come on, girls.'

They glanced at one another, looking shame-faced. They'd all been so involved in their own issues that they hadn't thought of their mum's life and what was happening in it. Apart from Fatti, of course, but even she didn't know *this*

266

was happening. Or *not* happening, as it were. Who could've predicted the sexual awakening of their mother? And who could've realized that the local hairdresser would know more about it than them? It wasn't as if their mum would be able to speak to any of their aunties about it, they were sure. She had no one and each of them was to blame.

'There,' said Cathy, pulling her fingers through to the bottom of Farah's hair and getting out another mirror. 'What do you think?'

Farah swallowed hard. 'It's lovely. Thanks.'

Her mum looked at her appraisingly and smiled. 'She looks very pretty, Cathy.'

'She *is* very pretty,' Cathy replied. 'Four gorgeous daughters you have. Now, let's do you, shall we?'

Farah got up and went and sat between Bubblee and Fatti, while Mae was on the stool, recording the entire fiasco. Their mum sat on the seat.

'For you,' said Cathy, 'we need something that is irresistible.'

'Who is this woman?' whispered Farah to Bubblee and Fatti as she glanced at Cathy.

They both looked at her, watching their mum, and had to be grateful for her speaking.

Mae rolled up to them on her stool, pointing the camera at her sisters. 'Pay attention, Faar. That's Cathy. Aka, Mum's new bestie.'

They all looked at the two, laughing at something their mum had said.

'Is Mum funny?' said Mae.

'God knows who she is,' answered Bubblee.

'Who'd have thought?' Mae put her phone away.

'Don't you dare do anything with that,' said Bubblee, pointing at where she'd put her phone. 'If I see any of that online I will kill you.'

'We all will,' added Farah.

Bubblee felt a sense of hope come to the surface.

'Are you mad?' said Mae. 'This is for my eyes only, but I think it's well useful when thinking about female interaction and the spaces relation-ships form.'

Bubblee patted Mae's leg, caught between pride and exasperation. The four sisters sat there as they watched Cathy style their mum's henna-dyed hair into a shoulder-length cut, curled in layers, taking ten years off her.

Their mum looked at her reflection, consider-ing each of her facial angles, lifting her chin and then smiling.

'What do you think, girls?' Cathy asked the four sisters.

Lovely, great, gorgeous, came all their voices.

'There you are,' said Cathy. 'Now go and show it off to your husband.'

'I don't care if he likes it,' replied their mum. 'I do.'

★   ★   ★

They dropped Mum home because she said she had to make dinner for their dad, but the sisters decided to go back to Farah's afterwards. Bubblee drove them all in silence, only exchanging glances with Mae in the rear-view mirror now and again. They went into the flat and Bubblee was relieved that after using the bathroom, Farah came in rather than getting back into her bed.

'Well,' said Mae. 'That was . . . interesting.'

Fatti stuffed two pillows under her back as she shifted her bulk from side to side on the sofa, trying to get comfortable. Bubblee watched her, not much looking forward to the coming months of her own expansion. Mae had her phone out already and pressed the play button on her recording. The sisters listened to it, all wincing anew at each nauseating sentence.

'Who'd have thought it?' said Bubblee.

'At least now we know why they finally got rid of the bunk bed,' replied Fatti.

'Ewww.' Mae stopped playing the recording. 'It's too gross for words. Does this mean we have to include her in our WhatsApp group chat and give her advice on how to have . . . you know, with Dad?'

'God, no!' said Bubblee.

'Well, maybe no on the advice, but perhaps we should let her into the chat,' said Fatti.

The three looked at Farah.

'Well, what do you think?' asked Bubblee.

'Me? I don't know.'

Bubblee supposed she didn't care much, seeing as she hardly ever responded to the messages on chat any more. Then Farah shrugged.

'I suppose let her in. We can still have a separate sisters' chat, can't we?'

'I'll get her a phone,' said Fatti.

Now, if only Farah would look at Bubblee for more than a split second, if only she'd allow her gaze to wander towards her baby.

'Ah,' said Bubblee, putting her hand on her belly. 'The baby just kicked.'

It hadn't really. In fact, Bubblee couldn't remember the baby ever kicking in Farah's presence. She wondered whether this was a sign, but told herself not to be so silly and superstitious. Fatti would have other views, if she knew. She might be telling Bubblee to give it time, but Bubblee could tell by the look on her face that even she was beginning to worry about Farah's lack of interest in her own baby.

Mae lunged forward to put her hand on Bubblee's stomach. 'Ugh. Typical. It's not doing it any more.'

Bubblee waited for a flicker of interest to appear on Farah's face. Fatti seemed to be doing the same, her face creasing into a worried look.

'Well, it certainly does enough of it during the night,' said Bubblee.

Farah was looking at her hands, rubbing her palm and fingers as if massaging them. Mae also glanced at Farah.

'You guys thought of any names yet? Boy and girl. So weird you didn't want to know the sex of the baby.'

Farah got up. 'I'm going to change.'

'It's only four o'clock in the afternoon,' said Fatti.

'These leggings. They're uncomfortable.'

With that Farah left the room.

'Give it time,' said Fatti, without Bubblee even saying anything.

'I mean, yeah, obvs, but it's kind of ticking, isn't it?' replied Mae.

An hour later Farah still hadn't come back, and they knew she'd probably crawled into bed. They'd have to think of another way to get her out tomorrow.

★ ★ ★

Bubblee had been up since five o'clock in the morning. She'd been staring out of the kitchen window, mostly, decaffeinated coffee in one hand, stroking her protruding bump with the other.

'Your mum's going to be fine in the end, Sprout,' she said.

Bubblee looked over her shoulder to make sure the baby's mum wasn't listening to what had become her favourite pastime.

'It'll just take a little while.'

And maybe a sizeable miracle, she thought. There was no point in being frustrated about it; how was anyone meant to get over finding their partner in their bed, lifeless of their own accord? Bubblee shuddered and took a sip of coffee. Her feelings towards Farah would dip and swerve. There were times she'd want to shake her back into the present day, into life that was going on around Farah and inside Bubblee. Then there were times when her frustration would settle into a resigned calm, an understanding that there were some things you never got over. This

271

thought filled her with so much dread she'd taken to giving herself words of comfort by talking to the baby. Because what if Farah never did get over it? What if the baby was born and she didn't look at it — no longer wanted it? What would happen to the poor thing?

'Hopefully it won't be longer than you coming into the world,' she added, draining her last dregs of coffee and putting the mug in the sink.

Just then her phone rang. It was only seven o'clock in the morning — what was Mae doing calling her at this time?

'What's going on?' she asked urgently.

'Oh, Godddd,' cried out Mae on the other end of the line.

'What's happened? Is it Fatti?'

There was another groan from Mae and Bubblee wondered whether her sister had got food poisoning or something.

'I just can't believe it,' Mae said finally, desperation in her voice. 'I swear to God, whoever's done this, I'm going to find them and I'm going to shove their phone right up their — '

'Mae, what are you talking about? You're not making any sense.'

'I only sent it to one friend, honestly. Because, well, there was no reason not to. As a piece of media case study, it was pretty interesting, you have to admit. Anyway, I told her — I said: *Don't you dare forward this on to anyone.* Why do people not listen to me?'

Bubblee swallowed hard. 'Mae,' she began in the same tone she used whenever she or her family suspected Mae of wrongdoing. 'What was

272

this someone meant to have listened to?'

Mae let out another groan. 'She says she only sent it to one friend of hers, but this friend, right, well, her boyfriend had her phone and saw it, and then he sent it to this WhatsApp group of his and one of those guys, they . . . I don't know. They must've done some weird remix to it and then stuck it on Facebook, and then people shared it on Twitter and now . . . Oh, dear God.'

'Saw what, Mae?'

Silence.

'Saw *what?*'

Bubblee's phone beeped. Mae had sent her a link. She clicked on it while still on the phone. A YouTube page came up and Bubblee's heart sank. No good ever came out of Mae and her use of social media. There it was: the familiar scene of yesterday's hairdressing salon. Bubblee's hand went to her forehead. She pressed the play button and R. Kelly's 'Ignition (Remix)' began as she watched an edited version of yesterday's trip to the hairdresser's unfold before her eyes. This time with background music.

'Oh, God,' she said as the lens zoomed in on their mum's face.

Bubblee knew what was coming, but she had to see it through to the end. The video went into slow motion as her mum's mouth opened, the music approaching the choral line, and then stopping just as their mum exclaims: 'I want the — I want the — I want the sex, sex, sex.'

'Oh, my *God*, Mae.'

'*I know.*'

Bubblee didn't even stop the video as she

started shouting at Mae down the phone, R. Kelly singing nonchalantly in the background.

'How stupid do you have to be?' exclaimed Bubblee. 'How many people have shared this? You need to stop this *right now.*'

Mae's words spilled out, protesting and lamenting: 'I didn't know. It was an accident. I'm going to kill my friend.'

Bubblee told her to get off the phone and deal with the situation.

'There's no way to stop it,' Mae said.

'What do you mean? It's *your* video.'

'I sent the video but someone else uploaded it on YouTube,' explained Mae. 'With the soundtrack. It was quite inventive of them, if you think about it.'

Bubblee had to rub her eyes and take a deep breath. This was all they needed. She looked at the video again — their mum's face in clear view, contorted in desperation, which only served to make the whole thing worse.

'How many people have seen this?'

Mae paused. 'A lot.'

'*Mae!*'

'It's not my fault,' she retorted. 'Okay, it's my fault for sending it to my friend but how did I know she'd go and send it on to another friend, who'd send it to another, whose boyfriend would see it and who'd pass it along to his mates?'

'Because it's university and no one cares what you ask them not to do — you do it anyway. And because social media is evil.'

'*What* is going on?'

Bubblee turned around to see Farah, wrapping

her dressing gown around her, a frown etched into her brows. Bubblee was lost for words. She simply stomped up to Farah and shoved the phone in her face, saying to Mae: 'Here, *you* explain it to her.'

As Bubblee looked on, she saw Farah's expression change; closing her eyes, shaking her head. Bubblee watched her go through the same steps as she just had, playing the video, watching their mum . . . remixed. Asking for *the sex*.

'Oh, *Mae*,' whispered Farah, looking at Bubblee. 'This is *awful*.'

Bubblee heard more muffled pleading coming from the phone.

'Okay, okay, calm down,' said Farah. 'Go and see if your friend's friend's boyfriend's friend can take it off YouTube.'

'Don't see!' shouted Bubblee. 'Make it happen!' She snatched the phone from Farah. 'Did you hear? *Make it happen*.'

Farah took the phone from Bubblee, turning away. 'Fix this, Mae. It's the last thing Mum needs. The last thing any of us need. If any of our friends or family see this, it's going to be a disaster.'

Farah put the phone down.

'*Disaster?*' said Bubblee. 'Mum's not going to be able to show her face. This is just absolutely typical of Mae.' Bubblee began pacing the room. 'She's at university but completely irresponsible and of course nothing is ever her fault.'

'It wasn't intentional,' reasoned Farah.

'It never is with her. Somehow these things just happen to her magically, don't they? Or have you forgotten that time she put up the blog about Mustafa's accident, which went viral?'

Bubblee looked at Farah and saw the muscles on her face contract. Why had she brought up Mustafa when Farah was actually interacting with her? But she knew it was too late to take it back. Farah had already turned around and made her way back into her bedroom, and Bubblee heard her shut the door behind her.

Fatti: I think we should all stay calm while Mae tries to sort this out.

Bubblee: Calm?? Like hell.

Mae: IM SORRY. Im on it, im on it. I promise. Tho, uve gotta admit the remix was pretty epic.

Bubblee: I'm blocking her from this group.

Fatti: Mae . . .

Mae: Ok! Soz. ON IT.

13

It wasn't what they had expected. When Fatti had found out about the video, she insisted they all go over to their mum's house and fix this together. At first, Farah said there was nothing she could do to help, they should go on without her, but this time Fatti had put her hands on her hips and said: 'You'll find you *can* help, actually,'

Farah looked at Fatti, framed in the doorway of her bedroom, feet in the passage, belly in her room.

'I don't see how,' Farah added, tucking herself further under her covers.

'By being a concerned daughter,' said Fatti.

It was so unlike Fatti to conjure up this commanding voice, to tell anyone to do anything, least of all Farah, that it prevented Farah from any retort. She could've argued with Bubblee, shouted at her, avoiding her gaze and especially her bump, but she couldn't bring herself to do it with Fatti.

Their mum didn't seem to know that her face and voice were crawling over the Internet, that, sitting in Wyvernage, she had managed to go viral. Fatti had given her a phone and was setting it up for her while Mae was keeping track of the comments section, which was getting longer and longer.

Get in there, aunti ji!
#Brownwomenrule

Iz this real?

Why isnt tht my hairdresser or mum?

Hahahahaha. Best ting since samosas bro.

'Mum's a hit,' she kept whispering, to which Bubblee would shoot her a look and Mae would retreat and put her phone away.

The sisters gave sidelong glances to their dad as well, as he watched the news or went out into the garden, checking on his begonias.

'Faru,' he called out to her from the garden. 'Come and help me.'

Farah seemed to have forgotten the 'yes' and 'no' part of her brain functionality and let herself be led by her dad's suggestion. Ever since Mustafa's death, he had seemed to have got over the surrogacy. How was that for irony? They both stood in front of the flower bed. Farah noticed the neatly mowed lawn, the pine tree that grew into the next-door neighbours' garden, the tulips and hyacinths that grew alongside the begonias.

'They're doing well, yes?' said her dad, patting her shoulder.

She didn't know why this made her want to cry. She almost reached out to put her hand over his. Farah nodded.

'Hand me that sack of mud,' he said, getting his gardening fork and gloves.

Farah did as he asked and watched him put down new soil, dig up the weeds as she squatted next to him.

'It's a lot of work,' she said. 'When you know they're going to die come winter anyway.'

He looked at her and smiled, his jet-black hair

almost gleaming in the sun.

'But see how they make the garden beautiful? And how happy your mother is to see them too?'

It had never occurred to Farah that her father did anything to please their mum. She was immediately embarrassed, recalling the day at the hairdresser's and the subsequent video, which Mae was still trying to take offline. Thoughts she'd rather not have to deal with came flooding into her head, so she offered to help her dad with the weeding, taking the pair of gardening gloves that he handed her.

'You like keeping Amma happy?' she asked.

He looked at her a little surprised, flushed even. Farah suspected it was because she had never asked her dad such a frank question — none of the sisters did. Somehow, talking about feelings wasn't part of their family set-up.

'Oh, I only try,' he replied.

Farah wondered if he knew how unhappy her mum was with him, and . . . what she wanted from him. She let out an involuntary groan.

'Are you okay?' asked her dad.

She nodded and carried on weeding.

'What if she isn't happy?' asked Farah.

Her dad dug the fork into the soil and looked at her, concentrating on her face in such a way that she wondered if he could read her thoughts.

'Happiness comes from within,' he answered.

Farah shook her head. Typical of her dad to give a stock philosophical answer; it was a stupid question to ask him anyway. Of course it doesn't just come from within — you have to have a world around you that you're happy to be in too.

Mustafa did not have that world. Perhaps it was because Farah hadn't given it to him. Somehow she'd sapped happiness out of him and it was this thought that brought tears to her eyes, which tumbled down her cheeks into the soil. It was too much, though. How could she have created happiness in their world when he'd done so much to destroy it? She wiped her eyes before her dad noticed. He cleared his throat.

'We have been married a long time now,' he added, staring at his flower bed. 'What happiness there was to give, is given. The rest we just . . . top up.'

'With gardens?' said Farah, pouring in some fresh soil.

She should say that their mum wanted more than a garden, but how could she without going bright red and also experiencing an acute sense of nausea? But she knew how it had felt — your own husband not wanting to sleep with you — and she was sorry for her mum; even sorrier that she couldn't do anything to help her in some way. Her dad simply nodded, looking at Farah's handiwork.

'With gardens that my daughter is helping me grow,' he said.

* * *

An hour later Farah was tired and her dad said he was meeting a friend, so she went inside to find Fatti, Bubblee and Mae, whispering furiously.

'Where's Mum?' asked Farah.

280

'Bathroom,' said Mae.

'He's not taking the video down,' exclaimed Bubblee to Farah. 'None of these little shits is listening because of all the hits the link is getting. They'd better watch out for the hit they get when I get my hands on them.'

Fatti didn't look too happy.

'I *tried*,' cried Mae.

'You didn't try hard enough,' replied Bubblee through gritted teeth.

'Hi, Amma!' exclaimed Farah.

Their mum looked around the room, frowning. 'What is happening?'

'Nothing, nothing. Like your new phone? Do you want some tea? I've made a courgette cake,' said Mae.

'She's baking. Can you believe it? At a time like this she's actually baking,' said Bubblee, shaking her head while Fatti tried to tell her with a simple look to calm down.

'Where is your abba?' asked their mum.

'Gone to see his friend,' replied Farah.

Their mum scoffed and the girls looked at each other.

'Yes, his friends are very important.'

'He's doing the garden for you,' said Farah, trying to be encouraging.

Anything to stop this conversation going where it was headed. Fatti, Bubblee and Mae were all looking at their mum.

'Yes, yes. The garden is all for me. Okay, I am making fish curry, Faru. You will help me.'

Farah was a little taken aback by the change of subject when the phone in the hallway rang.

Their mum picked it up. The way she was talking it seemed to be an obscure aunt, but then the colour from their mum's face appeared to drain. The sisters all looked at each other.

'No, no. I haven't seen it,' said their mum, looking around at the four of them, her eyes resting on Mae.

Oh, no. All the talking came from the other end of the phone as their mum simply listened, first drained of colour, now with her cheeks flushed.

'I don't know. I don't know. These girls, you know?'

She stayed listening on the end of the line, her cheeks getting redder by the second.

Farah noticed her sisters all looking at the ground at this point as their mum put the phone gently back on the charger and went into the kitchen without looking at any of them. Farah followed her mum dutifully into the kitchen, looking back at her sisters. A few minutes later she came out and said: 'Mae, add Mum to our WhatsApp group. *Now*. At least start making all of this right.'

With which she turned around and walked back into the kitchen.

★ ★ ★

Bubblee and Fatti were both sitting on the bed, Mae on the floor, when Farah came in. They all fell silent. Had they been talking about her?

'We thought you might be Mum,' explained Mae. 'Did she say anything about the phone

282

call?' She clutched her stomach. 'I bet that stupid aunt's told the world about it.'

'She couldn't even look at me,' said Farah. 'It was awful. Any progress, Mae?'

Bubblee shot Mae a look, which clearly meant no.

'It actually gets worse the more you watch it,' said Mae, ignoring Bubblee's looks.

Farah looked at Fatti, sitting upright against the wall, three pillows behind her back.

'How are you?' she asked.

'Only seven weeks to go,' she said, shifting uncomfortably.

Farah knew it was the moment to also ask Bubblee how she was, how her bump was, but she couldn't quite get her head around the idea of it being her baby now that Mustafa was gone. It was as if he was the cord that strung them all together and she'd never even realized it. But one thing she had realized — she hadn't just wanted the baby, she'd wanted their family. Without him, none of this seemed to make sense. She was so used to him being around — so intrinsic was he to her daily living — that she had never quite understood he was a separate person and so could be separated from her. Yet this was the same man who had started to annoy her so often she wasn't sure whether she even loved him any more. This only made things worse. As if she had betrayed him by doubting her feelings for him. Maybe it wasn't the fact that she wanted to have a baby with him — perhaps it was just the idea of being a family, as if that equalled happiness. Nothing was clear-cut any more. Not even her feelings.

'You know,' said Fatti, who'd stolen a glance at Bubblee before looking at Farah. 'We could do with some more help at the driving school. Ash's planning his holiday with his son before the baby comes and anyway, it'd be nice, the three of us working together. Wouldn't it?'

Mae cleared her throat as she swiped through her phone, sending messages and checking for any updates on the YouTube link being taken down. Farah shrugged.

'Sure.'

Fatti beamed and patted Bubblee's leg.

'Can I come?' said Mae.

'No,' they all said in unison.

'Fine,' said Mae, hardly seeming surprised by their reaction. 'But maybe you can help me with my project,' she said to Farah.

Farah furrowed her eyebrows. Mae never asked any of them for help.

'You know,' said Mae. 'Women, solidarity. That kind of thing.'

'I can't believe that you can even think about more projects when your last one is doing international rounds,' said Bubblee, shaking her head.

'It's called being a professional about things,' replied Mae. 'Anyway,' she added, looking back at Farah, 'I'd rather not have those two around complaining about their nausea and blah blah blah.'

'You have nausea?' Farah asked Bubblee.

'I *am* pregnant.'

Farah gripped the doorknob and looked back

at Mae. 'Fine, yes. I'll come along. Though I don't know what use I'll be.'

Just then their mum's voice called out for Farah because more onions needed chopping, and their dad walked back into the house, calling for her to help him with the new flowers he'd just bought. Farah had a vague sense of being overstretched by all these requests. She'd rather be lying in bed.

'Come, come,' called out her dad. 'Look at these petunias.'

That evening, Farah was in the kitchen with Mae, tidying up, and Fatti was getting ready to leave while Bubblee napped in the bedroom when voices emerged from the living room.

'You say this all to me as if it's my fault,' they heard their mum say.

'Who else should I say it to?'

Farah couldn't help but look at Mae. Was this it? Had he found out?

'People are talking, talking, talking. And you speak to the hairdresser. Of all people.'

That answered that question.

'It is not proper,' he continued, lowering his voice further, 'to talk about such things. Especially with our daughters around. Especially with strangers!'

'Who else am I meant to talk to?' replied their mum, her voice rising. 'You carry on in your garden with your flowers, and I carry on in my kitchen — I cook for you, I look after you, I do everything and you don't listen to what I want.'

Fatti had crept past the living room and into the kitchen, resting her bag on the kitchen table.

285

'Looks like my husband's going to have to wait.'

'What kind of example is this for our daughters?' he said.

'Ugh. Dad is so cliched sometimes,' said Mae.

'I think you should hold your tongue.'

It was Bubblee. She'd clearly been woken up by their parents' voices and was in the kitchen doorway, rubbing her eyes with one hand, and her bump with another. Farah wondered whether she had her hand on her belly so often just to make a point. She wasn't even showing that much.

'You think our daughters don't know these things?' said their mum.

'Shhh,' they heard him say. He obviously didn't realize how loud his whispers were. 'The whole community is talking about it — people are laughing at me.'

'Yes! This is why you are worried. Because people are wondering what kind of a man . . . '

The sisters all had to rush to the kitchen door to hear the rest of the sentence since their mum decided to lower her voice too. They only managed to catch: ' . . . his wife.' And then: 'Let everyone talk about it,' said their mum evenly. 'I am a woman. I have needs.'

Fatti's phone beeped. 'It's Ash. I think he kind of misses me being around at weekends. I spend most of my time here.' Fatti looked apologetic as she said it. 'Not that he says anything,' she added quickly.

'Just go,' said Mae, looking miserable as she slumped at the kitchen table. 'No reason we should all have to suffer.'

Fatti gave each of her sisters a quick kiss. She tried to leave without being noticed but her dad caught sight of her walking past the living room.

'Ah, Fatti, you are leaving.'

He glanced at her mum who put on a smile.

'I'll see you later this week,' she said, then kissed them swiftly and dashed out of the house.

Fatti's departure seemed to have dampened their parents' argumentative fire. Farah left the rest of the dishes in the sink as Bubblee handed Mae the rubber gloves.

'Since you can't clear up the YouTube mess, you can clear up the kitchen,' she said.

'Please, take me with you,' said Mae as she watched them get ready to leave too.

'This is your penance,' replied Bubblee.

Farah managed to give Mae a sympathetic look. 'Make sure you actually finish the dishes. Mum could probably do with a rest.'

Mae loomed over the sink, picking up a plate and looking at it in resignation as the sisters left her to it.

Farah and Bubblee got in the car, Farah in the driver's seat. The air seemed to always change when it was just the two of them.

'Honestly, that Mae is always making trouble,' said Bubblee, fastening her seat belt.

Farah paused before replying: 'Bit like someone else I remember.'

She felt Bubblee's gaze on her as she pulled out of the parking space.

'Generally the stuff I put up didn't go viral,' said Bubblee.

Farah chose not to respond. They drove the rest of the way home in silence and went to bed with no other words exchanged except a simple goodnight.

★ ★ ★

The following day, Farah and Mae went to the park with Mae's phone camera fully charged for recording.

'People think the park is all couples and kids and people who go running, but now and again you'll notice a bunch of women together. See? Look at them.'

Mae focused her camera on four women, probably in their sixties or seventies, power-walking together. One of them was using hiking sticks. They all had different-coloured bum-bags, caps protecting them from the sun, their grey hair jutting out in curls, wearing luminous colours and radiant smiles. One of them called out to another, apparently called Betty — the one with the hiking sticks: 'You'd think after twenty years you'd have sped up.'

They all laughed. Including Betty. Farah looked at them and smiled. Fatti was probably Betty. The one who shouted would be Mae, of course. She couldn't decide which one was Bubblee or her.

'What's that meant to show?' Farah asked.

Mae considered it for a few seconds. 'I'd call it sisterhood through the ages.'

'Through what ages? You only see glimpses — how can you make up a story based on just a few minutes of observation?'

'Imagination,' replied Mae. 'And anyway, look. It's pretty easy to make up a story for those women, isn't it?'

Farah watched them laughing and teasing each other as they hobbled on, some fitter than others, but all of them in it together.

'I'd have thought you'd have had enough of taking videos after the hairdressing saga.'

Mae let out a groan. 'Can't we start pretending that didn't happen?'

'Not likely. I don't suppose the house phone's stopped ringing all morning.'

Mae pretended to be engrossed in recording the old women.

'I'll take that as a no,' said Farah.

'Here, you record,' said Mae, handing her the phone.

'What am I looking at?' she asked, reluctantly taking it.

Mae was looking at the women and smiling. 'Capture it.'

'What?'

'The moments they're sharing, obviously.' Mae rolled her eyes.

'Right.'

Farah kept hold of the phone, waiting for the ladies to make another round before passing Farah and Mae, focusing on the way they smiled and laughed, the way Betty seemed to struggle with the walk, the way they helped her and made fun of her. This was life, happening around her — other people's happiness in the face of her own tragedy. But for some reason, as she sat and recorded them, their happiness soothed her. It was still in the world. Even if it wasn't hers.

★ ★ ★

'Don't tell me it's not ridiculous,' said Bubblee, putting down the phone to another person enquiring about how much ten lessons would cost him.

Fatti seemed to forget what she was doing. 'Where's my orange juice gone?'

'I mean, did you see the way she just ignored me when I said: *I am pregnant?*' said Bubblee, getting up and handing the orange juice to Fatti, which was in front of her, on her desk.

Fatti looked at it and decided to throw it in the bin.

'Why don't you have baby brain?' Fatti asked.

'I'm too sensible for that,' replied Bubblee, just as she tripped over.

'That's made me feel better. You're too composed for a pregnant woman.'

'The other day I couldn't find my keys and was looking for them for twenty minutes. I got thirsty and opened the fridge for some juice and there they were, on top of the hummus.'

'Yep,' said Fatti.

'How much longer am I meant to put up with this?' said Bubblee, getting back to the subject at hand.

Each day her grievance multiplied, not least because no one seemed to be worried that Farah was paying no attention to the person carrying

290

her baby, or the actual baby.

'Just practically, even,' added Bubblee. 'Won't the baby need a nursery? Clothes? Toys? When exactly does she think she'll be doing all that? When it's born?'

Fatti gave Bubblee a sympathetic look. 'And you're not going to NCT classes?'

'No! Why should I? When the mother of the baby's not bothered?'

Fatti's silence spoke a thousand judgements.

'So I'm the one in the wrong here?' demanded Bubblee.

'I shouldn't have thrown that juice away,' said Fatti, looking at it in the bin.

'I'll get you another one — just answer my question.'

Bubblee could feel the rage push to the surface of her rationality.

'I can't pretend I know what you're going through,' said Fatti, looking at the floor, apparently considering her words carefully. 'But then you can't pretend to know what Farah's going through.'

Just then, Farah walked through the door.

'Oh, great, you're here,' exclaimed Fatti, heaving herself off her chair and taking a moment before standing up straight.

Farah gave a weak smile, looking around the office, the two desks at which Fatti and Bubblee sat, the filing cabinets against the wall, which was decorated with L plates.

'So . . . ' Farah began. 'What am I meant to be helping with?'

'Taxes,' said Fatti, opening the back door. 'Do

you mind sorting receipts and putting them all on an Excel sheet?'

'Sure,' Farah replied, walking into the cramped back-room office.

'We'll keep the door open,' said Fatti. 'So we can chat. Maybe we should've let Mae come and help too.'

Bubblee banged a file on the desk as the phone rang. She barked into the receiver before hanging up.

'Or perhaps Bubblee can do the taxes and, Farah, you can answer calls.'

Bubblee gave Fatti a disdainful look as she and Farah swapped roles. 'No orange juice for you,' she whispered as she passed Fatti.

Bubblee decided to slam the door behind her, cooping herself up in the small room with nothing but tax receipts and rage.

The following day Bubblee said to Farah she wouldn't be going into the office with her.

'Oh, right. Are you feeling okay?' asked Farah, checking her bag for her phone.

'I might go to an NCT class,' Bubblee added.

Farah ignored her, saying something about leaving her phone upstairs.

'Have a good day,' she said, not returning to the living room, but leaving for the office without breakfast or a coffee.

Bubblee wanted to call someone and shout about how wronged she was, but even she could tell she'd come off as the unsympathetic one. *Give her time*, people kept saying.

'There's not much left, is there?' she said, looking at her bump and stroking it.

What happens if a child's mother no longer wants it? What if Farah never came around? Who'd look after the baby in the meantime? What if years passed and Farah refused to look at it, just as she refused to look at Bubblee nowadays? Whose responsibility was it now, anyway? Bubblee had a flash of the baby being born; her holding it with no one else around; it crying in a room with her alone. The walls seemed to be closing in on her. It got rather hot. Bubblee felt beads of sweat form on her forehead as she began taking deeper breaths. It felt as if her heart was contracting, her breath coming faster, she felt her throat constrict. *What was happening?* The room began to swim in front of her eyes, even though she was seated, gripping her stomach as she leaned forward to try to calm the pacing of her heart. *Was she having a heart attack? Where was her phone? Would Farah come home and find her here, dead, with her unborn baby inside her?* She closed her eyes and continued to take deep breaths. They began to become more even. It took a while before she was able to lift her head and open her eyes, the beads of sweat still trickling down her temples. She got a tissue and wiped her forehead before leaning her elbows on the table and putting her head in her hands. She had not signed up for this. Bubblee could not, would not, be the mother of this child.

'I'm sorry, baby,' she whispered to it. 'I'm sorry.'

Mum: heklo girks

293

Mae: Dont worry dont worry. Im showin her the whatsapp ropes

Fatti: Hello, Mum.

Bubblee: Great. That fills us all with confidence.

Mum: ☺

14

Things seemed to have calmed down at home. Their parents were still talking in clipped tones to one another but the shouting had stopped. Bubblee was sure that Mae was probably counting down the days for when the Easter break would be over and she could return to the sanctuary of her university. At least the house phone wasn't ringing quite as much and their mum being part of their WhatsApp group seemed to have had a pacifying effect on her mood, at least.

After that morning when Farah had left for work at the driving school, Bubblee decided not to spend any more nights in her home. What was the point? Whatever had happened to Bubblee in that kitchen, there was no use sharing it with anyone. But she couldn't be around her sister without wanting to shake her, or shout at her, and that would probably help no one.

When she told Farah she was leaving she merely said, 'Oh, okay. If you want.'

There was no apparent need on her behalf for Bubblee to stay, no asking Bubblee whether she was sure, no saying that Farah liked having her there. Nothing. Her parents of course had a lot of opinions about it: *Leaving your sister alone like that. We don't need you here, she needs you there.* But Bubblee, as with most things when it came to her family, just ignored them. What did they know about living with Farah? About the ill-feeling that was probably being fed to the baby through Bubblee's own anger?

The doorbell of her parents' home rang but Bubblee remained in her bed, staring at the ceiling, wondering just how she was meant to piece back together the puzzle of her life to create something new. The doorbell rang again. Where were her parents and Mae? She got begrudgingly out of her bed, and stomped down the stairs to open the door.

'Oh, Jack, hi.'

Jay's delivery friend gave her an awkward smile. 'Sorry, you have to sign for it.'

Bubblee took the electronic pen and machine, signed it and gave it back. 'Why didn't Jay just bring it?'

Jack cleared his throat. 'Busy doing another route. Your brother said it was for you.'

'Me?'

Jack shrugged. 'One of you.'

Bubblee shook the box and saw that it was just addressed to Ms Amir. Jack said a very quick goodbye and was back in his van before Bubblee could respond. Perhaps it was for Mae. But Bubblee was the only one who insisted on being called Ms. Maybe it was from Sasha in London? Bubblee couldn't remember the last time she had been sent a present and her heart fluttered at the thought of it. Who knew her heart could flutter? She ripped open the box, only to find another box, this time bright blue with a weird kind of sculpture on the front of it. Was this Sasha's way of giving Bubblee some hope for the future of her career? She had to shake her head because it was a very odd sculpture and her eyes couldn't quite make out what it was. She turned the box around and gasped as she let it go, and it fell to the floor.

'*Oh, my God.*'

Bubblee then shook her head and grabbed the box, checking her eyes hadn't deceived her, and rang Sasha's number. She tapped her foot on the floor impatiently as she waited for her to pick up.

'Well, thank you very much for that,' began Bubblee without even waiting for Sasha to speak. 'It's very funny. Well done. Wouldn't have been quite as funny if my mum or dad had opened it, thinking it was for them. You know my dad never reads who things are addressed to.'

'What?'

'The package has arrived. I mean, come on, Sash. You know me better than that.'

'Bubs,' replied Sasha. 'What the hell are you talking about?'

'The *dildo*.'

'The *what?*'

'Dildo,' Bubble repeated, getting increasingly exasperated with her friend. 'This is the kind of thing other friends do. Not us. It's really not the way I want to be cheered up right now.'

Sasha paused before Bubblee heard laughter down the phone. 'Are you joking?' she said. 'This is excellent. Who's this mystery person gifting you such exciting things?'

'Oh, stop it,' said Bubblee.

Sasha laughed some more. 'I can't. I wish I could take credit for it, but you're right, it would've been in poor taste for us. Still, I'd like to shake the hand of the person who did send it.'

Bubblee stopped tapping her foot. 'Are you telling me it wasn't you?'

'And there's you blaming *me* for not knowing *you* well enough,' said Sasha. 'You know I'd at least have sent you a card with it. I'm thoughtful like that.'

'Oh, my God,' said Bubblee, looking at the box again.

'It has your name on it?' asked Sasha.

'Yes! Well, it says Ms Amir, and I'm the only one called that in this family.'

Who would send such a thing? It didn't make any sense.

'Well, Ms Marple. You have some investigation to do.'

Bubblee said her goodbyes to an amused Sasha and realized it was too late to run out and flag down Jack and tell him that he'd probably delivered the item to the wrong family. Why on earth would any of them order a *dildo?* But of course Jack was long gone and then there was the family name on the box. She picked up the box and looked at the phallic shape. Surely there had to be some kind of mistake. Thank God her mum hadn't opened it by accident. She began reading the directions when someone cleared their throat. Bubblee jumped. It was Mae. She instinctively hid the box behind her back, although she wasn't sure why.

'What's that?' Mae asked.

'Where were you?' said Bubblee, wondering how guilty she looked on a scale of one to ten.

'We ran out of soya milk — went out to get some. What have you got behind your back?'

Bubblee felt her face flush and she wasn't even sure why. 'Oh, nothing. Wrong delivery. I think.'

Mae gave a non-committal shrug. She went to put the milk in the kitchen as Bubblee made to go upstairs with the newly delivered package, but then Mae bounced back out and snatched the box.

'You little . . . ' exclaimed Bubblee as she saw Mae look at the box and take in its content.

Mae looked up at her in surprise and, of course, amusement.

'Hahaha, oh, my God. This is just brilliant,' said Mae, laughing, wiping her eyes. 'Are times hard then, Bubs?'

'Shut up, Mae. It's not mine.'

'Hang on,' Mae continued, 'if you're using this then are you really technically a virgin? Because, you know, there's a definition for being a virgin and if you've used one of these then I'm not sure it applies.'

Bubblee snatched the box back. 'I told you, it's not *mine*.'

'Oh, right. Is it a '*friend's*'?' said Mae, using air quotes. 'You're lucky it's me who saw this and not Farah or Fatti — they wouldn't be able to look you in the eye. And, let's face it, Farah's already having trouble there, anyway. I don't know why you're looking so mortified, Bubs. I thought you were a feminist.'

'I'm not mortified. I'm merely pointing out that I didn't order this, nor do I need it.'

'Oh, yeah. I forgot — you're emotionally and physically independent.' Mae folded her arms and leaned against the wall, not even trying to suppress her smile. 'But, my dear Bubs, biology gets the better of us all sooner or later. Can't hide it.'

'How many times do I have to repeat it? *It's not mine.*'

Bubblee felt the colour in her cheeks rise and she wasn't even sure why. Probably because she was standing there, having to explain herself to her little brat of a sister.

'Methinks the lady doth protest too much. Anyway, how come it's addressed to Ms Amir then, hmm? Don't worry, I won't tell anyone. Now at least I have something to bribe you with next time you bring up Mum's YouTube video.'

Bubblee was just about to retort with something when the keys rattled in the door and Farah and Fatti came through. Bubblee hid the box behind her again, edging for Mae to take it, who stood behind Bubblee and was far too amused to want to help out.

'What are you both doing here?' asked Bubblee.

'Mum told us to come home for lunch,' said Fatti, waddling through the door. 'Not that I can eat. What's that box you're hiding behind your back?'

'Oh, for God's sake,' mumbled Bubblee and handed it to her.

'Eww, Bubs!' exclaimed Fatti, throwing the box to Farah who had to do a doubletake.

'What are you doing with this?' asked Farah, looking distressed.

'*It's not mine!*' shouted Bubblee.

'It's a '*friend's*',' repeated Mae with the air quotes.

'Anyway,' added Bubblee, 'even if it was, it's a perfectly fine expression of a woman's sexuality, thank-you-very-much.'

'You tell 'em, Bubs.'

The keys rattled in the door again. Farah threw the box to Fatti, who threw it back to Bubblee, who threw it to Mae, who didn't even bother trying to catch it as it fell to the floor.

'Hide it,' exclaimed Bubblee, looking at Mae.

Mae rolled her eyes and sighed as she took the box and was about to sprint up the stairs when their mum walked through the door, their dad a few steps behind.

'What are you all doing in the passage?' she asked, looking at Mae.

Then her eyes travelled to the box in Mae's hands and her face flushed a fiercer red than the girls had ever seen. Their mum slammed the door behind her, right in their dad's face.

'Why do you have this?' she exclaimed, taking the box from Mae.

Their dad knocked on the door.

'It's not *mine*,' said Mae, pointing at Bubblee.

'Of course it's not yours, you silly girl, it's *mine*,' said their mum.

What in the name of God? It was impossible. It couldn't be. Their mum didn't even know how to use WhatsApp! How had she gone online to order a *dildo*? And how in hell was she actually going to operate it when she couldn't even use her phone properly?

'Jay's amma!' called their dad from outside. 'Open the door.'

But the look on their mum's face said it all. It was hers, all right. Cathy! Of course! It was Cathy giving their mum all these ideas. Well, Bubblee supposed it was better her than any of them having to order it for their mum. Thank God for Cathy.

'Go and put it in your room and don't look inside,' said their mum.

As if the huge picture on the box wasn't a dead giveaway! Mae ran up the stairs as their mum opened the door to their rather perplexed-looking dad.

'What happened?' he said, looking around. 'Why are you all standing here?'

A bang came from upstairs.

'I'm okay,' shouted Mae from upstairs. 'Just tripped.'

'We came for lunch, Abba,' said Fatti, putting on a smile.

Her father beamed at the sight of her, pushing past the others, and put his arm around her.

'We have lunch in the kitchen, Fatti.' He looked at Farah and took her by the arm too. 'Come, my good daughters. A shame you can't come to your auntie's for dinner tonight.'

Bubblee groaned at the thought of being forced into a family dinner as she and her mum trudged along behind them. And how would she keep a normal composure, knowing who the dildo belonged to! She looked ahead at her dad with Fatti and Farah and felt a pang of sympathy for her mum. For once, Bubblee thought she knew how she must feel, always being sidelined.

★ ★ ★

'What the actual hell?' said Mae when the sisters went upstairs to her room. 'Someone has got to be pulling my leg.'

'No wonder Jay didn't make the delivery,' said Bubblee, still feeling slightly dazed by the unearthing of the dildo belonging to their mum.

'What do you think Mum was thinking when she bought it?' said Mae.

Bubblee shook her head. One thing she was very grateful for was maternity jeans.

'I mean, there's nothing wrong with a woman expressing her desires,' said Bubblee.

Yet, even as she said the words, she felt them stick to her throat and they came out tasting bitter. It was their *mum*. Did she want to use it with their dad? Did she want to use it alone? Bubblee shuddered dramatically and sat on the bed, leaning back on her palms. She'd swear her belly had grown since yesterday.

'I think I'm going to be sick, and for the first time it has nothing to do with my pregnancy,' said Fatti.

She looked down at her swollen feet.

'God, they're enormous,' said Mae, looking at her feet too. 'You're actually an elephant.'

'Do we . . . ' began Farah. 'Should we talk to Mum about it?'

'No way,' exclaimed Mae, as Bubblee and

303

Fatti both retorted with: 'No, thanks.'

Bubblee looked at Farah and almost laughed. If they cut out all the things that had happened to them over the past few months, everything outside this room, her sister was still the same — the one who, for so long, had been the only person she wanted to confide in. In this moment, Farah wasn't the grieving widow or the detached mother-to-be. She was simply her sister who was looking for some kind of understanding.

'Maybe I'll talk to her,' Farah added.

'She's clearly having troubles,' said Fatti.

'So, see a therapist,' interjected Mae.

Bubblee was sorry for it, but she rather agreed with Mae.

'I mean, can you imagine if Dad ever finds it?' said Farah.

Fatti pursed her lips, suppressing a laugh as Mae snorted. Even Bubblee had to laugh.

'That's assuming he's not about to become acquainted with it,' said Bubblee.

'He'd probably think it was a gardening tool,' replied Mae.

This time Bubblee's shoulders shook with laughter. Fatti let out a laugh, which must've put pressure on her bladder as she made a dash for the toilet. Farah looked at Fatti waddling out of the door and bent her head so low that no one could tell what she was doing. When she looked up, Bubblee saw that her eyes were streaming with tears as she took a deep breath and let out a laugh.

★ ★ ★

Fatti and Farah both hugged their mum goodbye after lunch. Farah gave her a knowing look, squeezing her hands. She cringed internally as she did it, but she also knew what it felt like not to be desired, and how nice it might've been to have talked to one of her sisters about it. Maybe they could've helped somehow, and it would've all had a cosmic effect, which meant that Mustafa would still be alive. Farah couldn't help but bring everything back to him and his life. Or his death, in this case.

'Have fun tonight, Amma,' said Fatti. 'Send our love to Auntie.'

Mae scrunched up her nose and went to hug Fatti, who later told Farah that she'd said they were undoubtedly only invited because the aunt had seen the video, and was probably planning some kind of public denunciation.

★   ★   ★

After a few hours in the office Fatti said she wasn't feeling too well and went into the staff room to rest for a bit. Farah noticed that she kept clutching her stomach but she thought that was what women carrying children did. It was certainly something Bubblee did a lot of. After half an hour Farah went in to check on her. As soon as she looked at her face she knew something was wrong.

'I'm fine,' said Fatti, though she didn't seem able to move without experiencing pain. 'Baby's just being wriggly today.'

Farah paused at the door, unsure, but was

about to take Fatti's word for it when she let out a cry.

'What do contractions feel like?' said Fatti through gritted teeth.

'You went to all the classes,' exclaimed Farah. 'Shouldn't you know?'

'My water's not broken yet.'

'But it doesn't have to.'

'No,' replied Fatti. 'You're right.'

'You can't be having the baby yet, you're not due for another six weeks.'

'Exactly.' Fatti tried to stand up and lean over. 'It's probably noth- ah!'

Farah rushed up to her, taking her hand. Fatti squeezed it so hard Farah almost cried out herself.

'It's not right,' said Fatti.

'Right, let's get you to the hospital.'

'But the office.'

'I'm getting you in the car and I'll close up. It'll take five minutes.'

Fatti nodded as Farah helped her to the car, told her to hold on and quickly grabbed their bags before locking the office. She got into the driver's seat and pulled out quicker than she ever had done as she sped towards the hospital. Fatti was leaning into her seat with her eyes closed, breathing in short jagged breaths.

'You're going to be okay,' said Farah. 'It's all going to be okay.'

As Farah parked, Fatti opened her eyes. 'Phone. Tell Ash.'

It wasn't as if there was much he could do since he wasn't even in the country but Farah scrambled for Fatti's bag, looking for her mobile. It wasn't there.

'Shit. I left it at the office,' said Farah.

She lunged for her own bag to get her mobile, frantically looking in all the pockets.

'Tell me you have yours,' said Fatti, between breaths.

Farah covered her face with her hands and let out a muffled scream. 'I'll go back.'

But then she looked at Fatti who shook her head.

'We'll call Mum and Dad when we get in, okay?'

Every time Farah had been into this hospital — and it was a lot of times — there had been wheelchairs everywhere. Now, when she needed one for her sister, she couldn't find any. Farah looked frantically around the corridors as Fatti limped through the doors behind her.

'Okay, okay,' Farah said, rushing to support her. 'Can you walk?'

Fatti nodded.

'If I said, *can you fly*, would you say no?'

Fatti gave a small smile. Farah had a bout of admiration at how nothing seemed to phase her sister. They approached the maternity ward and Farah left Fatti at the door to rush to reception.

'Something's happening to my sister. She's pregnant,' Farah explained. 'She needs a doctor.'

Fatti had come up to the desk too and took a deep breath. 'I'm getting sharp pains here,' she said, putting her hand at the top of her bump. 'I don't think they're contractions, but I'm due in six weeks.'

The nurse came around to inspect Fatti. 'How often are you getting these pains?'

'Every few minutes, I think. I haven't kept count.'

Farah looked at Fatti's face — it was strained, yet at the same time an ethereal calm appeared to have possessed her. It seemed nonsensical for there to be any calm right now.

'What's happening?' asked Farah. 'Is she going to be okay?'

The nurse ignored her as she asked them to wait to be checked out.

'Wait?' exclaimed Farah. 'How long?'

'Someone will be with you very soon.'

Farah sat Fatti down and rushed to one of the pay phones in the hospital. She was calling their mum and dad but no one was picking up when she remembered they'd all probably left to go to their aunt's. Who knew what her number was. She rushed back to Fatti.

'Do you know Mae's number off by heart?'

Fatti gave her an incredulous look, as she bent over and scrunched her eyes shut again.

'No one's at home. I don't know anyone's mobile number.'

Farah stood as if poised to race somewhere, except she didn't know where, when Fatti's name was called. They both went into a room where the midwife examined her.

'Well, Ms Amir,' said the midwife snapping off her gloves. 'It looks like you're having the baby.'

Fatti looked at Farah — the shadow of dismay passing over her face.

'You're five centimetres dilated, but we'll keep

an eye. In the meantime, try to pace the room to help your waters break, or we'll have to break them for you.'

Farah stood up as she took in all this information.

'But her husband's away,' said Farah, grabbing Fatti's hand.

The midwife made some notes on Fatti's chart, and without looking up, replied: 'Then it's just as well she has you.'

Mae: OMG. Y do aunties put so much oil in food?

Bubblee: It really is rather grotesque. I don't think the baby's enjoying it.

Mum: Isthiswatugirls tlk abuot on here

15

Minutes felt like hours. Farah tried to call home repeatedly, leaving messages, but knew they wouldn't be back until late at night. She racked her brain for how else she could get a message to Ash and her family. She wasn't equipped to be in the room with Fatti; to be present at the birth of another life. Watching Fatti double over in pain every few minutes made Farah weak at the knees.

It was another two hours before Fatti's waters broke and she was eight centimetres dilated. The midwife would come in, check, and leave without giving any information as to when the baby might come; how much longer until Fatti was ten centimetres. Fatti knelt on all fours, leaned forward on to the bed, pushing her hands against the edges, sat on a massive ball, but nothing seemed to help the pain she was in. Not even the gas and air, which made her feel light-headed and spaced out. Farah kept telling her to take an epidural but Fatti insisted she wanted to be fully aware of what was going on when she was giving birth. The midwife shook her head.

At around ten o'clock in the evening Farah tried the house phone again, in the hope that the family had come home earlier than anticipated — perhaps the aunt had brought up the YouTube video, there'd been a huge argument and her parents and sisters had left in a fury of indignation. Or maybe Jay would be home from his shift? The phone rang and rang. Maybe not. Farah left another message and went back into the room. Fatti was lying flat on the bed as the midwife was doing another check.

'Okay, we're nearly there.' She paused as a frown appeared on her brow. 'Right, you're doing well considering the baby's breech.'

'Breech?' exclaimed Farah. She rushed to Fatti's side. 'But the baby's going to be okay?'

The nurse said that they'd have to keep a close eye on the heartbeat, which for now seemed normal, but they'd remain vigilant. It was a footling breech, which meant the feet were positioned to come out first. She left the room, telling them that she was getting the doctor, as Farah looked into Fatti's now rather sweaty face.

'You never told us,' exclaimed Farah.

Fatti gave another weak smile. 'There was enough going on. And it'll be fine.'

Farah wiped Fatti's forehead with a cloth, pushing back the strands of hair that stuck to it.

'Yes. It will be,' said Farah.

The more she said it, the more she felt it might not be. What if something went wrong? What if the baby's heartbeat slowed down, or — God forbid — stopped altogether? Farah swallowed hard and muttered a prayer under her breath. A doctor came rushing in, putting on her gloves and checking Fatti.

'Right, you're almost ready to start pushing. When I say push, you push, okay?'

Fatti nodded. Farah felt her heart race.

'What? No,' said Farah. 'We're not ready,' she exclaimed.

How could this be happening? Fatti deserved someone who wanted to be there, who could be the support she needed. Farah wasn't ready for this — any of it.

'I'm afraid that the baby is, which is all that matters in this case,' said the doctor firmly.

'You're doing good, Faar,' said Fatti to her. 'Remember each second. Ash'll want a full description.'

Poor Ash! Poor Fatti! Farah gripped her sister's hand even tighter. Trust Fatti to be consoling her when she was the one in need of consolation. Her words seemed to do something to Farah, though. It was as if she'd been given a verbal shake. *Let this be over soon, please. Let it all be okay.* She kissed Fatti's forehead and stepped towards the bottom of the bed.

'Don't tell me what it looks like,' said Fatti.

Farah tried to ensure her face didn't say it all.

'Push,' said the doctor.

And Fatti did. Farah rushed to her again.

'You'll have to go harder if you want the baby to come out,' said the doctor. 'The next contraction you push with all you have, okay?'

She looked up and smiled as Fatti nodded. Fatti pushed once more and Farah rushed to the bottom of the bed again. Farah hadn't seen any births before apart from on television, but she was sure they didn't look like that. She noticed the beating of the baby's heart on the monitor slow down.

'The baby's in late deceleration,' said the doctor.

'What? What does that mean?' asked Farah.

Things were going wrong. The air in the room changed and there was now an urgency in the midwife and doctor's actions that Farah didn't like.

'Can you change position?' the doctor asked Fatti.

Fatti nodded as she sat up.

A fear gripped Farah's heart as she looked at Fatti's placid face. She felt tears surface her eyes. *Please, God, no. Not another death. Let this baby be the beginning of something that's better. Please.*

'We're in the last throes here,' said the doctor. 'You're doing fine. Nurse, get her some more oxygen.'

'Okay. I'm here,' said Farah, gripping her knee. 'I'm here, okay?'

Farah couldn't look. Instead she kept her eyes on her sister's face, stroking her hair, holding her hand, watching her go through pain for which she could do nothing. It occurred to Farah how useless human beings can be, even when they want to help. How timing and chance could change any given situation. Ash was meant to be here, and yet Farah was there instead. Any one of her sisters, or her mum, could be here but they were beyond reach. She recalled the day she found Mustafa — how he'd never seen the picture she sent him of the baby scan from the hospital and how perhaps it was inevitable, because you can't know anything beyond what you know in any given moment. Fatti let out a cry of pain.

'I'm fine, it's okay,' she said, looking up at Farah.

At that moment, Farah felt that if she could have the baby for Fatti, to help her through it, she would — without a second thought. Farah thought of Bubblee.

'Sick,' said Fatti through laboured breaths.

Farah rushed to pass her the vomiting bowl as Fatti threw up just clear water and mucus. Farah had to look away; the sound of vomiting made her gag and want to take another bowl for herself.

'I'd no idea I could get so queasy,' she said to the doctor apologetically.

'I've seen worse,' the doctor replied, snapping on a new pair of plastic gloves.

How could this be happening without Ash here to help Fatti through it? And how long was Farah meant to shy away from the life that was unfolding before her? She took a deep breath and gripped her sister's hand again.

'Tell me,' said Farah — her voice coming out clear and strong this time. 'What else can I do? How can I make this okay for you?'

Fatti opened her eyes. 'You're here. That's all that matters.'

Mae: Fats since ur husbands away ur getting the pleasure of my company 2nite.

Mum: is this how people at universaty rite English? Tst tst

16

'Okay,' said the doctor, looking up at Fatti. '*Push.*'

Fatti's face went red again and her eyes scrunched up; every ounce of energy she had seemed to be going into that push. Farah stood up and looked over to the bottom of the bed.

'That's it, Fats. That's it,' she exclaimed, tears rushing down her cheeks.

'We're getting there,' said the doctor as Fatti exhaled.

'One more time,' said the doctor. 'Can you do that?'

Fatti nodded and with the next contraction pushed with all her might.

'That's it. Yes, you're doing it, Fats. Come on, *push.*'

And with those words out came Fatti's baby boy.

'Oh, my God,' whispered Farah.

Farah looked at Fatti who seemed as though she'd fallen asleep, but had a smile on her face.

'It's a boy,' said Farah. 'Oh, my God,' she repeated. This time, taking a closer look. 'What . . . ?'

Farah looked at the doctor who'd given the baby to the nurse to be taken into the premature unit.

'Your baby has the biggest, blackest testicles I've ever seen!' exclaimed Farah.

Fatti was looking at her baby in the incubator, a tear running down her face.

'We're going to take him to NICU to check he's all okay,' said the doctor.

Fatti nodded. She watched as they wheeled the baby away from her.

'I'm going with him, okay?' said Farah.

Farah gave Fatti a huge smile, kissed her sister and promised she'd be right back to give her an update. As she rushed out she saw her family rushing into the maternity unit, Mae at the lead, Bubblee next and her parents holding hands as they hurried behind.

'Jay called to tell us about your messages and we came straight here,' said Bubblee.

'Where is he?' asked Farah.

'Having a cigarette outside,' said Mae, as if it were just typical of him. 'Has she had it?'

Farah nodded, smiling, unable to speak without her voice breaking.

'She's had the baby? But so early,' said their mum. 'Is it okay?'

'Yes,' replied Farah. 'He's great.'

'Oh, thank you, Allah.'

Their mum looked up at the hospital ceiling and joined her hands together.

'It's healthy?' said Bubblee. 'Where is it? Where's Fatti?'

Farah explained what was going on and told them to check on Fatti while she went with the baby. Everyone followed Farah's instruction as she rushed into the lift and pressed the button towards the neonatal unit, watching them all walk towards Fatti's room.

She saw the doctor and nurses huddled around her little nephew. One of the nurses came out and informed her that he'd managed to swallow his own poo.

'Oh,' said Farah, disconcerted.

'Don't worry,' replied the nurse. 'It happens.'

Farah laughed at the sheer unpredictability of having a baby — how there were no rules, how it was impossible to control anything — not even whether a baby ate its own poo or not.

'The little shitface,' she said to herself, smiling.

She knew she should go back to see Fatti, but she was transfixed by his little face; the bald head and scabby little hands and feet. He weighed four pounds and one ounce. It wasn't long before they took him away to clean him up. There wasn't much Farah could do but her family was with Fatti now and, however illogical it might be, she thought if she left her nephew then there was no knowing what might happen to him. It was a while before another nurse came out.

'His heart rate is regular now and there aren't any signs of the distress impacting him. We need to keep him here for observation, though. He's still very early.'

'He's really going to be okay?' Farah asked.

She realized she wasn't used to good news. She'd become a pessimist and, without even realizing it, it had taken any possible joy out of her. All positive things in her life had been dampened by this feeling that something bad was just around the corner. And this was long before what happened with Mustafa. His name was on her lips — how could it not be? This was the same place he'd been in a coma; the place he'd been brought when the life had already left his body. Now, in this very same place again a baby had been born to her sister, just as one would be born to Bubblee. No, by Bubblee, *to* Farah. The idea terrified her. She knew that Mustafa would have thrived on being an uncle. The bond between him and Fatti's baby would've been something special, because Fatti was his sister by blood, after all. Farah thought of all the things he'd miss out on, all the memories she wouldn't see him make with the new member of their family. She didn't think it was possible to feel your heart hurt in such a way without giving way to grief, but it did. Except she was still standing. She was learning to carry the heaviness with her, without allowing it to weigh her down — shifting it so it was manageable.

'We'll call you when it's all done, but you can go and see your sister now, if you want.'

Farah looked at the nurse and hugged her. 'Thank you. Thank you so, so much.'

The nurse smiled. 'All in a day's work.'

★ ★ ★

When Farah went into Fatti's room she could tell Fatti could barely keep her eyes open.

'Come on, guys,' said Farah, clapping her hands. 'Let her rest. Out. And you . . . ' she said, pointing to Jay. 'I don't want your tobacco smell in this room.'

Fatti let out a small laugh and said it was fine.

'Which obviously means, it's not,' said Mae, giving her sister a kiss on the cheek. 'We'll come tomorrow, first thing, okay? Can't we see the baby?'

Farah shook her head, explaining that the staff were still fixing him up, but that they'd be able to see him tomorrow.

'Ash is already getting the next flight home,' added Mae.

'He's going to be so upset,' said Fatti.

'He'll get over it once he sees how perfect his little boy is,' added Farah.

She caught Bubblee's eye as Mum, Dad, Jay and Mae made to leave the room.

'Why don't you stay?' she said to Bubblee.

'Yes, you stay,' said their mum who'd already grabbed their dad and Mae and was pushing Jay out of the room.

'I'm going to spend the night here, I think,' said Farah. 'You can keep me company. If you want. And can,' she added, glancing at Bubblee's belly.

Bubblee seemed to hesitate. 'Fine,' she said eventually.

★　★　★

The two sisters stayed in the room with Fatti until she'd fallen asleep. Bubblee had been up to see the baby and came back looking slightly pale.

'He's so small, isn't he?' said Farah.

'If he's that big coming out six weeks early what will mine — I mean, the labour — be like?'

Farah looked at her sympathetically, but couldn't bring herself to offer any comfort. After a while Farah said they should maybe go for a walk and stretch their legs so Bubblee followed her out of the room. They walked towards the café and got some coffee, eventually tiring of the same hospital scenes so they thought they might as well tire of it sitting down and went into the waiting room. They stared at the blue walls on which noticeboards hung with all kinds of information on pregnancy, flu jabs, post-natal care. Farah could tell that Bubblee was taking it all in.

'Is your nausea better?' asked Farah.

Bubblee looked at her. 'Concerned now, are you?'

Farah looked down at her black coffee. Neither of them spoke for a few minutes.

'This isn't how it was supposed to happen,' said Farah.

'No. I'm carrying your baby inside me. Clearly not.'

'I mean the rest of it too.'

Tears stung her eyes. She should be getting used to them, but these tears felt different. They weren't a symptom of how Farah was feeling, but rather a release of something within her — perhaps that's why they seemed to hurt.

'I know,' said Bubblee, her voice softening.

'He just left me,' said Farah.

A tear fell into her coffee. She wiped her runny nose.

'Not intentionally,' said Bubblee. 'It was never about you. It was about him. You might not feel it yet, but it wasn't your fault.'

Farah looked at her sister. 'How was it not?'

'Maybe it was a little of everyone's fault. But the medication didn't help either and you have to remember that.' She paused. 'The thing with time is there's no going back and changing things. You can regret things as much as you want, but I'm not sure how that helps matters.'

'No.'

Farah looked back at her coffee again.

'He's going to miss out on the rest of our lives,' said Farah, this time looking at Bubblee's stomach. 'Every small detail, every big occasion.'

'I know.'

Bubblee put her arm around Farah and let her sob. She took the coffee cup and held it out, trying to soothe her sister by rocking her, while not spilling her coffee. They were locked like that for such a long time. Once Farah began she couldn't stop because she was crying for all the things that had gone wrong, all the small ways Mustafa had let her down and the multiple ways in which she'd let him down for which she could now never say sorry. How was she to move on without one last conversation with him? Without him knowing that she knew she had also played a part in how things unfolded? She would have to find a way to relieve herself of her guilt, because she knew she couldn't live like this for ever. Perhaps she should, as penance, but she couldn't. She didn't want to. And, what's more, she knew that Mustafa wouldn't want her to either. It took a while before Farah was able to compose herself.

'He's beautiful, isn't he? Fatti's baby.'

Bubblee furrowed her brows. 'I don't know. Newborns are always a bit alien-looking.'

Farah hit Bubblee as she wiped her nose again with the sleeve of her arm. Bubblee gave her a tissue.

'She didn't complain,' Farah added. 'Not once.'

'We should rename her Fatti the Martyr.'

'How'd she get like that? Who does she get it from?'

Bubblee shrugged. 'Not sure. Maybe it helps that we don't have the same biological parents.'

Farah let out a small laugh. 'Maybe.' She paused. 'I'm not sure if you can learn that kind of calmness. Although, I remember Mustafa used to have it.'

It was the first time she'd mentioned his name in a way that didn't descend into grief. A knot formed in her stomach. It felt like a hurdle, saying his name so casually. But she had to or his memories would be buried and she didn't want that.

'Well, we can all stand to try, I guess,' said Bubblee.

'Yes. We can try.'

★   ★   ★

After a few hours Farah insisted that Bubblee take her car and go home to get some proper sleep. It was bad for the baby otherwise. Bubblee hugged Farah, taking her face in her hands, and said: 'Welcome back.'

Farah went up in the lift to the neonatal ward again, looking for her little nephew. She couldn't remember how long she was standing there, but dawn seemed to have broken between Bubblee leaving and Farah staying.

'How's he doing?' she asked a nurse who'd come in to check on the babies. She gave her his tag name.

'Just fine. He's awake, see?'

He was lying there so quietly that Farah didn't even realize.

'Can I . . . can I hold him?'

The nurse smiled. 'I'm afraid not yet.'

Farah felt an ache. She wanted to feel his little hands in hers, wanted to stroke his brow and watch his face; the way he blinked, the small black hairs on his forehead, the blue veins showing through his skin.

'Come inside,' said the nurse.

They went in and Farah leaned over her nephew. He was so small Farah thought that if she were allowed to hold him she'd probably break him, so instead she just stared; his brows knitted together as his tongue came out, like a little lizard's. Farah laughed.

'Getting the taste of poo out, are you?' she whispered to him.

She couldn't believe it. Farah had seen this boy come out of her sister, into the world, kicking and screaming, and yet he was here flicking his tongue, frowning at her. Fatti had managed it all, but he'd also done the work, borne the brunt of pain that he'd never remember. What a miracle that he should've made it. That in this hospital, even now, there were babies being born and they were all making it. Their mothers too. Survival seems to be the one thing everyone fights for. Except for Mustafa. He didn't want to survive any more. Farah wished she could forget her own pain, but then reneged. Perhaps remembering was the best way to honour those who weren't around any longer. Mustafa might not have survived but she'd have to make sure the memory of him did.

'Hello, Little Shitface,' she said to her nephew. 'I love you.'

Perhaps remembering was also the only way to be grateful for happiness, which could also come your way. And, of course, to remind her to never make the same mistakes again. To be present. Just like her nephew.

> **Farah: Here. I sneaked a picture of little shitface for you guys.**

> **Mae: Best. Name. Eva**

> **Mum: wat nam isthis?**

> **Bubblee: Don't you think he has Mustafa's eyes?**

> **Mae: Totes.**

> **Fatti: Was thinking exactly the same thing. Xxxx**

> **Farah: Yes. He does. Xxx**

17

It wasn't like Fatti to remind a person — especially Farah — how much she needed Ash, but when she saw him come through the hospital door she cried. She still hadn't held her own baby and so being able to hold Ash somewhat allayed what she was missing.

'He's perfect,' he said.

Fatti couldn't believe her luck in life. She had a family — one that loved each other. A mum and dad and sisters — even a brother — who she adored. She felt a passing sadness about Mustafa. It didn't matter that they never really developed a relationship, despite finding out they were biological brother and sister, but it felt like a missed opportunity; something she wished she had tried to work better at. People kept feeling sorry for her while she was pregnant because of how ill she was, how much her baby had to go through and how awful it must've been, but throughout it she was just filled with gratitude. Fatti related the whole story to Ash, not leaving out any details — apart from perhaps Farah's panicking — while he held her hand.

'I can't believe I missed it,' he said, looking crestfallen.

'I had my sister.'

Fatti would never betray that she wished he had been there too, but also realized that perhaps this had been good for Farah.

'How was she?' he asked with uncertainty.

Fatti paused. 'Exactly what I needed.'

Ash looked incredulous, but Fatti felt that it was true: she had wanted Ash, but she had probably needed Farah too. They had needed each other.

There was a knock on the door and Farah appeared, looking brighter than Fatti had seen her in a while. Ash shot up off his seat and hugged her.

'Oh,' said Farah, clearly taken by surprise.

'You were here,' Ash said to her. 'You helped her through it. I don't know how I'm meant to thank you.'

Farah glanced at Fatti who laughed at the look on her sister's face. Farah gave a small smile. 'It's what sisters are for. By the way, the nurse says Shitface is doing well.'

Ash leaned back, furrowing his eyebrows.

'Didn't I mention he ate his own poo?' said Fatti. 'And wait until you see him without his tiny nappy.'

'He's all okay . . . down there . . . isn't he?' said Ash.

Fatti laughed. 'Oh, yes. He's fine. You'll see.'

Farah suppressed a smile.

'Is Bubblee coming later?' Fatti asked Farah.

'Yes, probably,' Farah replied. 'Anyway, I just wanted to see SF.' She looked at Ash. 'He's the best thing I've seen in my life.'

'Me too,' Ash beamed. 'Apart from my wife, of course.'

'I'm going to go. Let you guys spend some

time together, but I'll come by later, or tomorrow. Okay?'

Farah went and kissed Fatti on the forehead and left the couple, on their own, to count their blessings — of which they felt they had more than they deserved.

A few weeks later, they were back home, cradling their newborn baby, Adil, in their arms, where they gave up keeping up with counting their blessings. They knew there were just far too many.

* * *

Farah found herself finally being able to look Bubblee in the eye for more than a split second, and what's more, at her stomach. There was still an awkwardness there, which neither of them seemed to be able to overcome. It didn't help that Mae was back at university and with Fatti being busy with the new baby there was no one to distract them from each other whenever Farah came to her parents' home. Everyone had noticed a marked difference in the way their mum spoke to their dad, but no one liked to think about why that might be. Who knows what had happened to that dildo? Whether it made an appearance in their parents' room and was there to stay or not. All they knew was that something had changed and they were happy to leave the details a mystery.

Bubblee and Farah would help out at Fatti and Ash's driving school in turns, giving the happy couple time to rejoice in their new arrival, and get some sleep, which Ash was only beginning to realize how much he treasured. Even Fatti couldn't put a positive spin on middle-of-the-night feeds. All this baby talk only magnified the elephant in the room, which Farah still wasn't ready to address, but something had begun to blossom within her. It was desire. Not for the husband that she had lost, but for a future. When she woke up in the mornings, the sadness was there, but it was layered with other things: shopping for milk and toilet paper, paying a bill, learning to cook a new recipe in the kitchen with her mum. She'd even begun to take a continuing interest in the garden with her dad. There was something therapeutic about watching things you had planted grow.

One day Farah got out of bed and realized that she'd stopped getting back into it so regularly after using the bathroom. Bubblee was at the driving school that morning, so she didn't have to go in. She opened the curtains and looked at the oak trees lining her tiny road. She walked around the flat taking in its walls and furniture, remembering Mustafa sitting at the table, on the floor, fixing a lamp, in the kitchen making coffee. Going back into her bedroom she sat in the corner on the floor, staring at the bed in which she had found him. She didn't feel immobile any more, as if her body had given up the ability to move. She got up, changed and drove to her parents' house.

'Faru, Faru,' said her dad as soon as she entered. 'The flowers are coming out very nice.'

Her mum was on the phone to Fatti, asking

what she should make them for dinner, and waved at Farah. 'Go and look at his garden,' her mum said, putting her hand over the receiver.

Farah was pleased that her mum didn't look so stroppy any more. Maybe it was because she'd become a grandmother, or maybe she was finally getting *the sex*. Farah didn't really want to ask. Instead, she went out into the garden and after a twenty-minute conversation with her dad about the PH levels of his soil, came into the house again.

'I'm making some fermented fish and beef curry for Fatti and Ash,' said her mum, tying the ends of her sari around her waist. 'You can take some home as well.'

Farah went and got some vegetables out of the fridge to make a salad for everyone too.

'How's Bubblee?' she asked her mum.

'She is your sister; you should know better than me.'

Farah began chopping a red onion, giving her mum a sidelong glance. She wondered just how much their mum revealed and how much she kept to herself. It was an art to interfere without seeming to; guiding someone without them asking.

'*Amma.*'

Her mum turned to her, spatula in hand.

'Faru, she is having your baby. She is being sick sometimes, but not a lot. She now likes to eat chocolate and drink fizzy drinks, and is thanking God Mae has gone because every time she looks at anything green she wants to be sick again.'

Farah smiled. This was all the familiarity that she'd been missing out on these past few months.

'She misses her sister,' her mum added.

'Did she say that?'

'I'm your amma. I know these things.'

Farah paused. 'Amma . . . I think I want to move house.'

Her mum nodded. 'Yes. I think you are right.' After a long pause, she added: 'You should come and live with us.'

'What? No,' said Farah.

She had to smile at her mum for suggesting it, but the idea of being back home with her parents and brother filled her with dread. She wasn't quite sure how Bubblee, of all people, was managing it.

'But you must think what you will do on your own, Faru. How will you raise the baby? How will you cope?'

Farah carried on chopping the onions. These were exactly the questions she didn't want to ask herself because it involved thinking about her baby. The truth was, she wasn't scared of being on her own as much as she was at the idea of raising a tiny human being by herself. She knew she would, and somewhere inside her she knew she'd even be good at it. But somehow, just the two of them would feel as though something was missing and she didn't want the baby to grow up thinking that the picture of its life was incomplete.

'You must talk to your sister,' said her mum. 'You know she speaks to the baby when she thinks no one is listening?'

Farah looked at her mum. 'Really?'

The idea amused Farah. She tried to imagine Bubblee sitting in her room, reading, intermittently having conversations with the baby. She laughed. 'Are you sure?' she asked. 'It doesn't sound like Bubblee.'

'I have ears, Faru. And Bubblee isn't as quiet as she thinks she is.'

'She's anything but,' said Farah under her breath.

'But she is also alone.'

Farah began chopping the peppers as she put the onions in a bowl. 'Don't start on her, amma. She likes it that way.'

'She doesn't understand yet what being alone for ever means. She is too young for that, but she is also getting too old to find a husband who will take her.'

Sometimes Farah wondered whether her mum realized what century they lived in. At barely thirty-three, Bubblee's life was full of potential and options. She guessed both of their lives were. In any case, her mum would never really understand that Bubblee didn't want to get married or be tied to any institution. Maybe Farah didn't understand it either, but she was learning to respect it.

'She doesn't want to be *taken*. She just wants to live by her own rules. That's all.'

Her mum smiled at her. 'Then why don't you make some new rules? Together?'

Farah had to ask her mum what she meant.

'Faru, my daughter, I was never close with my

331

sister, even though she gave me her own daughter to adopt. She always lived in Bangladesh and to her Fatti was just a burden because she was a girl. But you girls are different. Look at what Bubblee has done for you.'

'What are you getting at, Amma?'

'Why don't you both move in together?' she said.

Farah almost guffawed. 'Are you joking? That's the last thing Bubblee would want in her life.'

'Have you seen how she is recently?'

Farah shook her head. People don't really change. Bubblee had never wanted a family, so why would she start now?

'Did you think you'd be able to think about your baby since . . . since Mustafa?'

Farah carefully cut the aubergine into slices, almost measuring their width. She shook her head again.

'Things happen and they change people. I am not the woman I was ten years ago. Or even one year ago.'

God, Farah really hoped her mum wasn't referring to the dildo.

'But, Amma, she's never wanted these things. Why would she start now?' asked Farah.

'Maybe not. Maybe I am wrong and she will say no, but sometimes we don't know what is good for us. You think she can go back to living her life in London when she has left her . . . what was it?'

'Art, Amma.'

Her mum just shook her head in confusion, as if art as a concept didn't even exist and Bubblee had actually been away chasing unicorns.

It didn't seem like a very good idea to Farah. But perhaps Bubblee needed something to hold on to until . . . until she decided what she *did* want to chase.

'Faru,' added her mum, 'what is the harm in asking?'

Farah half-smiled. 'You don't think it's going to stop her from getting a husband?' Surely her mum would be panicking about that.

Her mum sighed, lowering the heat on the hob. 'She has a baby growing inside her and she isn't married, Faru. I think those chances are already slim. But maybe it is time to think of new ways of living. If I had the options you girls have — maybe I would've taken them instead too.'

**Mae: hows my nephew? I miss him.
Does he stil hv really big black balls?**

Farah: YES

Mae: Awwww. Too cute.

Bubblee: They really are huge.

Fatti: Ash still isn't sure if he should be proud or worried.

Mum: Baby is too yung to play wit balls. Stop givi him this.

← ● **SISTERS**

Mae: Oops. Thot Id written that in our sister group. Dare I of u 2 tell mum to stop playing wiv dad's 1ˢᵗ. Hahahahaha.

Bubblee: You are grotesque.
Mae: Yeh. Luv u 2 Bubs.

18

When Bubblee came home from work, she wanted to get into the bath and just *think* about things. She'd been home so long now that she hardly remembered her time in London and felt it was so far behind her that there was no returning to it, no matter how much she wanted to in principle. Hearing voices in the kitchen, she sneaked up the stairs so she wouldn't have to deal with any mundane questions about the day and her mum's need to fill her in on what Fatti had been doing with the baby. She heard enough about it directly from Fatti.

'You're an all right kid,' she said to her bump. 'But if that's what a person turns into when they have a baby — nothing for conversation but baby-chat — your mum and I might not be talking to each other a whole lot.'

Bubblee got into the steaming bath, the flowery scent of lavender and jasmine filling and relaxing her senses.

'That's more like it, isn't it, Sprout?' she added.

She closed her eyes for a while before opening them and looking at the way her belly protruded above the surface of the water, the silvery lines that stretched over her stomach now. Her very first stretch marks. The cocoa butter wasn't quite doing its job but Bubblee didn't care so much about that. Those things never had really

335

bothered her. The marks to her were mesmerizing. She'd look at her breasts in the mirror more closely than she ever had done before. The shifting of the shape of her body seemed to tell a story. If anything was art, it was this.

'You're getting bigger by the day.'

She felt it kick and laughed, laying her hand on her stomach. 'Calm down. You'd better not give me a hard time when you're coming out of me. Your mum's giving me a hard enough time already.'

Bubblee closed her eyes again, and realized the only time she ever smiled or laughed was when she felt the baby. Was this maternal instinct? Had it got to her? And yet, she still rolled her eyes when Fatti went on about her nephew. He was fun to look at and even pick up for a while, but it's not as if she relished watching Fatti feed him on her breast, or that she felt she could look at him for hours. Not the way Farah seemed to be able to do. She realized there was only ten weeks until she gave birth and the idea of not being pregnant any more made her feel, quite literally, empty. *I am more than just a vessel to propagate the human species.* Yes, she knew this on an intellectual level, but perhaps she'd underestimated the emotional aspect of it. Her thoughts were interrupted by a light knock on the door.

'There's someone in here,' she called out.

'It's me,' came Farah's voice. 'Can I come in?'

Bubblee sighed deeply, got out to unlock the door and climbed back into the bath again.

'Oh, sorry. Am I disturbing you?' Farah asked.

'Why would you be disturbing someone who's

in the bathroom?' said Bubblee. 'I didn't know you were here,' she added.

She realized that Farah could see her belly pop through the surface of the water and was staring at it before she turned away.

'You can look at it, you know,' said Bubblee. 'It *is* your baby.'

Farah put the toilet lid down to sit on and looked at the bump again. She seemed transfixed by it.

'Sorry about the stretch marks,' she said.

Bubblee shrugged. 'I don't care. People's obsession with perfect bodies is just another way to distract us from the important aspect of living.'

Farah folded her legs. 'What's that then?'

Bubblee thought about it. 'The fact that we have a brain and we should be using it. That there are a million and one things happening in the world at any given moment and that we choose to focus on our bodies is, honestly, the crisis of humanity.'

She shook her head as if it was the most illogical thing people ever did. Bubblee wanted to tell the baby to make sure it never got trapped by its human counterparts' foibles, but she couldn't say anything, not with Farah in the bathroom. Farah smiled at her.

'I've not been a very good mum, have I?' she said after a few moments.

Bubblee poured some frothy water over the bump. 'You've had things on your mind.'

It had become a lot harder for Bubblee to hold on to grudges. She thought she was toughening up with time, but this baby was softening her emotions and reactions as well as her figure. It was a lot more difficult to deal with the former than the latter.

'Yeah,' said Farah. 'But still . . . '

Farah got up and knelt in front of the tub, eyes fixed on Bubblee's bump. 'What do you think of a water birth? I've been . . . well, I've been reading up on it again.'

Bubblee added more bath foam to the water. 'I don't hate the idea. I've been looking into it too.'

Bubblee thought she saw Farah hesitate. Was it too much? Was Bubblee going to have to carry on being careful about how much they talked about the pregnancy?

'I've just been speaking to Mum,' said Farah. Bubblee noticed her swallow hard. 'She has the craziest idea of you and me living together and bringing up the baby.'

Bubblee almost slipped down under the water. She laughed out of sheer shock.

'Just when you think you know a person, Mum goes and says something mad like that,' said Bubblee.

Farah's face seemed to fall.

'You didn't . . . ' Bubblee began. 'You don't actually think it's a good idea, do you?'

Farah shrugged. 'Last year we both thought you carrying the baby was just as ridiculous and now look. Things change. People change.'

Bubblee sat up, folding her arms over her boobs, which in the past month or so had started giving way to gravity.

'I'm still the same person, thank you,' said Bubblee.

'Don't worry, Bubs, no one's thinking that you'll suddenly be Mother Teresa.'

Bubblee scoffed. 'You know, not everything you read is true about people.'

'It's just . . . something Mum said and, well, I didn't hate the idea,' replied Farah.

'You and me? Living together and . . . what? Being a couple.'

Farah shrugged. 'Something like that. Co-parents, I guess.'

It was absurd! Bubblee had her life to consider once this pregnancy was over: what she was going to do, where she was going to do it. Bringing up a baby was nonsensical, and how could her twin sister, of all people, think that she'd ever want to do such a thing? She'd spent her whole life telling her parents and sisters that she never wanted a family. But that was before she had this little thing inside her, before she'd got used to talking to it, having it around, thinking about what it might look like when it came out; who he or she might grow up to be, what presents she'd send it for birthdays and Eid and other celebrations.

'I did tell her you'd hate the idea,' said Farah, looking disappointed.

'But don't *you* hate the idea?' said Bubblee. 'Give me my robe.'

Farah handed it over to her, helping Bubblee out of the bath.

'Well?' said Bubblee. 'Don't you?'

Farah couldn't lie. 'No. I don't.'

Bubblee tied the robe around her. 'Oh.'

'But I knew you would. It's fine, I know.'

'Yes, but Faar, it's not exactly how you wanted things to be either. That's not the life you planned for yourself.'

Farah sat back down on the toilet lid. 'Maybe not. But after all that's happened . . . who says what I've wanted was the thing that I needed? And anyway, since when do things ever go according to plan?'

Bubblee felt as though she needed to rest and left the bathroom. She lay down on her bed and Farah followed her into the room. Her sister, who had been unable to get out of bed until recently, was beginning to sound . . . reasonable. Grounded, even. It was disconcerting.

'I'm sorry. I know it's not for you, but you know Mum,' said Farah.

The truth was, the thing that kept occurring to Bubblee was: *I'll be with the baby.* And it knocked her for six. Floored her. The impact of the realization literally had her lying on her bed. She had only ever wanted one thing in life, and that was to be a successful artist. She didn't realize she had room for wanting anything else and it was this that surprised her the most. That she was capable of wanting other things.

'What happens if you meet someone?' said Bubblee.

Farah put her hand on her chest. 'I don't even want to think about it.'

'Not now, sure. But in a year's time. Or two years' time. Then where does that leave me?'

'What if *you* meet someone?' replied Farah.

Bubblee scoffed. 'We all know I'm not tying myself to anyone. Ever.'

Surely her family should know by now that relationships held no appeal for her.

'You say that . . . ' began Farah. 'But who knows. You might meet someone who you don't hate the sight of and decide to give the relationship thing a whirl. Stranger things have happened.'

Bubblee sat up in frustration. 'This baby is yours by blood. It'll always be *yours*.'

'It's yours too,' said Farah. 'It'll be your niece or nephew. Just like Fatti is to Mum.'

'This is crazy.'

'Is it, though?' said Farah, rushing to sit by Bubblee's side. 'Is it really that crazy? Says who? The same people who said this surrogacy was an awful idea? The people who said I should leave Mustafa to his moods — that he was a man and would deal with it in his own way?'

People tended to know very little about others' lives.

'This is what I know,' said Farah. 'I want to move out of that house. I want to start afresh — a new life for me and this baby. And I want you to be a part of it.'

Bubblee leaned away from her sister. 'What if I change my mind? I hate it when babies cry. I mean, it's all very well right now, not minding the baby kicking, the idea of what it'll be like when it's born and the kind of fun things I'll be able to teach it, but that's rosy-eyed and I know it.'

Farah smiled. 'I know. I want to say you're

either in this or you're not, but things change, people change. Who knows what will happen tomorrow. But doesn't this feel right for now?'

'So what? We'd rent a place together?'

Farah nodded. 'I'd go out and earn our bread and butter. Or you could. We could share it.'

It was all so confusing. It didn't sound anything like what Bubblee had ever wanted, and yet, nothing Farah said made her averse to the idea. If anything, the panic of needing to know what she had to do with her life diminished somewhat. *Confused about life's direction? Have a baby!* That was also ridiculous.

'Maybe I will meet someone,' said Farah. 'Who knows? Maybe I won't. But I can't make decisions about life based on what might or might not happen. I can only make them based on what I know *now*. If life has taught me anything in the past year or so, it's that.

'It's a lot to take in,' said Farah. 'And I want you to do something because you *want* to. Not because you feel you have to.'

Bubblee looked at her incredulously.

'Right,' said Farah. 'Not that you ever would. But still. I'm going to go now, but if you want, we can talk about it more. Later. Or not. Whatever.'

'No pressure then,' said Bubblee, unable to move from her spot on the bed.

Farah made to leave the room before turning around and hugging Bubblee, putting her hand on her belly.

'Thank you,' she whispered in her ear. 'For all of it.'

Every time Bubblee wanted to use the bathroom in the middle of the night at least she was already awake. Sleep had escaped her. Just like the dreams she'd once had. Only this time it didn't feel as though she'd lost something. This time it felt as though she could be gaining something. Perhaps the only things she had to overcome were the expectations she had of herself.

She fell asleep just as dawn was about to break and woke up with a start. It was eleven o'clock in the morning and she felt invigorated. There was a contentment in her that she couldn't quite place until she remembered her conversation with Farah. Was this really what she wanted? Bubblee didn't want to be the woman who suddenly turned maternal in the face of pregnancy. But it wasn't exactly that. It was the idea that there was something bigger than her, or something that she could help shape, which ignited excitement in her.

'This is crazy,' she said to herself. Or the baby. She was beginning to forget who she addressed when she spoke now.

Bubblee washed in the bathroom before going to the kitchen where she found both her parents, sitting and drinking tea. She'd wanted to be alone and hoped that they'd gone out shopping or something. No such luck around here.

'Didn't get to sleep until late,' she explained before they asked questions about why she had woken up so late. 'Where are the decaff teabags?'

'Oh, yes, we need more,' said her mum, adding

it to her shopping list.

Bubblee huffed. She felt out of control here. As if not even the right kind of teabags were in her grasp. She saw her dad glance up at her from inserting new batteries in the wall clock, before looking at her mum.

'What?' said Bubblee.

Was she really a thirty-three-year-old woman, pregnant with someone else's baby, saying *what* to her mum and dad?

'Have you spoken to Farah?' asked her mum.

'About?' replied Bubblee.

Her dad cleared his throat, putting his ear to the clock. Bubblee saw her parents exchange looks again.

'You know?' she asked her mum.

Her dad put the clock down. 'Bubblee, this will always be your home.'

'But maybe,' her mum continued, 'it's also time to make a new one. Since you don't have a husband.'

'I don't *want* a husband,' she exclaimed. 'How many times do I have to say it for it to get through to you guys?'

Perhaps hysteria was hormonal. Her dad cleared his throat again, frowning at the clock. She thought her mum was about to retort with something, and Bubblee was ready for an argument again; ready to tell them she didn't have to do what others do, her life shouldn't have to mean servitude to a husband or family, but her mum simply finished her shopping list.

'You are a grown woman,' said her mum. 'You can make your own decision.'

Bubblee wondered if she really was a grown woman, what with her penchant to argue with everyone about nearly everything.

'Come on, Jay's abba,' said her mum to her dad.

Her parents got up and her dad put his hand on her head. 'Do you need anything else, apart from decaff teabags?'

'No, thanks, Abba.'

Bubblee suddenly had an image of Farah's son or daughter, getting ready for school, and Bubblee asking if they wanted anything else in their lunch box. Her day mapped out in front of her: send child to school, organize house, go to the gallery. *What gallery?* Bubblee shook her head at the nonsensical idea. But was it that nonsensical? Who said that with time and support she couldn't perhaps open one of her own? Housing her favourite up-and-coming artists. The ones with talent. If she couldn't create something herself, why not at least help nurture talent? Alongside nurturing something else.

* * *

Farah put on her jacket and took a deep breath, giving herself one last look in the mirror, before leaving the house. She got into the car and made her way down the small roads, before getting to the main one, leading away from the hospital. When she'd parked she had to take a few minutes. She gripped the steering wheel, her knuckles whitening from the pressure, and rested her forehead on her hands. *You can do this.*

It embarrassed Farah that she hadn't yet visited her husband's grave. It wasn't as if not going meant that she thought he'd walk through the bedroom door or anything. But the idea that the man who had once been flesh and bones was now buried under six feet of soil was absurd. And yet true. Farah got out of the car and made her way through the gates of the graveyard. She clutched on to her handbag — as if she expected to get pickpocketed any minute — down the flowered paths, looking at all the gravestones that lined the greenery. So many deaths. So many lost. Farah hadn't given too much thought to mortality until it was lying on her bed. Now, looking at the graves, the sheer volume of it overwhelmed her. How small her loss seemed in the face of all these. How many lives had changed just as hers had? All these months she'd felt so alone, and she had been, really — who else could understand? — but there were others out there who had felt the same things she had. There were men, women, children who'd found it hard to get out of bed, to whom the world no longer made sense because their loved one was gone from it. She walked up to a line of graves that was relatively new. Another line had already formed in front of it as she searched for his name. Then she found it. She thought it would be a profound moment, that she might even cry, but somehow she couldn't connect the grave to the man she had once loved and married. Farah stared at the gravestone for a while, confused by it. She noticed a few weeds growing at the sides and pulled them out, throwing them on the footpath. Daisies and buttercups were sprouting from the grass around it, and it made the grave seem almost friendly. She said a prayer, but that took no more than a few minutes. Once she'd done that she wondered: *What are you meant to do, standing next to a grave?* She looked around to see if there were people nearby. It was empty, probably because it was a weekday.

'The baby's doing well,' she said quietly, checking again if anyone was within earshot.

She'd seen people in films talk to their loved ones' graves, but she felt ridiculous — because it wasn't as if Mustafa could hear her. She stood and continued to stare at his name on the gravestone. The longer she stared, the more foreign it seemed to her. Then, finally, she said: 'I forgive you.'

She knew this wasn't true. But she also knew it was something that she wanted to be true. For all her guilt, she was still angry with him for leaving her — doing what he did. But perhaps one day she would let go of that.

'I'm sorry,' she added.

This was different. This she felt, more deeply, every day. The past few years played in her head as if on a loop. What if she'd asked him how he was feeling that day, after he'd lost his temper? What if she put her own feelings to one side and asked about his? Why hadn't she made that doctor's appointment that she knew he needed? But she also knew that it was like asking people not to be human. Why was it easier to relegate her own wants to one side to raise a child, when she often ignored how Mustafa had felt? She wished he'd left a letter. Farah often thought about the lack of one. He'd offered her no explanation, no final goodbye, no words for their baby-to-be, except it no longer angered her. He was thinking about one thing only and it made her feel sorrier for him than she ever had done when he was alive. What was the point in sympathy now?

'Our baby will know about the man you used to be,' she said.

Yes, that she could do for him. She had to let go of what he had or hadn't done, the wrongs that had been done to her, and move forward to the ways in which she could right her own wrongs. Farah was going to put pictures all over the house. Whatever house that would be. She'd talk about him as her child grew up, showing pictures of their dad who would've loved them if only he had the opportunity. It was time to put away blame. Farah smiled at a memory of when they first got married and moved into their big home. Mustafa had put his arms around her and kissed her neck.

'Just something small, until we can afford a bigger house,' he'd joked.

She'd laughed, scanning the huge French windows and high ceilings. When they'd started trying for a baby, and eight months later they still hadn't conceived, Farah was crying one day when he came home from work. He'd rushed to her, asking what was wrong. She'd sobbed into his arms because she didn't feel complete; as though there was a part of her missing and she didn't know how to fill it. He'd tucked a loose strand of hair behind her ear and said: 'You are complete to me.' She was so glad he hadn't said: *You complete me.* And yet, even if he had, she would've loved him for his affection, for always trying to make her happy.

'I'll remember those moments,' she said to his grave.

Farah would insist on playing these kinds of memories on a loop, rather than the last few years of her marriage to Mustafa. Though she wouldn't forget those, either. She'd keep them tucked away as a reminder that things change, that nothing stays the same; but that only meant you had to find new ways of dealing with it. You can't expect to have the same reaction to different problems. Farah bent down low, plucking some daisies from the grass and putting them on Mustafa's grave. They seemed full of humility and hope and reminded her of him.

'We'll think of a name for the baby. I'll make sure it's something you would've liked too.'

It felt wrong, turning away from him now. If she could take the grave with her, she would. But she'd be back. This time it wouldn't take her months. The only way she could stop being sorry for feeling as if she failed him was to remember him. She would forgive him. And then she would forgive herself.

When Farah turned into her road she saw a figure leaning against the front garden's brick wall. She got out of the car. Bubblee seemed to shift uncomfortably.

'Hi,' said Farah.

Bubblee looked Farah in the eye. 'All right, then. Let's do it.'

★ ★ ★

'Oh, my God,' exclaimed Mae, bringing in the last of the boxes. 'Bubs, man, you have a *lot* of crap.'

Farah looked at all the boxes in dismay as Mae put her arm around her. 'Too late now. Can't change your mind.'

Fatti called Ash for the third time in the space of an hour to make sure the baby was still okay.

'Yes, I know, okay,' she said down the phone, making a face at her sisters. 'You've looked after him before. What? No, they're all in the room with me right now.' Fatti seemed to struggle when, as if repeating a mantra, she said: 'It is absolutely normal for me to leave my son with his father and not expect him to have dropped him on his head.'

They heard Ash's mumbled voice come from the phone.

'Yes,' said Fatti. 'I trust you.' She looked at her sisters again and made a face that suggested she was lying.

She put the phone down as Bubblee watched her with eyebrows raised, munching on a bag of cheese-and-onion crisps.

'Why did no one tell me how good these were?' Bubblee said, looking at her third empty packet. 'Sure I can't help?' she added, without much conviction.

'No, no,' said Mae. 'You sit and get high on

salt and sugar while we do all the heavy lifting.'

'I like that this living room has more space,' said Bubblee, looking around the room.

'And two bedrooms,' added Farah, taking a bottle of sparkling water out of the fridge.

'Ugh, I need to pee,' said Bubblee.

She reached out her hands for someone to help her as Fatti came to the rescue.

'Thank God you've got your strength back,' said Bubblee to her, managing to get up and putting her hand on the small of her back. 'Make sure you never lose weight again.'

Bubblee waddled off to the bathroom and came back a few minutes later to see Mae on her phone and Fatti and Farah taking her old sculptures out of the boxes.

'Loft,' said Bubblee.

'Too right,' replied Mae, looking up from her phone at Bubblee's artwork.

'I quite like them,' said Fatti.

Bubblee felt unaccountably happy. Seeing the sculptures like that, to be relegated where she wouldn't see them, no longer filled her with despair. They gave her a sense of hope that she might do something better; as if they were the beginning of something and she was only now starting to see that.

'Are you okay?' asked Farah.

'Yeah,' replied Bubblee. 'You?'

'She's organizing boxes. Of course she's okay,' said Mae.

'Need to get them done by tomorrow because I can't have this hanging over my head when the baby comes,' said Farah. 'Plus, I have a feeling I won't get away with flexi hours with my new boss, so an early-morning start. Practise for when the baby arrives.'

Bubblee felt like lying down. 'Are you recording this, Mae? I swear to God if we end up on YouTube I will strangle you with my baby's umbilical cord.'

Bubblee had taken to calling it her baby now as well.

'I hope baby-cakes doesn't inherit your penchant for violence,' replied Mae.

Bubblee put her hand on one of the boxes and winced. 'It's fine. I'm fine. Back is killing me. I'm going to lie down.'

'Good idea,' said Farah, taking her by the arm. 'You should try and get as much sl — '

The number of times Bubblee had heard people recommending that she get sleep could actually put her to sleep. Why did people have to say the most obvious things to pregnant women? Mae laughed at the look Bubblee gave her.

'Unpack your boxes,' said Bubblee. 'I'll make it up the stairs mys — '

And then she felt a gush come from down below. *What was that?*

'Oh, God,' exclaimed Mae, looking horrified.

Bubblee's heart began racing. She looked at the floor, the carpet drenched in water as Farah and Fatti stared at each other.

'Have you wet yourself?' said Farah.

How was that possible when she'd gone to the bathroom three minutes ago?

'I'm so sorry!' exclaimed Bubblee, on the verge of crying. 'I can't believe I just did that. I

352

don't even . . . how . . . '

She hadn't felt any pressure in her bladder.

'Bubblee,' said Farah, her grip on Bubblee's arm getting tighter.

'I'll clean it up.' Bubblee made to get a kitchen towel.

'Bubs,' said Fatti, smiling.

'I'm sorry, okay? Have none of you ever wet yourself before?'

Bubblee felt tears sting her eyes and she wasn't even sure why.

'*Bubs,*' Farah repeated.

Bubblee looked at Farah who was supressing a huge smile.

'Mae,' said Fatti. 'Hospital bag.'

Mae jumped off the sofa. 'On it.'

Bubblee could see her reflection in Farah's eyes and was sure she looked as though she'd just seen a ghost, there was so much fear in it.

'It's okay,' said Farah.

'Oh,' said Bubblee. 'Oh, my God.'

She began taking deep breaths. Fatti had already grabbed her jacket, the car keys and was asking about contractions.

'No, nothing,' began Bubblee. 'I don't feel any — argh!'

Bubblee bent over, breathing deeply again, closing her eyes to try and shut out the pain. When it had passed she looked at Fatti. 'Do they *all* feel like that?'

'That's what medication is for,' said Fatti.

Mae had appeared, bag in hand, phone in her pocket. 'Well? What are we waiting for?' she exclaimed, making her way to the door.

'Make sure you give me drugs,' said Bubblee. 'Give me all the drugs.'

'We will,' said Farah.

'Especially if it means it helps you pass out,' added Mae.

'Come on, come on. I'm calling Mum and Dad,' said Fatti, already out of the door.

'This is it,' said Bubblee, looking at Farah.

Farah nodded, gripping her hand. Bubblee gripped back. It helped to steady her walk, somehow lessening the pain she knew would return. Marginally.

On the threshold of the door, just as Bubblee was about to leave their new home, she realized that they'd be returning, plus one.

'It's really begun,' she said to Farah.

'Oh, yes,' Farah replied. 'It has.'

We do hope that you have enjoyed reading this large print book.

Did you know that all of our titles are available for purchase?

We publish a wide range of high quality large print books including:
Romances, Mysteries, Classics
General Fiction
Non Fiction and Westerns

Special interest titles available in large print are:
The Little Oxford Dictionary
Music Book
Song Book
Hymn Book
Service Book

Also available from us courtesy of Oxford University Press:
Young Readers' Dictionary
(large print edition)
Young Readers' Thesaurus
(large print edition)

For further information or a free brochure, please contact us at:
Ulverscroft Large Print Books Ltd.,
The Green, Bradgate Road, Anstey,
Leicester, LE7 7FU, England.
Tel: (00 44) 0116 236 4325
Fax: (00 44) 0116 234 0205

Other titles published by Ulverscroft:

THE SECRET LIVES OF
THE AMIR SISTERS

Nadiya Hussain

Fatima, Farah, Bubblee and Mae, the four Amir sisters, are the only young Muslims in the quaint English village of Wyvernage. On the outside, despite not quite fitting in with their neighbours, the Amirs are happy. But on the inside, each sister is secretly struggling. Fatima is trying to find out who she really is — and finally pass her driving test. Farah is happy being a wife but longs to be a mother. Bubblee is determined to be an artist in London, away from family tradition. And Mae is coping with burgeoning YouTube stardom. Yet when family tragedy strikes, it brings them closer together and forces them to learn more about life, love, and each other than they ever thought possible.

THE GIRL IN THE LETTER

Emily Gunnis

1956: When Ivy Jenkins falls pregnant, she is sent in disgrace to St Margaret's: a dark, brooding house for unmarried mothers. Her baby is adopted against her will. Ivy will never leave. Present day: Samantha Harper is a journalist desperate for a break. When she stumbles on a letter from the past, the contents shock and move her. The letter is from a young mother, begging to be rescued from St Margaret's before it is too late. Sam is pulled into the tragic story and discovers a spate of unexplained deaths surrounding the woman and her child. With St Margaret's set for demolition, Sam has only hours to piece together a sixty-year-old mystery before the truth, which lies disturbingly close to home, is lost forever.

BAY TREE COTTAGE

Anna Jacobs

Once a row of abandoned houses, Saffron Lane is bursting with new life thanks to the efforts of owners Nell and Angus. Their plan to develop an artists' colony is fast becoming a reality, as is their idea to transform the secret wartime messaging room in one of the houses into a museum. Ginger finds a place to call her own in the fledgling community, taking refuge from her bully of a son. When she meets Iain, sparks fly between them — the first time she's been attracted to anyone for years. But will her son succeed in spoiling it? Meanwhile, Emil is in charge of readying the messaging room for the public and, despite an interfering councilwoman, is determined to face his challenges head on. Will the newcomers manage to find happiness?